SOUTH DEERING

Coming Of Age In The Mob

STEVE ESPARZA

*For Carmen, without her, there would be nothing. I Want You to Know:
We have talked, you and me, of what to do if one must leave. We've
talked of money, home and kids. Who to call…Who would care? But
while I can, I want you to know how much I love and care. For all you've
done and your support, for loving me with all my warts. For accepting my
apologies for things I've done, you are my life. You've been the one. I
wanted you to know before one must go.*

Acknowledgments

First and foremost to my good friend and neighbor, John W Wood, an author in his own right, for guiding me thru the whole business of trying to tell a story. His knowledge and experience were of great comfort. John always said, "Write it like you talk it, and let the characters speak for themselves," Mike and Anna Yurkovich, 2 good friends and better listeners, Christine Navarr. She told me to write a chapter a week. Rena Winters, also an author, transferred my handwritten manuscript to a thumb drive for my computer.

PART I

1953 - 1963

IN THE STILL OF THE NIGHT
By The Satins

Prologue

NESTLED ALONG THE SOUTHWESTERN TIP OF LAKE MICHIGAN is a highly industrial area called the Calumet Region. It is aptly named for the Calumet River that runs through it, stretching from 79th Street in South Chicago to northwest Indiana, stopping in Gary. It is known mainly for the big steel producers in the US. Steel South Works, US. Steel Gary Works, Inland Steel, Youngstown Sheet and Tube, Republic Steel, Interlake Iron and Coke Works, and our neighborhood mill, Wisconsin Steel Works.

There were factories such as Lever Brothers, also known as the "Rinso Factory," General Mills, Chicago Steel and Wire, and the Calumet Canal and Dock Company. Located at 130th and Torrence Avenue was the vast Ford Motor Assembly Plant. Bounded by 103rd Street to the north, 111th Street to the south, Torrence Avenue to the east, and the Chicago West Pullman Rail Yard to the west was the quiet little neighborhood known as South Deering. Founded in 1875 along with the Joseph H. Brown Iron and Steel Company, it became known as Irondale. It stayed that way until 1903, when the community leaders renamed it, South Deering.

International Harvester, an agricultural machinery manufacturer, acquired Browns Mill in 1902 and constructed a new facility, Wisconsin Steel, to produce steel for its tractors and combines. With the influx of workers, the neighborhood blossomed.

Trumbull Park opened to the public in 1907 at 103rd Street and Yates Avenue. In 1914 the field house was constructed along with most of the landscaping. It was relatively quiet until 1936 when the Chicago Housing Authority built the Trumbull Park Homes, which were for people looking for affordable homes. All the calm and serenity ended on a summer night in 1953.

The Federal Government, citing civil rights legislation, banning discrimination in hiring and housing, moved a black family into the homes. It sparked a decade-long period of violence and protests by the neighborhood residents. When my mom and I moved upstairs, above my sister Mary's store, the neighborhood's south end was quiet and peaceful. My older brother, Raul, was already working in the mill. My mother and I helped downstairs in the store, so I always had a few bucks in my pocket.

Chapter 1

7/14/53

I met Tommy Stetich in the summer of 1953. He and some of his friends were playing softball on the playground of Orville T. Bright Elementary School. We had just moved to South Deering, and I was starting my first year at Chicago Vocational High School. As for Tommy, I never knew if he went to school or not. I don't remember ever seeing him at the bus stop or saying anything about high school or which school he attended. I figured it was none of my business. I just knew that I had a new best friend.

We went and did almost everything together. I met the other guys who hung out in front of Jerry's store, most of whom played softball. Our main occupation in the summer was playing ball and drinking beer in the alley. Nobody had a car, so most nights, we sat around in front of the store. That was our routine: stay home in the winter, play ball, drink beer, and hang out in the summer.

Not much changed in the next four years. We got older and drank more beer, but things changed that summer of 1957. Three weeks before graduation, I met Augie Vargas on the bus coming home from school. In the following weeks, we talked about what we were doing that summer. Augie said he and some friends were starting a softball team. They would be at Trumbull Park at about 6:30pm if I wanted to try out. I couldn't wait to get home and tell Tommy.

After our first day of practice, I knew it was not something Tommy wanted to do.

His idea of practice was playing "hits and homers" at Bright School ground. I, myself, wanted to be on the team, and that, I'm sad to say, was the beginning of the end of our friendship. I began spending more time on 108th and Torrence Avenue, in front of South Deering Billiards. There, I met the other two guys who, along with Augie, would become my three best and closest friends. They were Mike Kowalski and Larry Szymanski. Larry wasn't into sports, but he knew everything there was to know about cars.

We hit it off and began to hang out together when we weren't playing ball. We would either be drinking beer in the back of the pool hall or shooting pool. No matter how often I asked Tommy to join us, he always had an excuse, even when I went to Jerry's store. I finally realized that things were not the same anymore. The rift between us was palatable to everyone on the corner. We hardly spoke to each other. Sometimes Tommy would just walk away and not come back. We never knew where he went or why. I found out later that he was hanging out on the east side. It was then that I realized what I thought was a great friendship wasn't that great, and though I still had good friends there, the thought of Tommy being there kept me away.

Roland (Fat Rollie) Jacinto owned the pool hall, the building, and the buildings on either side. He was about 5 feet 7 inches tall and weighed close to 300 pounds. His black curly hair was always cut short, with a few gray hairs above each ear. He was never seen without an unlit cigar in his mouth.

Needless to say, he was the sponsor of both our softball and bowling teams.

I don't think we ever saw him lose his temper. He was always in a good mood, even when we lost. In one of those good moods, he gave me the nickname "Flacco." At first, I didn't like it, but then I realized he didn't mean anything by it.

We played ball Fridays at Trumbull Park and Sundays at Calumet Park. Lil Joe, Pete, and Bobby all had cars, so we would meet in front of Rollies and carpool to the games. That's how the summer, fall, and winter went by, one turning into the other. The talk around the neighborhood that February in 1959 was that Wisconsin Steel Works had started hiring. The four of us were there bright and early Monday morning, and after filling out the paperwork, we started working the next month.

I started working on March 24th and was fortunate to work the day shift with the weekends off. Larry, Augie, and Mike were all stuck on shift work with a few weekends off. We were all working then, and by the beginning of May, we were all driving our cars. There was no more carpooling; even though they were not new, we treated them as if they were.

Things changed that summer. Now we all had a set of wheels to go to and from the games. Another change was that Augie, Mike, and Larry were spending more time with their girlfriends, and me not having one of my own. I spent a lot of time at Rollie's whenever I did a double date. For whatever reason, things just never seemed to work out.

Most of them just wanted to be friends; sometimes, I felt like a third wheel, just taking up space. Soon I just didn't feel like it was worth it.

All that changed the second weekend in May. We were sitting in Rolllie's backyard; I was in the middle of the yard, sitting on a cooler full of cold beer. It was about 9pm under a full moon, with a cloudless sky.

We were discussing our game and why we lost when we suddenly noticed car headlights coming down the alley.

Mike and I walked into the alley and stopped when we noticed it was Larry's car. Tommy Stetich was in the back seat with his arm around the most beautiful girl I'd ever seen.

I know this might sound corny, but looking at her, I knew I would love her for the rest of her life. Larry broke the spell. "I've got another case in the trunk."

"We'll get it," Mike said, looking at me. Taking a couple of steps, he opened the trunk and walked back into the yard.

Standing there looking at her, I felt stupid, and when she smiled, my heart skipped a beat.

When I got my voice back, I told Larry, "Park the car in front, and come and have a beer."

"Okay," he said, "I could use a cold one."

Now back on the cooler, I was facing the gangway. I just wanted to see her again. Maybe she would smile at me.

I kept berating myself between those thoughts and thinking, "What good would that do? She's with Tommy."

I was about to get up and get another beer when Larry, followed by his girlfriend Jeannie, walked into the yard and towards me. Getting up, I noticed that my legs were shaking, and I had this weird feeling in the pit of my stomach.

Without waiting to ask for her, I asked Larry, "What happened to Tommy?" He stopped to talk with Bobby and Pete out in the front.

Just then, Jeannie observed her friend come into the yard. I turned to look, and there she was. It was as though someone had set a spotlight on the whole yard.

She looked about 5 feet 10 or 11 inches, with long chestnut hair pulled back into a ponytail, a sleeveless print blouse, tan Capri's, and flat sandals. How she carried herself when she walked was like looking at a model walking down a runway. As she walked toward us, she smiled at me, and my heart did double flips, and I started shaking again.

She was standing next to me, and all I could do was stare and hope I didn't do anything stupid. I felt I had taken root and had lost my voice.

Larry, with a beer in hand, was walking toward the stairs. Before joining him, Jeannie turned to me and said: "Jesse, I'd like you to meet Molly, a friend of mine."

I stood there as if in a fog, not knowing what to say or do. I don't know how long I stood there in that fog.

"Aren't you even going to say hi?" Molly asked.

Swallowing my mouth full of cotton, I croaked out "Hi" and sat back down on the cooler.

After the fog lifted, I noticed that Larry and Jeannie were sitting on the stairs with Mike and his girlfriend, Joyce. I also noted that Tommy, Pete, and Bobby were now in the yard talking to Larry and Mike.

I turned and looked up only to see Molly still standing, only now with a quizzical look. "What?" I said, shrugging my shoulders.

"I'm so glad you can talk," Molly said with a smile. "Do you think I can have a beer?"

"Are you old enough?" I challenged.

"Are you?" she shot back. We looked at each other and laughed. For me, that broke the ice and brought me back down to earth.

Feeling better, I got her a beer, opened it, and sat back down.

Towering over me and looking down with that beautiful and radiant smile, Molly asked: "Is there room for both of us?"

"Aren't you with Tommy?

"Right now, I'm with you. You don't mind, do you?"

"No, I don't, but I saw you sitting in the back seat together."

"Well," she said, sitting next to me, "we stopped at Jerry's store looking for you, and before we knew it, he was in the back seat with me."

"You were looking for me?"

"Yeah, Larry wanted me to meet you," and "oh, are you cold?"

"No," I said, looking down and noticing my legs shaking.

"Listen," Molly said, "if this is too close, we can go sit on the stairs."

I stood up, helped her to her feet, took out two more beers, and sat on the stairs. After lighting up a Salem, I asked, "Do you live close to Jeannie?"

"No," Molly replied, "I live in a small town west of Philadelphia called Upper Darby."

"You were born there?"

"I was born here in Chicago, right down the street from Jeannie's house

"How'd you end up in Upper Darby?"

"Well, my father's a lawyer, and about five years ago, he went to work for a law firm in Philly."

"I thought you lived in Upper Darby?"

"We do, but my parents didn't want to live in the city. My aunt lives in Upper Darby, so we moved there."

"Oh," I said. "Before I forget, what's the Molly for?"

"My name is Mary Catherine Malone. Molly is just a nickname, like yours, right, 'Flacco'?"

When she said that, something went off in my head, and before I knew it, I was on my feet and walking to where Tommy was standing. Coming up behind him, I gave him a shove, so he would turn and face me.

"Thanks a lot," I said.

"For what?" he answered.

"You know what," I said, getting madder by the minute. "You just had to tell Molly, right?"

"Oh, that. It's only a nickname."

"Yeah, well, fuck you, Tommy!"

"Well, fuck you too, Flacco!"

With that, I landed a roundhouse right to his left cheekbone. He went into the railing with a loud crack. He came off the railing, and I landed another shot below his rib cage.

He doubled over, I stepped back, then he rushed me, and we both went down in the dirt. We flailed at each other on the ground, and he clipped me on my mouth with his elbow. I tasted blood, and I wanted to really kick his ass. All I could see was red. I just wanted to keep hitting until I couldn't swing my arms.

Somehow Tommy got my head in a hammerlock with his left arm, hitting me a couple of times, once on my right cheek and the other on my forehead. We were rolling around until Mike, Augie, and Larry finally pulled us apart.

Mike stepped between us, looked Tommy in the eye, and said, "I think you should leave now." Tommy then stole a quick glance around the yard and walked to where Molly was standing with a grin.

Dusting off his shirt and pants, he said, "You ready to go?"

"Go where?" she answered.

"Back by Jerry's."

"I came with Larry and Jeannie."

With disbelief, Tommy walked toward the gangway, entered, took one last look around, and declared loudly, "Fuck all of you!"

While everyone was watching him, I quietly walked into the alley, turned left, and made my way home.

It was about 11:30pm when I finally climbed the stairs and walked into the house. My mom was watching TV in the front room and saw my bloody lip, bruised cheekbone, and torn shirt. She rose from the couch, rushed over to me, and asked, "Que Paso?" (What happened) with a worried look.

"There was a little excitement by the pool hall."

"What kind of excitement?" she asked.

"It was a fight," I said. "Me and Tommy."

"I thought Tommy was your best friend?" she said.

"We were," I answered, "until I started playing ball with Mike, Augie, and the other guys, and we got Fat Rollie to sponsor us."

"Isn't Tommy on the team?" she inquired.

"They didn't ask him."

"That's too bad," she said. "I always thought you two were best friends."

"So did I," was my answer. With that, I turned and walked toward the bathroom.

Once inside, I took off my shirt and T-shirt, checked my mouth, and saw that it was just a split lip. Most of the blood had dried, but my cheek was another matter. It was going to be a beautiful shiner.

After washing up, I gave my mom a goodnight kiss on the cheek, went into my room, flopped on the bed, and tried to get some sleep.

I tossed and turned until 3 o'clock. I kept seeing Molly's face, how she smiled, how she looked at me. I was shaking, just sitting next to her. It was so easy to talk to her, and how we joked and laughed together. All the while, I kept thinking, "Did she actually come looking for me?" It seemed too good to be true. "She is so beautiful," I thought to myself. Maybe it's just a beautiful dream. I'll wake up in the morning, and I won't have a split lip and no shiner.

After my breakfast of chorizo, eggs, beans, and flour tortillas, I finished my second cup of coffee with the Sun-Times when the phone rang. "It's Larry," my mom said, standing in the dining room.

"Hey, Lar," I said. "What's up?"

"Where the fuck did you go last night? We were waiting for you to come back."

"I came home to wash up and change my shirt. I knew I couldn't go back when I saw my face."

"Why not?" Larry asked.

"I feel like I made a big fucking fool of myself. I don't know why I went after Tommy," I said. "He used to be my best friend. Maybe because he told Molly to call me Flacco or I was trying to impress her, whatever it was, it didn't work."

"Maybe it did," Larry said with a short laugh.

"What ya mean," I said anxiously.

"Well," he said, "you have to promise you won't tell her."

"Tell her what?"

"We waited in front of Rollie's till 12 o'clock, and she kept asking me to tell her where you lived."

"Why," I asked, a little confused.

"You'll have to ask her."

"Listen, Lar, do me a favor and don't bring her to the park or Rollie's, okay?"

"How come?" Larry asked.

"I wanna lay low until this fucking shiner is gone."

"Okay, but I don't think it matters to her."

"Why not?"

"Because she told Jeannie that she likes you a lot."

"She does?" I asked, not believing what I had just heard.

Larry chuckled, then added, "That's what Jeannie told me this morning."

"I still need some time."

"Don't take too long," he said. "She leaves in September,"

"Really?"

"Yeah, she's only here for the summer."

"Okay," I said, "I heard you."

After we hung up, I got dressed and went out to wash my car.

Chapter 2

Saturday

IT WAS ABOUT 10:30 THAT NIGHT WHEN AUGIE BANKED THE 8 ball in the corner pocket, ending the game.

I walked in the back door and nodded to Rollie, who was at his usual spot behind the counter. He nodded back and motioned for me to come up to the counter. "Hold on, Fat Man, I'll be right there."

Larry, Augie, Mike, and Lil Joe had just finished; Pete, Eddie, Bobby, and Butch all turned when they heard my voice. They all noticed my shiner and split lip but didn't say anything.

"Rack 'em, Mike," Lil Joe said. "That's one game apiece,"

"Who's got winners?" I asked.

"Yeah, me and Butch," Bobby answered.

"Okay," I said, "but I got' um after that."

I turned, took about ten steps, stood at the counter, and asked: "What's up?"

"Hey, Flacco," Rollie said, "I heard there was a little scuffle in the back last night. I hope you got in a couple of shots."

"Yeah, that fucken, Tommy. I can't believe we used to be best friends."

"I heard she's beautiful," Rollie said with a twinkle.

"You know, Rollie, sometimes I don't know what comes over me. All I see is red. Last night I wanted to hurt Tommy real bad."

No sooner had I said that Larry was standing next to me.

"Hey," he said, "can I talk to you for a couple of minutes after this game."

"Sure," I said, "I'll be in the yard. What's on your mind, Rollie?"

"We'll talk after the game, okay?"

Having lost the game, me and Larry were sitting on the stairs. We both lit up. After a couple of drags, Larry turned and looked at the end of his cigarette. "I know you don't want Molly to see you right now, but we're going to the show tomorrow, and she wants you to go with us."

"Naw, man, I need some time."

"She doesn't care about your eye."

"How does she know about my eye?" I asked, getting a little pissed.

"I guess I must have said something."

"What the fuck, Lar, She didn't have to know about that," I almost shouted. Now I was really getting fucking pissed.

"I'm sorry, man, I was just trying to help. Besides, we're only going to the show!"

After thinking about it and knowing she would be leaving in a couple of months, against my better judgment, I said, "Okay."

"All right," Larry said rather happily.

"Oh," he said, "one more thing, Tommy called her today and asked her out."

"What did she say?"

"She said no. I think because she's waiting for you to call."

"If she wants to go out with him, that's up to her."

"Besides, as you said, she'll be gone in a couple of months, right?"

"Yeah, I guess so."

"Okay then, let's go shoot some 8 ball."

Once inside, Rollie motioned me over to the counter. "What's up?" I asked.

"I wanted to ask how you felt about making a couple of bucks, watching the place on Saturday and Sunday?"

"Yeah, sure," I answered, "what time are you talking about?"

"How about from 6pm till whatever time you want to close. It'll be alright. The guys will be here with you."

"That's great, man. When do you want me to start?"

"How's tomorrow sound?"

"I got a date tomorrow. How about next week?"

"Okay," he said, "I hope it's with Jeannie's girlfriend."

"It is," I answered with a smile of confidence.

"Try to get here about 5:30. I'll show you what to do."

"Fine," I said. "Now I'm gonna shoot some pool."

Chapter 3

Sunday

ON THE RIDE OVER TO JEANNIE'S HOUSE, I WAS A BIG BUNDLE of nerves, my hands were shaking, and my heart felt way out of whack. I kept telling myself, "It's only a movie," what could go wrong? Just go with the flow, and it'll be over in a couple of hours.

What do I say when I see her?

Do I put my arm around her in the theater

Should I try and kiss her?

Why, I thought, was I asking myself all this shit? Hadn't I been a fill-in before with Augie and Mike?

Not to worry, I told myself, one date and she'll be gone.

I parked at the curb and was about to get out when I noticed Larry, Jeannie, and Molly come out the front door. When they got to the sidewalk, Larry walked up to my car, leaned in, and said, "Let's go in my car." He had that sneaky smile, and I went along with it.

Putting my sunglasses on, I climbed out, locked the door, and was about to step up to the curb. Instead, I stopped and looked at where Molly and Jeannie were standing.

Jeannie said, "Hi," but I don't even think I heard her; all sound and motion seemed to stop. Molly was more beautiful than I remembered, just standing there looking at me with that beautiful smile. All I could think of was, "Why me?"

Finally, Molly walked up to me with a slight frown and asked, "Are you all right?"

"You are beautiful," was all I managed to say.

"Don't say that, please," Molly answered, looking down at her feet.

"Why not?

"Because you don't know me that well."

"I don't have to know someone to know they are beautiful."

When Molly finally looked up at me, there was this wondrous and almost magical expression. I felt frozen to the spot. My arms and legs were not responding to my commands.

Molly reached up and, taking my sunglasses off, said rather shyly, "I've seen bruises before. It's not that bad," looking at my split lip, "I'll have to be careful with that."

"Are you guys coming or not?" Jeannie yelled, standing next to Larry's car.

"Come on," Molly said, taking hold of my hand.

We were sitting in the back seat no sooner than Molly laid her head on my shoulder, whispering, "Why did you hit Tommy? Was it because of—?"

"We'll talk about it later, okay?"

"Okay," was all she said.

Walking out of the Avalon Theater after three hours of "South Pacific" was a welcome relief. We were standing by the curb, waiting for Larry and Jeannie, when Molly asked, "Would you mind if we walked back? It's such a beautiful night, and we've been sitting for the past three hours."

Larry and Jeannie were on their way to the parking lot. "Hey, Lar," I said. "We're gonna walk back."

"Okay," he said, "I'll see you at the house."

Molly and I turned and began walking west on 79th Street. "You don't talk much, do you?"

"Look, Molly, what happened between Tommy and me had nothing to do with you."

"I know," she said. "But I was the one who called you Flacco."

"Yeah," I said, "but he gave you the name, right?"

Soon we were standing at the intersection where 79th Street, South Chicago Avenue, and Stoney Island Avenue meet at different angles. When the light turned green, and we stepped off the curb, Molly reached over and took hold of my hand, crossing the street. My whole arm was shaking, and I couldn't wait to get on the sidewalk.

Letting go of my hand, Molly walked a few steps ahead, turned, and said, "I can go back by myself now."

"What's that mean?"

"That means," she said, "I don't think you really want to be here."

"Why do you say that?" I said, astonished.

"Why?" she inquired, sounding a bit angry. "You act like you don't want to get close to me. We just sat for three hours and could have sat in different rows. What are you afraid of?"

We had passed under the Railroad Viaduct and were standing beneath the Skyway Overpass.

"You don't like me very much, do you?" Molly inquired.

"I think it's the opposite," I responded, taking hold of her hands.

"You have a funny way of showing it," she said, looking directly into my eyes.

"Can I tell you something without you laughing at me?"

"Okay," she said, interlacing our fingers.

"I want you to know this is my first real date. I don't know how to act or what to do. I wanted to put my arm around you in the show, but I didn't know how to do it.

Even now, crossing the street, just holding hands, I got the shakes."

"You mean that?" Molly asked, now with that radiant smile. "You really get the shakes?"

"Yeah," I answered, looking down at my shoes. Looking up, I saw she was smiling.

I tried to match her smile but couldn't, so I kissed her instead, pressing my mouth to hers too hard. I could feel her lips crush beneath mine. She cried in mild pain.

"What do you think now?" I asked.

Her hands were fingering her bruised lips. "You hurt me," Molly accused.

"I'm sorry, Molly," I pleaded. "That's the first time I've ever kissed anyone before."

"You know what," she said, "I believe you."

"I'll never lie to you, Molly."

"Promise?" she asked.

"I promise," was my answer.

"Okay then," she said. "Let's try that again."

She came into my arms again, and this time the kiss was tender but with meaning. I don't know how long we stood there, holding on to that kiss, but after some car horns and a few 'get a room' comments, we finally pulled apart, but not before Molly ran her tongue across my split lip. "That didn't hurt, did it?" she asked with a smile.

"Molly, I—"

"Don't say anything," she whispered. "Just hold me a little while."

So there we stood in the shadow of the Skyway on a beautiful night in May. I felt as if time had stood still. I didn't want to move, thinking I might break the spell. I could have stood there all night.

I was so busy inhaling her beautiful scent that I almost didn't notice the little shiver. "Are you cold?" I asked, not wanting to let go. Molly pulled back a little, lifted her head, looked deep into my eyes, and, smiling, replied, "Not really. I've never had this feeling after kissing anyone before. I can't explain it."

Somehow we ended up in front of Jeannie's house. I noticed that Larry's car was nowhere in sight. I was about to suggest that we sit in my car when Molly said, smiling, "I noticed you're still holding my hand."

"I don't want to take a chance that you'll disappear."

"I'm not going anywhere," she replied, "and I just want to say I had a great time tonight."

"So did I," I said, taking hold of her other hand.

"Really."

"Yeah, really."

"I know," she said, "you didn't really like the movie."

"I'm not big on musicals."

"Neither am I," Molly mused. "Jeannie wanted to see it."

"I enjoyed just sitting next to you."

"Well, maybe you can put your arm around me next time."

"That sounds like a plan," I said.

"When will the next time be?" she asked, squeezing both hands.

"How about I call you?"

"Okay," she answered, looking past me to the street where Larry and Jeannie had just pulled up to the curb. I knew that look. I'd had it myself a few times. It's when you know you're being let down slowly so as not to hurt your feelings.

Slowly, Molly let go of my hands, waited until Larry and Jeannie finished their goodnight kiss, then walked to the curb. Jeannie exited the car and walked to where Molly was standing.

"Enjoy your walk?" she asked, looking directly at Molly.

"Yeah," Molly replied. "It's a beautiful night."

"I'll see you upstairs then," Jeannie said on her way to the front door.

"I have to go in now," Molly said, searching my face. "Will you call me?"

"Okay, I'll call."

"We can talk some more, okay?"

"Yeah," I said, "we'll talk."

I stood as if rooted to the spot, watching Molly slip through the front door. Back in my car, I lit up a Salem.

Letting out a plume of smoke, I thought, "Man, I really fucked that up. I really hoped that it was the right thing to do."

Chapter 4

Wednesday

As I turned the corner at 109th Street, I thought, "It's been three days now, and although I haven't stopped thinking about Molly, I'm feeling good about myself. I won't get hurt this time, she'll be gone, and things will return to normal again."

I know all about getting hurt and caring about someone who doesn't feel the same. It's happened quite a few times before.

Halfway down Torrence Avenue, I noticed Mike's car parked in front of Rollie's. As I approached, he got out and met me at the curb.

"Hey, Mike." I smiled.

"Where the fuck have you been? Nobody has seen you since last Friday."

"I've been feeling a little down since last Sunday."

"Things didn't go well with Molly?"

"Mike, can you stick around for a while? I have to see Rollie, then we can talk, okay?"

"Okay," Mike said, "I'll be out back."

Rollie came around the counter, unlocked the door, and ushered me inside.

"What's up, Rollie?"

"Same old shit, Flacco? Next, you lock the front door and turn off the sign." Walking behind the counter, Rollie opened the register, took out the drawer, turned, and said: "If there are any big bills, they'll be underneath. Take the drawer back to my bedroom and open the closet."

As we walked into the bedroom, Rollie reached, flicked on the light switch, and opened the closet door. I followed him in and watched as he opened the locked cabinet in the wall. He called me over and showed me where to put the drawer and the two guns on the lower shelf. One looked like a 45 caliber automatic, the other a snub-nosed revolver.

"Only two people will have a key, me and you. I trust you, Flacco. I only hope you never have to use either of them. They are both loaded, so be careful when you handle them, okay?" Taking the extra key from his key ring, he handed it to me, saying, "You're one of the older guys, so I trust that you'll always do the right thing."

We finally sat down across from each other at the little dinette set. I lit up one of my Salems. He had his cigar.

"Well," Rollie said, handing me a slip of paper. "That's my phone number at home, don't give it to anyone, but call me if you need anything."

"Yeah, sure, Rollie," I said, and with that, we both stood up and shook hands.

"We'll talk about the money later, okay?"

"Whatever you say, Rollie."

"If you guys want some beer, you'll have to stock up the fridge, just don't drink out in front. Lastly, there's a spare key for the front door under the register. Take it with you. That's about it," he said. "You can start Saturday, okay?"

"Okay," I said. "Mike's waiting for me in the back."

Mike was sitting on the stairs when I walked out the back

door. I had two beers, which I took out of the fridge, offered him one, and sat down beside him.

He looked apprehensive and nervous, taking deep drags on his cigarette.

"What's up?" I said, trying to sound cheerful, hoping to put him at ease.

"I got some news last night, and I don't know what to do or who I can talk to."

"You know you can always talk to me. Now, what's up?"

"Joyce's pregnant!" he blurted out.

"Wow!" I said. "How far is she?"

"About six weeks, give or take. Her father told her either to get married or leave the house."

"What do you wanna do?"

"I always knew we'd get married, but I don't know if I'm ready right now."

"I'm sure everything will work out, and you know I'm here for you. If there's anything you need from me, it's yours."

"Thanks," Mike said already with a look of confidence. "Just two things, though," he said, smiling a little.

"Shoot," I smiled back.

"First, I want you to be my best man, and second, if you could ask around and maybe get me in your department at work."

"Done," I said. "But why?"

"Can't work nights. Joyce's afraid to be alone at night."

"Okay, then, I'll see what I can do."

"You're the best," Mike said. "I'm gonna go tell Joyce the news."

We finished our beers and walked through the gangway to the front.

After a hug and handshake, Mike left. I turned and walked home, needing food and thinking about what had just happened.

Chapter 5

Friday

WE SAT IN THE BACKYARD AFTER OUR FRIDAY NIGHT GAME THE following week. I hadn't talked to or seen Molly for over a week. She wasn't at our games, and neither Jeannie nor Larry had mentioned anything to me.

As much as I wanted to see her, I was determined to keep my resolve and not get hurt again. I had lost count of how many times I'd heard, "Can't we be just friends!"

My train of thought was broken when Mike stood up and said too loudly, "I've got something to say." It wasn't like Mike, bringing attention to himself, so we all turned silently and listened.

He smiled a little sheepishly but with a twinkle in his eye and announced: "In two weeks, Joyce and I are getting married!"

So we celebrated our victory on the ball field and their engagement in the backyard.

Chapter 6

Saturday

WORKING SIX DAYS A WEEK IN THE MILL. OPENING AND closing the pool hall Saturday and Sunday, plus playing ball on Friday and Sunday, I didn't think I would have time to think about Molly. But how could I not think of somebody who had become so prominent a part of my everyday life? I wanted to see her so bad that I thought I would go nuts.

She was there as much as I tried to keep my mind occupied. Everywhere I went, I kept expecting to see her. I couldn't stop thinking of her, how it felt to hold her in my arms, and how she fit perfectly. It was all I could do, not to call or go to Jennie's house. A couple of times, I even drove by on the chance that she might be sitting outside. The only thing that kept me in place was that neither Jeannie nor Larry said she had mentioned me.

I felt empty, as if I was living in a shell. There was such an aching inside. I had a hard time sleeping and couldn't concentrate at work. I had become a wreck. The aching and longing seemed to get worse with each passing day. I knew that no matter what, I had to see Molly. Maybe I could tell her how I fucked up and could take back everything I had said.

She could tell me to "Get lost, go away, or it's too late," I didn't care. I just wanted to hear her voice again, even if she told me she was leaving next week. I had to take that chance.

I was sitting behind the counter, so deep into my reverie that I didn't hear Augie knocking on the big plate glass window. As I got up, I noticed it was 5:30am and time to open up.

"Hey,"

"Hey, Aug, what's up?"

"Just thought you might want to know that I talked to Davey Cinchler at work yesterday."

"And?" I asked, not knowing where this was going.

"And he said Tommy had come around a couple of days ago, and Molly was in the car with him."

I almost doubled over, as if someone had hit me in my stomach. I could hardly catch my breath.

"You all right?" he inquired, grabbing my arm.

"Yeah, gimmie a minute."

It took me a couple of minutes to get my bearings back, then I asked: "Are you sure?"

"He introduced Davey," Augie replied, "said she was his girlfriend."

Suddenly I realized my worst fears: I pushed her away, and now she was with Tommy. The worst thing was that I knew I couldn't compete with him.

Tommy had everything going for him, talent, good looks, plus a magnetic smile; he had it all over me.

We were interrupted by Lil Joe, Pete, Bobby, and Butch walking in and, after nodding, moved to the back table.

"I'll be at Barb's house, okay? I'll see you later."

"Later then," I said to his back as he walked out.

I was sitting behind the counter an hour later when Larry and Mike walked in and sauntered over to the counter. They both said, "Hey." I answered with my own, then motioned Mike over. "What's up?" he asked.

"Watch the place for a while. We're going in the back."

"Okay," he said.

"Let's go," I said to Larry, walking toward Rollie's apartment.

We got a few beers from the fridge, walked out, and sat on the stairs. After lighting our smokes, I turned to Larry and asked, "How come you didn't tell me about Molly being with Tommy?"

"I thought you didn't want to know."

"I did," I said in reply, "but now it's probably too late."

"I'm sorry," Larry said with a trace of sadness.

"It's all right, Lar," knowing how he was feeling. "It's all my fault."

We went back inside when we were done with our beer and cigarettes.

I was standing by the counter talking to Rollie when Larry came in, "Hey."

"What's up?"

"Must be Wednesday night, right?"

"Yeah, I guess. How's Jeannie?"

"I just took her home. She's alright."

"Looks like we got a wedding coming up soon.

"Yeah," Larry replied. "That's what happens when you go bareback."

"They were going to get married anyway. Just a little sooner than they expected."

Just then, the phone rang. Standing next to the booth, Pete called out, "I got it, Rollie," after a couple of seconds, poking his head out, he said, "It's for you, Larry."

"Can I take it in the back?"

"Yeah, okay," Rollie answered.

When Larry ducked into Rollie's apartment, I turned, looked at Pete, and asked, "Who was that?"

"Jeannie, she wanted to talk to Larry."

"Didn't he just take her home," Rollie asked, looking at me.

"Yeah," I looked at Rollie, "that's what he said. Maybe she forgot something."

"Maybe taking that ring out of his nose," he laughed.

"Give' um a break, Fat Man," trying to keep a straight face.

We both turned to see Larry standing in the doorway, motioning to me.

"What's up," I asked, sensing something had happened to Jeannie.

"Let's go out back, okay?" Larry asked, looking a little nervous.

I turned to Rollie, saying, "We'll be out back!"

"You got it, Flacco," he said. "Just shut the door."

Sitting on the stairs, lighting up a smoke, I broke the silence. "Is Jeannie all right?"

"It's not Jeannie. It's Molly."

"What'ya mean?" I said, getting a sinking feeling in the pit of my stomach.

"They were parked at Muttsen's Beach, making out when Tommy went a little too far."

"What'ya mean, too far," I said, starting to glimpse a red mist forming in front of my eyes.

"When Molly stopped him, he had his hand between her legs."

"That Mother Fucker," I almost shouted, the red getting brighter.

"He told her to get out of the car and just left her there."

"Is she still there?"

"No, she walked from Cal Park to 101st and Ewing, a place called Duke's 101 Pizza."

"You think he might be by Jerry's?"

"Why?"

"Because I'm gonna go beat the shit outa him."

"What'll that prove?" Larry insisted.

"I don't know, maybe just because."

"Because of what?" Now Larry had that little look of maybe knowing something. "I thought you weren't interested. You haven't called her in over a week."

"Right now, I'm a little confused, but I think I love her."

Now Larry was really smiling. "Wow!" he said. "That's great, but are you sure?"

"Yes, I am, you dumb fuck." Now I was smiling.

"I think maybe you should go get her."

"Yeah, I think I will. Besides, a friend of mine works there. I'll give him a call."

We walked back inside. I nodded to Rollie, stepped into the phone booth, looked up the number, and dialed the phone.

"Duke's Pizza," a voice said after the second ring.

"Is Alex Gleason working tonight?"

"Yeah," he said. "Hold on."

A couple of seconds later, Alex came on the line.

"Hello," he said. That's all it took to recognize his voice.

"Hey, Alex, it's me, Jesse."

"What's going on, Flacco? Long time no see."

"Listen, buddy, I need a big favor."

"You don't have to ask me, just tell me, you know that."

"Thanks, Al. I knew I could count on you."

"All the time, Flacco."

"So tell me, Al, is there a beautiful girl who looks a little nervous?"

"Yeah," he replied. "She looks like she's about ready to run out the front door. About fifteen minutes ago, she made a phone call to someone named Jeannie."

"I know," I said. "Just give her some pizza and a Pepsi while she waits for her ride."

"She's stunning, Jesse. I'd make a play myself if it was anybody but you."

"I really appreciate it, Al," I answered.

"Just do me a favor, alright," he intoned.

"Anything I can," I answered.

"Maybe you can bring her back one day, and we can split a pizza."

"I promise, Buddy. Just tell her to wait inside until her ride gets there."

"You got it, Jesse. See you when you get here."

"One last thing, Al, don't tell her it's me, okay?"

"You got it, Buddy."

"I'll explain everything when I get there."

"Don't forget, we close at midnight."

I didn't hear the last part, as I'd already hung up and was on my way outside. Ten minutes later. I turned off Ewing Avenue at 101st Street, parked at the curb, crossed the street, and stood looking through the open doorway.

They were sitting at a table against the wall. Molly had her back to me and didn't hear me come in. After motioning for Alex not to say anything, I stood next to Molly and addressed Alex.

"Hey, Alex, how's it going?"

"Alright, Flacco, good to see you."

Turning to Molly, who was looking up at me with surprise, "You all right?" I asked.

"I'm alright, but where's Larry?"

"I told him I'd take you home."

"Alex," Molly turned to him, "could you do me a favor?"

"Today must be my favorite day."

"Would you call a taxi for me?"

"I'll take you home," I said. "That's why I'm here."

"Thanks, Alex. I'll wait outside."

"What the fuck's going on, Flacco?" Alex asked as we watched Molly walk out the door.

"I'll explain it some other time, Al. Just hold off on the taxi, okay?"

Molly was standing about ten feet from the door when I walked out. She had her back to me, so she didn't notice when I walked up behind her and put my hand on her shoulder.

Jerking away, she whispered, "Don't," and walked a few feet away, turning to face me. With tears running down her cheeks, she asked, "Again, Jesse, why are you here?"

"I was worried about you."

"Seems like every time you say something, I ask, why?"

"Molly, I —"

"No, let me finish, you said that you would call, and we would talk about us, but you never called."

She turned, walked to the curb, and stopped directly under the street light. Seeing her standing there, Molly never looked more beautiful or vulnerable.

I stopped at her side and offered her my handkerchief. After wiping the tears away, she faced me with a questionable look, and I felt I had to say something.

"Can I at least take you home?"

She nodded, and we crossed the street to my car. Once inside, Molly turned and faced the side window. The half-hour drive seemed to take an hour.

Finally, we were parked in front of Jeannie's house.

"Can I ask you a question?" she asked, her voice choking on the words.

"Sure," I said, "you can ask me anything."

"Why didn't you get mad when Alex called you Flacco?"

"I've known Alex a lot longer than Tommy, so when he calls me Flacco, it's out of friendship, not as a put-down."

"So you think that's what Tommy meant?"

"Maybe, I don't know, but I've been friends with Tommy since I moved to South Deering, and he never once called me that."

"Why would he do it now?" she asked, her voice a little evener.

"I think he was trying to impress you."

Molly looked at me as though she was waiting for me to say something.

"One last thing before I go in, and I want you to be truthful, okay? Why did you come for me?" Now she had a determined tilt to her head, and her eyes were a little puffy from the tears, but she never looked more beautiful.

"I wanted to make sure you were all right, but I had to see you most of all."

"Again," Molly said, "why?"

"What do you want me to say?"

"Just how you feel, that's all."

"How I feel, okay," I said, "I'll tell you how I feel! When I saw you that Friday night, something came over me, it was a feeling I'd never felt before, and I knew right then that I would love you the rest of your life."

"You guys are all alike." There was a different tone to her voice, almost like a dismissal. "The last time someone told me he loved me, he had his hand between my legs."

"I can't believe you compare me with Tommy." Now I was getting mad. "That's not who I am."

"You're all after the same thing. I just thought you were different. I guess I was wrong."

With that, Molly opened the door, ran up to the front, and disappeared inside without looking back.

I lit up a Salem, turned the ignition, and pulled away from the curb. I don't remember driving home, but I found myself in the driveway with the garage door up.

After pulling in, I lit up another Salem and tried to figure out how something so good had turned sour.

Not being able to sleep didn't help. I kept thinking that maybe my inexperience with girls was why I kept doing and saying the wrong things.

6am came early that Thursday. After two cups of coffee and a couple of doughnuts, I went to work. Thursday and Friday passed in a blur, I was in no mood for playing ball Friday, and I told Rollie I would stay home Saturday and Sunday.

I am really hurting now. It's almost an ache. I don't know what I'm doing when I'm doing anything, anytime. I feel like an addict. I have to see her. It's like she's in my blood. I can't get her out of my mind.

It's been over a week, and I still can't sleep.

I think I'm losing weight. I don't think I've had a good meal since last week.

Chapter 7

WALKING IN THE FRONT DOOR FRIDAY AFTER WORK, SITTING
on the sofa, and kicking off my shoes, I reached over and
clicked on the TV. I was just in time to see the kids doing the
Stroll on *American Bandstand*.

My mother called out from the kitchen, "Are you gonna
eat today?"

"Yeah, Ma, I think I can eat something."

I didn't think I had much of an appetite, but once I took a
bite, the pork chop, beans, rice, and four tortillas were gone.

"It's good to see you eating again," my mom said with a
concerned look. "What's the matter? I hear you tossing and
turning every night, and you hardly eat anything. Is it about
Molly?"

"How do you know about Molly?"

"I talked to Larry," she said. "I was worried."

"Larry should learn to keep his mouth shut."

"They're all worried about you. They're your best
friends."

"I know, Ma, but I'll have to get through this alone."

"Just so you know, they're all behind you."

Tommy was in a left-field later that day. Our game was

against the Trumbull Blues, and he's their left fielder. I got a little payback, as we beat them 14 to 8, and he made the final out.

It's about 9:30pm. I'm on my third Salem. Mike is standing next to me, giving me an older brother look. "What?" I ask.

"When you gonna get your head outa your ass and get your shit together?"

"Fuck you, Mike!"

"Wouldn't you rather fuck her," he said. "Come on, get your head on straight."

We would probably be throwing punches if it was anyone else but Mike. "I'm sorry, Mike, I can't seem to get her outta my mind."

"You said it didn't work out, so just let it go."

"I wish it was that easy."

"You know me, Larry, and Augie would do anything to help. But you're gonna have to get through this on your own."

"By the way, where is Larry? I haven't seen him since I went to pick her up."

"I talked to him a couple of days ago. He and Jeannie want to spend some time together. I need another beer," Mike said, moving around to the front of the cooler.

I got up and opened the top. Mike took two beers out, offered me one, then turned and started walking back to where Joyce was sitting with Augie and Barb.

"Mike," I said.

He stopped and turned,

"Thanks," I said with a smile.

"Anytime, boss," was his reply.

Chapter 8

Thursday

I WAS STRETCHED OUT ON THE COUCH WATCHING *BAND STAND* when I heard the phone ring. I sat up, looked at my watch, and saw that it was 4:10pm, and it was starting to get dark. I grabbed the receiver and growled, "Yeah."

It was Augie asking, "You going up to Rollie's?"

"Yeah, as soon as I wash up. I'll see you in about an hour, okay?"

"See you then, boss."

Walking into Rollie's, I noticed Pete, Lil Joe, Butch, and Bobby at the back table, shooting pool. Fat Rollie was at his usual spot behind the counter.

I walked over and nodded, saying, "What's up?"

"Same old shit, Flacco, different day." He had a knack for talking with that unlit cigar never falling.

We both laughed as I turned and walked towards the back. After the "Hey, what's up?" I sat down, lit up a Salem, and watched the game. A couple of minutes later, Mike and Larry walked in, nodded to Rollie, and joined me at the table.

"Where's Augie?" was the first thing Mike asked.

"He should be here anytime now," was my reply.

As if on cue, Augie walked in, nodded to the Fat Man, walked over to the stick rack, declaring, "Whose partners?"

Friday evening, we played and lost our softball game, sat in Rollie's yard, drank our beer, and bullshitted about one thing or another until about 12 o'clock. After finishing the beer and one last cigarette, we called it a night. Once out front, everybody was going their separate way.

Mike was about to climb into his car when I called, "Hey, Mike, you got a minute?"

As I approached, he inquired, "What's up?"

"I've got something I want to ask you."

"Okay," he answered. "What's on your mind?"

"How come you, Augie, and Larry never call me Flacco out of all the guys?"

"I think that's because the four of us are closer, and just because the Fat Man gave you that name doesn't mean that we have to use it, and besides, I've never heard you call Larry or me Pollocks

"And what's with the 'boss' bullshit?"

"That's better than 'Flacco,' right, and you know you are between the four of us."

"You know, Mike, you're probably my best friend. I think I could trust you with my life."

"I know that," he said, "and I'll always have your back."

"Thanks, I'll never forget that."

We shook hands and gave each other a hug. Mike got in his car and drove off. As I neared the corner of 109th, I heard Augie come up behind me.

"Hey," he said, falling in step with me.

"What's up?" I inquired.

"I just got one thing to say and won't ever mention it again, okay?"

"Just one thing, Aug?" I laughed. "You always have a profound statement."

"Yeah." With a serious look, he suddenly turned and said, "I'm sorry it didn't work out between you and Molly."

"Thanks, Aug." I really appreciate giving him a hug.

"Anytime, boss." We both stood there, looking at each other, and I could tell he meant it.

With that, he turned and made his way back to his car. I walked over to the front steps, sat down, lit up a Salem, and pondered my situation.

I knew then that I loved Molly more than anything in my life. I wanted to see her so bad it was as if my insides had been torn out. But on the other hand, maybe, as hard as it would be, I should try and get over it. After all, she was leaving soon.

So with those troubling thoughts, I went upstairs and tried to get some sleep, which was not going to come easy that night. Every time I closed my eyes, I saw her face. It was so close I felt I could reach out and caress that beautiful smile. With pain and yearning, I knew that no matter what, I had to see her, explain how I felt and that it was wrong to say I loved her. I would apologize, never mention it again, and maybe we could try again.

The sky was between light and dark when I finally fell into a deep and dreamless sleep. I didn't even hear my mother coming into my bedroom later that night to check on me.

Chapter 9

Saturday

I STAYED HOME ALL SATURDAY, TRYING TO WORK UP THE courage to call Molly and argue my case. "What if she wouldn't talk to me," I thought. "What if she hangs up on me?" How would I get a chance to say anything? Maybe go over there and knock on the door? "Naw, fuck that!"

That was my thinking all day. Finally, after dinner with my mom, I stumbled into Rollie's. I sat down behind the counter, taking a pat on the back from the Fat Man on his way out.

Most of the guys were there, some shooting pool, a couple sitting out front, and the rest out back drinking beer. After about ten minutes, Augie came in through the back door, sat at the table next to the counter, and lit up a Winston.

"Where's Larry and Mike?" I asked, lighting up one of my Salems and blowing a plume of smoke.

"I talked to Larry earlier. He'll be here in a little while. Mike's with Joyce making plans for the wedding and their little getaway."

"Where's the wedding taking place?"

"They're going in front of a judge downtown, and they'll stay someplace close by."

"Well, that sucks," I said. "We'll have to find a place to throw them a little party. Right?"

"That sounds good, boss. Oh, here comes Larry now."

Larry, as usual, sauntered in and stood directly across from me.

"Where have you been?" I almost demanded.

"Whoa," Larry replied, "what the fuck is this?"

"I'm sorry, Lar, I feel I'm wound up a little tight."

"Jeannie and I decided we wanted to spend a little time together. Ever since her friend arrived, Jeannie's been taking her everywhere."

After everyone left, we closed up, turned off the big sign in the window, put the money away, along with the 45, and went outback for a beer and a smoke. We chitchatted, smoked, drank our beer, and talked about Mike's wedding.

Standing out front, I watched as Augie crossed the street to his car. Larry was parked a couple of houses down. I stopped him before he even started walking.

"It's okay to mention her name," with which we both smiled.

Chapter 10

Sunday

IF YOU DRIVE EAST ON 95TH STREET, GO OVER THE CALUMET River, past Ewing Avenue and Indianapolis Blvd. You'll drive right into Calumet Park, or as we called it, "Cal Park." It's on the east side and has 198 acres of grass, trees, scrubs, a big field house, and two beaches. It lies at the southwestern tip of Lake Michigan, and it's been our "swimming pool" since we were kids.

Foreman Drive is the northern boundary; East 102nd Street does the same at the southern end. Our games are played on the diamonds south of Foreman Drive.

That Sunday was a beautiful summer day, with the temperature in the mid-80s and just a slight breeze coming off the lake. I parked by the curb. I got my spikes out of the trunk and to where the guys were already starting our infield warm-ups. When Mike approached me, I sat down on the grass and put on my spikes.

"Hey, boss," he said. "Are you ready?"

"What the fuck, Mike? Why do you call me that?"

"Because," he said, getting serious, "even if you don't admit it, you know you are between the four of us."

"Do Augie and Larry feel that same way?"

"The three of us have talked. And even though they never say it, they're on the same page."

"Now, hurry up, and let's play some ball."

As Mike walked away, I was getting up off the grass when I noticed Larry and Jeannie walking across the field toward us. As they neared, I walked up to them, said "Hey" to Larry and gave Jeannie a little peck on the cheek.

She took my hand and led me away from the others. After about ten steps, she stopped, turned to me and said in a not-so-friendly tone, "Why haven't you called her?"

"Called who?" I said, trying to sound nonchalant.

"You know who," she said, "so don't try and act dumb."

"Look, Jeannie, I really messed up the other night. I said something that maybe I shouldn't have, and now I don't even know if I'll be able to talk to her again."

"Maybe," Jeannie said, "that's what she wants to talk to you about. We were up all that night, and after she stopped crying, she told me about it."

Molly told Jeannie she could not remember ever being that scared after Tommy left her alone in the park. Then she just walked, not knowing where she was going, and finally ended up at Duke's Pizza. Molly felt a little better after calling me. Knowing that Larry would pick her up, or how happy she was to see you standing behind her, with that worried look on your face, and asking if she was all right.

"Everything was going good," Jeannie said, "until you told her how you felt. Did you really tell her you loved her?"

"Yeah," I said, "but I didn't mean it that way."

"You know I wasn't just looking for a piece of ass."

"Well, she knows that now," she said, "so why don't you tell her."

"Okay," I said, "I'll call her after the game, okay?"

"Why don't you tell her right now? She's sitting in Larry's car."

"What!" I almost shouted, then I turned and could barely make out someone sitting in the back seat. "Really," I said.

"Go talk to her," Jeannie said, giving me a little shove.

"Mike," I yelled. "Come here!"

"What's up?" he asked, walking up to me.

"Take my place at 1st base."

"For how long?"

"As long as you want," I said. "Just don't fuck up."

I turned and took about ten steps when I started getting that feeling in the pit of my stomach. I was nervous as hell, and my mouth was full of cotton. "What do I do? What do I say?" without making a complete fool of myself. I looked up to see her get out and walk around the car.

She looked (if it was possible) more beautiful than I remembered. As we drew closer, I noticed that her long chestnut hair was pulled back into a ponytail, with a whisper of bangs across her forehead. We both stopped at the park bench; she was in the front, and I was in the back.

She said, "Hi," but I don't honestly think I heard. I was too busy looking at this most beautiful girl standing on the other side of the bench, smiling at me. I was drinking it all in, the high cheekbones, with just a dusting of freckles across the bridge of her nose. Her full lips didn't need any lipstick. The piercing blue eyes and the breasts that sat high up on her chest made her sleeveless top seem a little tight.

She noticed my ogling and said, "Hi," again.

I swallowed the mouth full of cotton and croaked, "Hi." My heart was beating like a bass drum, and I still didn't know what to say. Molly sat down on the bench, and I followed her lead, close but not too close.

She turned to me as I sat down. She was holding her hands in her lap and kept switching the left, holding the right, then the right, holding the left.

I wondered if she was as nervous as I was, so I asked, "How are you?"

"I think I'm alright, though I'm a little nervous now."

"Why are you nervous?"

"Jesse, look," she said, "I'm almost eighteen years old, and I have these feelings that I don't know what to do about."

"If it's my fault, I am sorry. I don't know how you feel about me, but I meant every word I said."

"I know that now," Molly said, "even though we've only known each other for a couple of weeks, I want us to get to know each other because I want to be with you. I'm happy when we're together. But I don't want to say anything that I might regret, so maybe we can start again a little slower, okay?"

"Okay," I replied, thinking, "Here we go again, just friends."

She held out her hand and said, "Hi, I'm Mary Catherine Malone. My friends call me Molly."

I took her hand and said, "I'm Jesse Cruz. My friends call me Flacco." With that, we both laughed, shook hands, looked into each other's eyes, and found something that made us hold on to each other's hands a little longer. I just couldn't keep my eyes off her face.

"Why do you look at me that way?" Molly asked.

"Because I can't believe how someone as beautiful as you wants to be with me."

"If you don't stop putting yourself down, I'll have to do something."

"Oh," I said, "and what's that?"

All of a sudden, before I knew it, we were kissing. Molly had the softest lips. When we were finally apart, we both opened our eyes slowly. She looked at me with that beautiful smile and said, "Now will you believe me and stop that?"

"Okay, boss, whatever you say." I couldn't believe what had just happened. I felt so excited. I just wanted to kiss her again, which was what I was about to do when I heard Augie call me.

"Come on," I said, getting up from the bench and holding out my hand.

We were walking back, holding hands, when Augie said: "You gotta go in now. Mike hurt his thumb."

"Is it bad," I asked.

"Naw," he said, "he just caught the ball wrong, and it pushed his thumb back."

"You all right?" I asked Mike, standing off the first base line holding his hand.

"I don't think it's broken. I can still move it a little."

I turned back to Molly, who was standing with Larry and Jeannie.

"Hold these for me, okay?" I said and handed her my car keys and my school ring.

"Okay," Molly said, "I guess I can stay and watch the game."

I walked up to her, gave her my ring and keys, then whispered in her ear, "You can stay as long as you want."

"You mean that?" she asked.

"Yeah, boss," I whispered, then ran out to the first base.

It was the fifth inning, and I was pretty sweaty when I stood next to Molly. We were holding hands when all of a sudden, she laid her head on my shoulder. I don't know if it was the shampoo or hair spray, but I just loved the smell of her hair. I looked down at her face, and she looked so happy, and when she smiled, I thought I could never be this lucky to have a beautiful girl, who I just couldn't stop looking at, like me.

"You shouldn't be standing so close to me," I said.

"Why?" was her reply, letting that smile slip a little.

"I'm all sweaty, and I probably smell."

"Well," she said, "I don't mind if you don't mind." (The smile was back).

I got to bat twice before the game ended, with the final score of 13 to 6 in our favor. We talked Mike into going to South Chicago Hospital and having his thumb checked. Augie and Barb were going to her house. I was picking up my spikes when Larry and Jeannie walked up to us.

"Hey, Jesse," Larry said, "would you mind taking Molly back to the house? We're going to take my mom out to dinner, okay?"

"Is that all right with you?" I asked her.

"Sure," Molly said with a smile, "I think I can trust you."

Larry and Jeannie walked away toward his car. I looked at Molly, who was just getting my car keys from her pocket, handed them to me, turned and started walking toward my car.

"Hey, didn't you forget something?"

"Oh, I'm sorry," she said, pulling the chain from under her top. On it was a small crucifix and my ring.

"That's all right," I said, "it looks better on you."

"But if you think it's too soon," I understand. "I don't want you to feel like I'm rushing you."

She walked up to me and took my hand in hers. I dropped my spikes as she took my other hand.

"I was hoping you'd say that," Molly said, then she reached up and gave me another soft, sweet kiss.

This kiss had a little more urgency to it. She came into my arms as easily as putting on a pair of well-worn gloves, and feeling Molly up against my body was almost more than I could stand.

Feeling her breasts against my chest, her leg in between mine, I didn't want the kiss to end. But when it did, she looked at me with a dreamy expression and said, "Wow!"

I could still feel her against me, so I had to ask, "Where'd you learn to kiss like that?"

"I don't know," she said, "I guess it just comes naturally. You didn't do too bad yourself."

"I thought we were going to take it slow."

"We are," Molly said, looking at me with a mischievous smile. We smiled as I bent down, picked up my spikes, and held hands. We walked to my car.

Sitting in my car and turning the ignition, I asked: "Do you have to be back right away?"

"What did you have in mind?' she said.

"I just want to show you something."

"Is it far?" Molly asked.

"No," I said, "it's here in the park."

"It's not the submarine races 'cause it's a little too early."

"I told you before, Molly, I'm not Tommy!"

When I turned to her, she saw that the expression on my face had changed.

"I'm sorry," she said. "I promise I'll never mention it again. I made a mistake. I'm sorry, okay?"

"It's all right," I said. "Come on, I'll take you back now."

She looked at me with a sad and confused look. "This isn't going to work out for us?"

"I don't think so, Molly," I said. "One minute, we're happy and can't keep our hands off each other, and the way you kiss makes me feel that this is really happening, but I don't think you trust me all that much. You know, Molly, I really care for you, and I'm not just trying for a quick piece. When we first met, I had difficulty figuring out why a beautiful girl like you would want anything to do with me. Look, we've only known each other for a couple of weeks, but ever since the first time I saw you, I felt something inside me that I never felt before."

I couldn't figure out why I was saying this. I was pushing Molly away when all I wanted to do was take her in my arms. I turned to look at her, but she was looking out the front wind-shield. Then she turned, faced me and said, "This is the first time anyone has ever told me that he loved me, other than

Tommy, and now I know he didn't really mean it," Molly said. "When I'm with you, I get a feeling inside that's hard to explain. I want to be with you because I'm happy. You make me smile. I love that crooked smile and how you laugh at yourself, but I don't know if I'm ready for anything serious right now."

"Okay," I said. "Now that we got that out of the way, maybe we can just do a little dating."

"That's not what I meant," Molly said.

"I know," I replied. "You'll be going home in a couple of months, so I didn't want you to say something you might want to take back. But just know this, my feelings for you will never change."

I put the car in gear and pulled away from the curb. When we got to the corner of Foreman Drive and Crilly Avenue, I stopped at the stop sign and turned to look at her. She was beautiful with the ponytail, the bangs, and the most beautiful legs I'd ever seen. Instead of going straight to 95th Street, I turned left, and after going about a block and a half, I pulled up along the curb.

"Come on," I said. I got out of the car and waited for her.

"Where are we going?" she asked.

"Just trust me this once, okay?"

She got out and gave me her hand as we crossed the street. Walking over a short grass space, we came to the sidewalk fronting the beach. There were benches all along the walkway, and we sat down.

"Just so you know, this is what I wanted to show you? I like to come here and just look at the water. Sometimes there might be one of those ore boats out there. It's even better now with the weather. There's nobody swimming."

"Where I live, you have to go to the coast to see anything like this," she said.

I reached my chest before realizing I still had my uniform on. "Shit."

"What's the matter? Molly asked.

"My cigarettes are in the car," I said, getting up.

"Wait!" Molly said, taking her sandals off and walking to the low wall that lined the beach.

She jumped down onto the sand and ran to the shore.

With my slip-ons and socks in hand, I jumped down and ran to where she was standing. Seeing her standing there with the water lapping at her feet was breathtaking.

"Let's walk a little, okay?" she said.

She took my hand, and we strolled until we reached the pier. Molly turned back, "I can see why you like it here. It's so quiet and calm." We didn't say much on the way back. I helped her up the low wall where she sat to put her sandals back on.

"I'm glad you showed me the beach," she said.

"Well, it ain't the submarine races, but I like it here."

"How many times do I have to say I'm sorry!" Molly said.

"Now, I guess it's my turn. What I said was stupid."

She looked at me with a sad, almost melancholy look saying, "Why do you keep pushing me away?"

"I don't know," I said. "Maybe because you don't feel the same about me. I know you said you like me, but that's like saying 'we could be good friends,' and I don't feel I could do that."

"I never meant it like that," Molly said. "Right now, I can't explain the feelings I have for you, but whatever they are, they're not just good friends. I don't feel like that when you hold me in your arms or when we kiss. I mean, it almost takes my breath away."

"Couldn't we just be together until then and see what happens?"

"No, Molly," I said. "The more we're together, the worse I'll feel. You'll go back home, to your life, and forget all about me."

"You're wrong, Jesse," she said. "No matter what happens, I'll never forget you."

With that, she turned and looked out the side window. Her reflection told me she was quietly sobbing.

"I don't have a handkerchief with me this time, putting my hand on her shoulder."

"Why do you always make me cry?" she asked, turning to face me.

"I don't do it on purpose," I said, feeling like a real jerk. "It's the last thing I want to do. I think it's time I took you back."

We drove out of the park, went west to Stoney Island, turned north, and drove to 84th Street. All the way there, she sat huddled against the door and never once looked at me. Parking at the curb, I was about to get out when she said, "It's alright." Got out and almost ran to the front door.

After she went in, I sat there, thinking, "What the fuck did I do?" We were just holding hands, walking on the beach, splashing each other, and now she couldn't wait to get out of the car. I turned the ignition on and was about to pull away from the curb when I saw Jeannie come out and walk over to the car.

"What did you say to her?" she asked, almost angrily.

"Why?" I said.

"Because she's upstairs crying her eyes out, that's why," she said.

"Look, Jeannie, I never meant to make her cry. I would never do that. I thought we both agreed that it wouldn't work out for us."

"Why," Jeannie asked, "because she didn't say she loved you?"

"How do you know about that?" I asked. "Did she tell you?"

'Yes, she did. Even though it scared her, she still wanted to see you. She also told me about her feelings for you, then I said to her that's the way I felt about Larry."

"Maybe, I can go and apologize?"

"I don't think she wants to talk to you right now," Jeannie said.

"Okay," I said, "then I'll call her later."

"Not right now," she said. "Just give her a little time."

Her tone was a little softer, so I decided to leave it there. "Tell her I'm sorry," I said and pulled away from the curb.

Chapter 11

Wednesday

IT'S BEEN ALMOST TWO WEEKS SINCE THAT NIGHT. I HAVEN'T called or tried to see Molly because I didn't know how to go about it. Molly hasn't been to any of our games.

Anyone who says "Time Heals All Wounds" is full of shit. I felt lost and out of place. Larry, Augie, and Mike did all they could to try and cheer me up. They even took me to East Gary, Indiana, and got me laid (it didn't work). I couldn't stop thinking about her and how I had "fucked things up."

Chapter 12

Saturday 27th

It was now Saturday night, the day before my birthday. We were all in the pool hall. Most were shooting pool or standing around watching. I was behind the counter, with Augie and Mike sitting nearby. 10:30pm, Larry came in, walked to the counter, and sat at the same table after all the hi's.

I wanted to talk to Larry, so I asked Augie and Mike to watch the counter. We were in the backyard, and after we both lit up, Larry asked: "What's up?"

"I don't know," I said. "Why don't you tell me?"

"What do you want me to say?" Molly hasn't said anything to me; I don't know if she said something to Jeannie, but Jeannie told me she's looking to get an earlier flight home.

"I'm sorry, Jesse."

"You didn't tell her it was my birthday tomorrow, did you?

"No," Larry said, "but I think Jeannie told her."

"Shit," I said. "Let's go back inside."

Chapter 13

Sunday 28th

SUNDAY AFTER THE GAME, WE GATHERED IN THE BACKYARD. The guys were all there, with their girlfriends and some with their wives.

Everyone pitched in, and we had some Heinies, shrimp, chicken, and French fries. Fat Rollie donated the beer, and his wife even baked me a birthday cake. We had a good time, eating and drinking. Even Fat Rollie wished me a Happy Birthday with a beer. (He doesn't usually drink.)

At about 8:30 that night, Larry and Jeannie walked into the backyard. Larry walked over to the cooler to get a beer. Jeannie approached me, handed me a box and said, "Happy Birthday."

"Thanks, Jeannie," I said.

"It's not from me. It's from Molly."

"What? Are you sure," I said, a little shocked.

Inside the box was a small bell jar filled with what looked to be sand. Taped to the jar was a white paper with writing, "Our Place."

"How'd she get this?" I asked, looking at both Jeannie and Larry.

"We took her!" Larry said with a big smile. "Read the note," Jeannie urged.

The note was just a folded sheet of paper. On it was written, "Happy Birthday, Flacco. Love, Molly." I couldn't believe what I was reading. "Did she really mean LOVE?" Standing up, I looked around the yard, finally settling back on Larry and Jeannie.

"She's not here?" I asked.

They looked at each other with big smiles; finally, Jeannie said, "She's out front." It felt as if I was out front and looking both ways in two steps. Glancing across the street, I saw her standing next to Larry's car. She had both hands at her mouth and seemed to be scared. I ran across the street, mindless of traffic, and walked around Larry's car.

She was standing there, looking at me, and me looking at her. She never looked more beautiful. We stared at each other for what seemed an eternity. When I couldn't stand it anymore, I walked up to her. "Hi," I said. She didn't say anything. She just walked into my arms and held me as tight.

"I love you, Molly," I said, kissing the top of her head.

"I know," she said. "It's taken a little while to realize and understand my feelings, but I know now that I love you too." We kissed then. First, it was sweet, turning into a deep, soul-searching meeting of lips. It was as though we both understood the meaning of what was said and felt.

Next, we were holding hands and looking into each other's eyes. Molly's eyes told me that she meant everything she said.

The way she was looking at me now, she looked like someone older than the last time I saw her. She didn't look 17 anymore, and I loved her even more.

"I missed you," I said, almost choking on the words. "I wanted to call you so many times and tell you that I didn't care when you were going back. I just wanted to see you and be with you as much as I could?"

"Jesse," Molly said, "I've been miserable the last couple weeks. The first week, I tried to get over what you said, but then I realized what Jeannie, Barb, Joyce, and even Jeannie's mom said was right that what happened with Tommy scared me. I had that trust in them and what they felt when they were told the same thing. The three of them told me how they'd known you for a long time, that you were nothing like Tommy. How sweet and kind you were, that you would never take advantage of me and do anything to hurt me."

She was squeezing my hands now and saying something I'll never forget for the rest of my life. I guess I didn't know it then. The same thing happened to me the first night we met. "I'll repeat it just so you'll be sure. I love you, Jesse."

I stood there like someone who didn't know the language and couldn't put two words together. Here I was, the master of the ad-lib, the teller of jokes, standing there as if I was deaf and dumb.

When I saw her smiling, I finally asked her, "What do you mean, Our Place?"

"From now on, that will always be our special place. You don't mind, do you?"

"Anything you say, boss," my face lit up with a big smile. "Now, let's go get a beer."

Crossing the street now, I had to be more mindful of the traffic; after all, Molly said she loved me and knew I loved her.

After the beer and food were gone, we were all standing in front of the pool hall. When Molly took hold of my hand. I felt the pressure of my school ring on her finger. We looked at each other. I could see the love in her eyes and the warmth of her hand in mine.

"I liked it better on the chain," I said. "It was closer to your heart."

"Really?" Molly said. "I thought when you went steady,

you wore it on your finger."

"I like it on the chain," I said, "because it's the first place you put it when I gave it to you."

Everyone except Barb, Augie, Jeannie, and Larry had left. Fat Rollie was locking the front door and turning off the sign. Larry turned to Molly, saying, "You ready to go?" Before she could answer, I said, "I'll take her home."

Before I could say anything else, Molly was already walking towards my car. "I'll see you guys later," I said, then turned and started walking to the car. About halfway there, I felt someone pulling my arm back. I saw it was Jeannie. She looked at me with a rather serious expression and said, "Jesse, do yourself a favor and don't fuck this up. She really cares about you."

I could tell by the look on her face and the tone of her voice she was saying something that I already knew. "I won't," I said and got into the car. When we stopped for the red light at 106th and Torrence, Molly turned and asked: "Are you ambidextrous?"

"Ambi-what?" I said.

"It means you can drive with either hand," she said.

"Yeah, I think so."

"Great!" she said, and slid over next to me, put my arm around her shoulder, and rested her head on my shoulder.

When we were parked in front of Jeannie's house, I asked her, "Do you have to go in now?"

"Do you want me to?"

"The way I feel now, Molly, I don't ever want this day to end."

We looked at each other, and I kept thinking to myself, how did I get to be so 'lucky' to have someone as beautiful as Molly want to be with me, let alone say she loved me. I pulled her in close and pressed my mouth to hers. She pressed right back. We kissed again, only this time it was short and sweet.

"I need a cigarette," I said, taking my Salem Menthols

from my shirt pocket and lighting up.

Exhaling a long plume of smoke, I turned the radio on, settling back on the seat. Molly took my arm and placed it on her shoulder. She cuddled up against me again. I took another drag on my cigarette, and that's when Dick Biondi's voice talked about "Skating Parties and Pizza." Taking my last drag, I flipped it out the window. Molly's eyes were closed, and she looked very peaceful.

"You sleeping?" I asked, almost afraid to move.

"No," she replied, lifting her head. "I like to cuddle."

When the commercial ended, he came back and, in a soft, soothing voice, said, "Here's one's for all you young lovers out there. It's the Satins with their big hit, "In The Still of The Night."

In The Still of The Night /, I held you,
Held you tight / cause I love, love you so
Promise I'll never let you go / In The Still of The Night,
I remember that night in May / the stars were bright above,
I'll hope, and I'll pray / to keep your precious love
Well, before the light / hold me again with all of your might
In The Still of The Night.

Somewhere between the "Doo-Wops" and the "Sax Solo," we were in each other's arms, holding as tightly as we could. Looking at each other, Molly, with tears in her eyes and me with a big lump in my throat, I still managed to croak, "You all right?"

"Yeah, I think so," was her reply.

"Are you sure?"

"If you stop squeezing me so tight," she said, "I think I'll be all right."

I couldn't stop looking at her and wondering what this beautiful girl was doing with me. As if to answer, she was in my arms again, searching for and finding my lips. We went at it again, only this time, it seemed we wanted to get to the same place. Our tongues danced to a rhythm, first in her mouth, then in mine. Hands were all over each other, seeking some-place to hold.

Finally, I took her hand and placed it on my crotch. She gave a little jerk and pulled her hand away. With that, I sat back and lit up another Salem. I was trying to calm down as I took another drag.

Glancing over at Molly, I noticed she was looking down at her lap, where she kept flicking her fingers. I was at a loss for words. Not knowing what to say or do, never been in this posi-tion before.

When she finally glanced at me, she had a hurt look, and I thought she was about to jump out of the car and run inside, and I'd never see her again. I kept thinking, "How do I make this right again?" I knew I had to do or say something.

I didn't know if she would believe me, but I had to tell her how I felt.

"I'm sorry, Molly," I said, taking her hand in mine. "I didn't mean for that to happen."

She put her other hand over mine and, looking at me with those beautiful blue eyes, said very softly, "It's all right, Hon. Don't worry about it.

"But I said I would never—what did you call me?"

"Hon," she said. "It's short for honey."

"I've never had anyone call me that before."

"Well," Molly said, "I like it better than Flacco."

"So do I, and what I was saying is what I told you before, that I would never try and make you do anything you didn't want to do."

She was getting her voice and composure back, and I could tell she was more or less back in control.

"I know what you said, but I keep thinking that if we keep going, I'm afraid I could get pregnant, and then what would happen?"

"Molly," I said, "if that were to happen, the best thing for me is that you would marry me.

"I'm only seventeen, and I still have to go back home and start college in September," she said.

"Do you want to go back?" I asked.

"Right now, I don't know," Molly said. 'I have all these feelings inside, pulling me in all directions, but the one feeling that I know now is that I love you, and I don't think that will ever change."

"You really mean that don't you," I said.

"Hon," she said, "could you turn off the radio? There's something I want you to know."

"Sure," I said, turning the knob, cutting off The Del Vikings singing "Come Go With Me."

"You have to promise not to say anything till I'm done, alright?"

I didn't know where this was going, so I said, "Okay." I felt at a loss for words, and not knowing what to say, I decided to just go along and hear her.

We sat there holding hands for what seemed like hours. Finally turning those big beautiful blue eyes at me, Molly said quietly, "I'm a virgin, and right now, I'm a little nervous and scared. I've never gone this far with anyone before." Her eyes never left my face, and I knew by the look on her face that she was telling me the truth.

"I've never French kissed anyone before."

"Never had anyone touch me the way you did."

"Never wanted to touch anyone before."

What Molly told me made me feel a little ashamed of myself. Here was the most beautiful girl I'd ever known, telling me how much in love she was, and I was trying to get a quick fuck.

Molly continued, "When you held my breast, rubbed my ass, and had your hand between my legs, I had all these different feelings inside. I knew more than anything in this world that I wanted them there. They were the most beautiful and wonderful feelings I've ever had."

She stopped there, looking at me as if she was waiting for me to say something when I didn't. She continued. "I've never seen a man's, let alone feel it. I was a little shocked and surprised. I didn't know what to do."

I looked at Molly, trying to gauge whether she was telling the truth, but one look at her face answered any doubts.

"You're telling me you've never seen a man up close!"

"I've seen pictures, but that's all," she said.

"Wow," I said. "That's kind of hard to believe!" (Boy, did I fuck that up.)

Sitting up straight and letting go of my hands, she asked, "Why, Jesse? Because I'm not like all the other girls, you know?"

"I don't know a lot of girls, and I'm sorry I said that."

"Are you really, really sorry, Jesse?"

"Yes, I am, Molly. You know, sometimes I open my mouth and then put my foot in, but I've never said that to you and didn't mean it. Look, Molly, I know I've said it before, and I'll say it as often as I have to. I love you, Mary Catherine Malone, and if you let me, I'll love you for the rest of your life!"

I had my arm on the front seat, so she had no trouble sliding over and snuggling next to me. Right then, I felt like the luckiest man alive. Molly had her feet tucked on the front seat, and with the shorts she had on, I couldn't help but notice her beautiful long legs. She was starting to tan, which made them all the more beautiful.

With the side of her face pressed against my chest, I hear Molly say very softly, "I'm glad I told you."

"You didn't have to," I said.

"Yes, I did," she said, looking directly at me.

"Why?" was all I could think of to say.

With her head back against my chest, she said: "I want

you to know who and what I am, and if you want to, we can do it here in the car."

While she was talking, she was moving her hand up my thigh.

"Molly, please stop!" I almost shouted. "Please."

"What's the matter?" she said. "Don't you want to?"

"More than anything in my life, but not like this, in the back seat. You mean much more to me than that."

"I'm so glad you said that," Molly said.

"You mean you would have done it, even if you didn't want to."

"Yes," she said, "if that's what you wanted."

"Why?" I asked, trying to understand.

"Because I get this tingling sensation when I'm in your arms and kissing you, and when you touch me, I almost lose control."

"I know what you're saying. I get a little excited myself."

"Yeah," she said. "Rubbing my crotch, I can tell."

"Molly," I pleaded, "you're only getting me more excited."

I lit up a Salem and blew out some smoke. I turned to her, trying to control myself, which wasn't easy, and said, "Molly, I want you to know that right at this minute, there's nothing more in this whole world that I want than to take you in the back seat. I'm a little nervous because I know you don't want to, and most of all, I'm afraid that you'll go back and later on, I hear that you had a baby, and I'm not ready for that."

"I am, too," Molly replied, almost with a sigh of relief. "Jesse," she took hold of my hands, "I was so sure I wanted to do it. I've had these feelings about how it would feel to have you inside me, to kiss you, and to be able to touch and hold each other. I thought I wanted it enough to even think about what might happen. I'm so glad that we were able to stop."

"Jesse," she continued, "we're both young and have our whole life ahead of us. We both know what our feelings are. Right now, I have to go back because of my age. Next year in

February, I'll be eighteen and be able to choose what I want to do."

"Do you think?" I asked stupidly, "maybe we should slow down and not be together so much."

"Don't you want to see me?" Molly asked tentatively.

"I didn't mean it that way. It's hard for me to be with you and not want to kiss and hold you."

"I know, Hon," she said. "I feel that same way."

"I'm gonna try, but I can't guarantee anything."

"Well, I'm glad to hear that," she announced.

"Come on," I said. "I'll walk you to the door."

We both got out, met on the sidewalk, and, holding hands, sauntered to the front door.

"Come inside," Molly said, pulling me inside. She didn't have to stand on the first step to give me a good night kiss; she was the right height.

"I'll dream about you and what we almost did."

"Why?" I asked, a little puzzled.

"Because I love you and want you to be happy."

"I'm happy just being with you. Everything else is a bonus."

We held hands and stared at each other until I couldn't keep it anymore and had to smile.

"I beat you again." She finally smiled. "Jesse," she said, "I hope you don't mind that I called you Hon."

"I always liked the sound of it, okay?"

She was halfway up the stairs when I stopped her with "Good night, Hon. I'll call you tomorrow after work."

Molly turned and, once again with that beautiful smile, blew me a kiss and mouthed, "I love you."

I walked back to my car, not really feeling the ground under my feet. Once inside, I lit up a Salem, started the car, and sat thinking, "How did I get this lucky?" Then I drove home, not really knowing how I got there.

Chapter 14

Monday

I DON'T KNOW HOW I GOT THROUGH EIGHT HOURS OF WORK Monday. I walked around like a fucking zombie, surprised I didn't get hurt or even killed. Finally, it was three o'clock, and I almost ran all the way, not even stopping at the pool hall.

Walking through the front door, I said "Hi" to my mom, walked to the front room, sat on the couch, and picked up the phone. As I dialed Jeannie's number, I kept thinking, "What do I say to her after last night."

On the third ring, I heard Jeannie's voice on the other end. "Hi, Jeannie," I said, "Is Molly there?"

"She's here."

"Can I talk to her?"

"Hold on."

When I heard Molly's voice, I closed my eyes and got the image of her sitting in my car.

"Hi," I said, "how are you?"

"All right, I guess," she said a little tentatively.

"Molly," I said, "what's the matter?"

"Nothing, I'm just not feeling so hot today."

"It's not about what happened last night, is it?"

"No," Molly said, "I would never—I mean."

"Can I come over?"

"I wish you wouldn't."

"I just want to see you."

"You wouldn't want to see me right now. I don't have any makeup on and am still in my pajamas.

"You know that doesn't matter to me."

"Would it be all right if we just stayed inside?

"Whatever you want is all right with me."

"Okay then, if you want, we can watch TV."

"I'll be there at about six o'clock, okay?"

"See you later then. Oh, hold on a minute. Jeannie wants to tell you something."

I could hear a little shuffling on the other end, and Jeannie was on the phone.

"Jesse, I know you want to see her, but she's not feeling that good right now."

"Is she sick or something?"

"No," Jeannie said, with a little laugh in her voice. "She got her period last night and has some cramps."

I still want to see her," I said. "So, I'll be there about 6 o'clock, okay?"

"All right," Jeannie answered, and with that, we both hung up.

After last night, I didn't think I would be nervous about seeing her, but I was by the front door, hoping I wouldn't show how anxious I really was.

I was so relieved when Jeannie's mom opened the door and invited me in.

"Hello, Jesse," she smiled. "How are you?"

"Fine, Mrs. Goodman," and, "How are you?"

'I'm good," she replied. "Mr. Goodman is in the front room." Walking away, she said over her shoulder, "I'll tell Molly you're here."

Irving Goodman was sitting in his usual spot, in front of the TV, watching the six o'clock news.

"Hi, Mr. Goodman. How are you?"

"Fine, Jesse, come on in and have a seat."

Before I could sit down, Mrs. Goodman, followed by Molly, entered the front room.

"Hi," she said, sounding a little timid. She never looked more beautiful. Even without makeup, her hair pulled back into a ponytail, Philly's T-shirt, and a pair of shorts, I couldn't take my eyes off her.

"Hi," I said. "How ya feeling?"

"All right," she answered. "We were just about to order a pizza. Are you hungry?"

After the pizza and a couple of Pepsis, we found ourselves in the front seat of my car.

"How come you didn't say it was your period."

"I wasn't feeling that great, and I didn't want you to see me like this."

"Now, who's acting like a kid," I chided her.

"What'ya mean?" she retorted, giving me a little shove.

"I remember a black eye and a split lip," I smiled.

She looked at me with the beginning of a smile and asked, "How do you do it?"

"Do what?" I asked, lighting one of my Salems.

"No matter how bad I feel, you always make me feel better."

"It must be my million-dollar personality." I smiled.

"And don't forget the good looks," Molly said, the smile becoming fuller.

"Do you think you'll be feeling better by Saturday?"

"I think so. Why?"

"Because I've something planned."

"Is it a surprise?"

"No, just someplace I'd like to take you."

"You mean," she said, "just the two of us?"

"Yeah," I said, "unless you want to invite Larry and Jeannie?"

"Okay, then, just the two of us."

Molly then looked at me with a very somber face saying, "Would you hurry up and put your arms around me."

Snuggling in, she whispered, "You know you never have to ask."

I never could get over the smell of her hair or the feel of her against me. I was barely hanging on, not knowing just what to do. I was lost in my thoughts when Molly lifted her head, then reached up and brought mine down.

Although it started as a soft kiss, she pulled back and, with a mischievous smile, said, "You can do better than that." We kissed again, only this time it was more intimate.

We were interrupted by the headlights of a car pulling up behind us. Looking in the rearview mirror, I could see Jeannie and Larry laughing behind us.

Before Jeannie and Larry got out of his car, Molly looked at me with the most loving look and whispered softly, "I love the way you kiss me!"

"You make it easy," I choked.

"I guess it's time I went in," she stated.

"Just a couple of minutes, okay?"

Larry and Jeannie were walking towards the house, so I had to ask, "I thought you didn't want to see me because of last night."

"How many times do I have to tell you! I said what I said not because I was pressured but because of my feelings for you. Look, Hon, I don't know if what I feel is love. I'm not even sure I know what love is. I only know how I feel when you kiss and hold me. I've kissed a few guys and seen the guys in high school, who my friends thought were hot, but I never felt anything, even with Tommy.

"Not until that night in the backyard at Rollie's pool hall. I didn't know why, but I felt attracted to you. Whenever you looked at me, I thought, 'Why do I have this stupid smile on my face.' After the first beer, and we started talking, I knew I wanted to be with you. I've never had that feeling before. There was never any doubt about how I felt. I just didn't know how strong those feelings would get."

"Are they as strong as I hope they are?"

"Maybe with a little encouragement, they could be."

We sat there for a couple of heartbeats, and I couldn't take my eyes off her. I sat there, holding her hands, trying to think of something to say.

"I really have to go in now," Molly said softly, reaching for the handle.

"Okay," I said. "Come on."

Soon we were standing at the foot of the stairs, and she turned to me and asked, "After everything I've said, you don't have anything to say." She had a somber and severe look, so I knew I would have to carefully choose what I would say to her. I was confident that knowing myself the way I did, I would open my mouth and stick my foot in. I also knew that what I was to say would put me at a crossroads as far as my feelings for Molly went.

I took her hands in mine and said, "Mary Catherine Malone, I love you."

With tears running down both cheeks, all she said before coming into my arms was, "Oh, Jesse, are you sure?"

"More than anything in my life," I finally expelled.

We clung to each other for a couple of minutes. I could feel Molly trembling against me, could hear her sobs.

"Why are you crying?"

"I never thought I could ever be this happy."

We looked at each other as if we could understand what we were thinking. Finally, we kissed, no tongue dancing, our arms just holding on. It was a warm and tender meshing of lips, conferring the love that we had expressed to each other.

I grabbed her shoulders, gently turned her around, and whispered, "Go to sleep. I'll call you tomorrow."

Walking out the front door, I stopped, lit up a Salem, then continued to my car. All the way home, I kept saying to myself, "She loves me."

Chapter 15

7/4/1959

BEING UP SINCE 6AM, I COULDN'T WAIT TO CALL MOLLY. I hadn't seen her since Monday night and was anxious just to see her. Talking on the phone is excellent, but it doesn't compare to seeing her. I love hearing her voice on the phone, how she laughs or calls me "Hon."

I can picture her holding the phone, with those blue eyes and a beautiful smile, but most of all, she is talking to me. These last four days have taken a toll on me.

I know now that I love her, but I'm also trying to temper myself, knowing she may leave. I want us to enjoy the time we have together and not mention anything about going back.

Molly picked up the phone on the second ring with a cheery "Hello."

"Hi, Hon," I answered, trying to sound the same.

Her following words were spoken in a more serious vein. "How come you haven't called? It's been four whole days."

"I promise I'll explain everything when we're on our way, trust me."

"Where are we going," her tone a little lighter.

"It's someplace I haven't been to in a long time. Just make sure you bring your swimsuit and a towel."

"Why so early?" Molly persisted, sounding a trifle suspicious.

"We should get there in time for breakfast; you haven't eaten yet, have you? See you in about one-half hour, okay?"

"I'll be out front," Molly acknowledged.

"Why out front?" I asked.

"They're all still sleeping."

"Okay, then, I love you."

"You remember," she almost shouted, "I love you more."

Seeing Molly standing in the early morning sunshine, I almost lost control of the car, going up on the curb. She had a red-checkered sleeveless top tied just below her breast. A pair of white short-shorts and open-toed sandals. The best and most important part was that she was wearing her hair down around her shoulders.

As she walked up to the car, I noticed something different. She gave me that million-dollar smile, but it wasn't the same. It took me a second, and then it dawned on me. She looked relaxed, confident, and, most of all, "mature."

It hit me, then. Molly didn't look seventeen anymore. I don't know if it was because her hair was down or the straightforward look. There just seemed to be an aura about her, maybe a glow.

I couldn't wait to go around and open the door for her. When I did, she said with a little laugh, "Don't you think you should get off the curb before I get in?"

We were in the car, off the curb, and I was about to put it in gear when Molly reached over, shut the ignition off, and turned to me, saying, "Okay, buster, where were you the last four days?"

"Buster?" I asked, laughing.

Molly finding it hard to keep a straight face, joined me in

my laughter. "It was all I could think of," she said, cuddling me.

"Good morning," I said, kissing her.

"Good morning to you," she said with her own kiss.

I couldn't imagine a better feeling than having her against me, seeing that smile, and being happy. I felt nothing I couldn't do with the smell of her hair and how she looked at me. The best and most important thing was that she was happy. I felt as though I was on top of the world.

"Hon," she said, can you pull over to the side? I want to say something."

"Okay," I said, turning my directional light on and riding up on the shoulder.

"I never thought I would say or feel this way all my life, but I want you to hold and touch me the same way I do. My only doubt is how far we go. Like you, when we go there, I want it to be someplace where we both enjoy it."

I looked at her new understanding of what she meant to me and whispered in her ear, "Mary Catherine Malone, I love you."

With tears in her eyes and a smile on her face, she whispered her reply, "I love you to Flacco!"

We spent the day at Warren Dunes State Park, swimming in Lake Michigan, climbing Mount Baldy and Tower Hill, and walking through the cabins where I spent my first summer camp. Seeing Molly standing at the water's edge reminded me of when Sean Connery first saw Ursula Andress in the film *Dr. No.*

I felt I'd done something right and good to have this beautiful creature say she loved me. I couldn't take my eyes off her until she turned, caught me, and gave me her unique smile.

"Why do I feel like you're undressing me when you look at me that way?"

"Well, it wouldn't take much with that two-piece you have on."

"Are you hungry yet?" I asked, thinking it must be close to four o'clock.

"Yeah," Molly answered. "A cheeseburger and some fries would hit the spot."

"Let's go change out of this wet stuff, okay?" I said.

"Do they have showers, so we can rinse off?"

"They should have. Let's go find out," I replied.

After shaking the sand off the blanket, we walked hand-in-hand back to the car. With Molly and her beach bag and me with my gym bag, we proceeded to the building at the end of the parking lot and changed clothes.

With the cheeseburgers, fries, and two Pepsis gone, we found ourselves back on our way home.

After dropping Molly at Jeannie's, I drove home. I took a quick shower, changed clothes, dropped my mom at the park (she loves fireworks), and rushed back to get Molly. We were standing near the corner of 103rd and Bensley Avenue when the fireworks ended.

Molly and I covered our ears, trying to keep out the loud thumping from the M-80s and Star Bursts. Finally, taking our hands down, we looked at each other and said simultaneously, "Wow, that was great."

"Would you mind if we took my mom home first?" I asked. "She's waiting by the corner."

"No, I don't mind, but I don't even know her. What do I say?"

"Just say Hi. It will only take a couple of minutes."

We dropped my mom off, and fifteen minutes later, we were sitting in front of Jeannie's house. I was on the second drag of my Salem when Molly turned and, with a loving smile, said, "Thanks for today, I had the best time of my life, and for a bonus, I got to meet your mom."

"I'm glad you had fun because I've got some other things planned," I said. "Some, just the two of us, some with the rest of the gang."

"I like it better when it's just the two of us."

"Really!" I asked incredulously.

"Really!" Molly said, showing me that beautiful smile.

"Who are you? Where did you come from? And why are you here?"

"Don't start!" she said, almost sternly.

"I keep forgetting," I answered lamely.

"You know who I am, I'm from Upper Darby, and I'm here because I want to be."

Molly then took both my hands in hers, looked me straight in the eye, and began to explain what had happened.

"I came here to spend the summer with Jeannie. It was a graduation gift from my parents. On my first night, I hadn't even unpacked yet. Larry came over and invited me to go with them to watch a softball game. I didn't know at the time that they wanted me to meet you."

"By the time we got there, the game was over, so we went by Jerry's store. One of Larry's friends, I think his name is Davy, said you were probably in Fat Rollie's backyard. We were just about to pull out when Tommy somehow ended up in the back seat with me," Molly relayed the story. "Tommy asked why we were looking for 'Flacco' and put his arm around my shoulders. 'That's not his name,' Jeannie admonished. 'Well, that's his nickname,' Tommy said rather smugly. Larry said we were going by Rollie's, and Tommy said he could use a cold beer. And that's how we ended up in the alley behind Rollie's." Molly stopped, took a deep breath, then continued.

"When I saw you standing there next to Mike, I felt an almost physical jolt through my whole body, I didn't know what it meant, but I couldn't turn away. I couldn't believe how your face looked or how your eyes were fixated on mine. It was a tingling sensation that went through my whole being."

"I gotta have a cigarette," I said.

"Not now, please," she pleaded.

"Okay. I'm sorry."

"After we sat and talked, I knew this would be different. I felt comfortable and at ease. I knew I could talk to you about anything, but I couldn't understand why you disappeared after the scuffle with Tommy. So now you know most of it, and though we've had our ups and downs, I think we might have something special."

"Now, can I have one?" I said, reaching for my pack of smokes.

"Okay," she said, "but I'm not done yet."

I exhaled a long plume of smoke and exclaimed, "That's better."

With that, we kissed once more. I walked Molly to the front door, then watched her climb the steps and into the house.

Home, I must have fallen asleep because the next thing I knew, my mom was shaking me, saying, "Mijo, are you all right?"

Opening my eyes, I answered. "It's all right, Ma, just a dream. What time is it?"

"It's 3:30. You kept calling for Molly."

"Okay, Ma, you can go back to sleep."

Once I was sure she was back in bed, I got up, put on my pants and shoes, grabbed my Salems, and went outside for a smoke. After finishing my cigarette, I went back upstairs, lay on the couch, and fell into a fitful sleep, but without any dreams.

Chapter 16

Sunday

7/5/59

I woke up to the smell of coffee brewing, got off the couch, washed up, and went into the kitchen. My mom was sitting at the table with her coffee. "Good morning, Mijo. Did you manage to get any sleep?"

I gave her a peck on the cheek. "I slept a little, Ma."

"I heard you going down the stairs. Is everything all right?"

"Yeah, Ma, everything is all right. I just have something to work out."

"Are you hungry?"

"No, Ma, just some coffee."

"If you're tired, Mijo, I can walk to church."

"We can't pass up our omelet, can we? We can still make ten o'clock mass." After pouring my coffee, I went into the front, sat on the couch, and called Molly. After the third ring, I recognized Jeannie's "Hello."

"Hello, Jeannie. I hope I didn't wake you up?"

"Hi, Jesse, no, you didn't. We've already had breakfast. Hold on, Molly's right here."

"Hi, Hon," she said, returning memories of the previous night.

"Good morning," I answered. "How are you?"

"I'm fine," Molly answered. "We just finished breakfast."

"Do you want to come to our game today?"

"Of course I do," she answered. "I can ride with Larry and Jeannie."

"No, that's all right. I'll be there at about one o'clock."

"Okay," she said, "I'll see you then."

Pulling up and parking at the curb, I was about to exit the car when Molly grabbed my arm and said very seriously, "What's the matter?"

"What'ya mean?" I answered.

"You haven't said two words since we left Jeannie's house."

"It's nothing."

"Yes, it is," Molly said, with a different tone.

"What's going on with you?"

"It'll pass."

"What will pass, Jesse? You call and ask if I want to come to the game. We walk to the car, but there's no 'Hi, how are you.' We don't even talk on the way. Now you park, there's no hug or even a kiss, and you say, 'It'll pass.'"

"I've got something on my mind that I have to tell you after the game."

"Oh no," she said. "Here we go again."

"It's not like that," I said. "I just have to figure out how to tell you."

"Well, for now, can I at least get a kiss."

"Gladly," I said, taking her in my arms.

"Now that's the Flacco we all know and love."

After the game, we drove to "our place." I got a couple of hot dogs and a couple of Pepsis and sat on our favorite bench. "Even with all the people, I still love it here," Molly said.

"Yeah," I replied. "It is kind of special."

When the hot dogs were gone, Molly turned, looking serious, and asked, "What did you want to tell me?"

I don't know exactly how to say it, so I'll just say it, okay?"

"What is it, Jesse?"

"After last night, I didn't know how I was going to act or what I was going to say."

"Oh, Hon, what I did last night, I did because I wanted to. I thought about it a lot last night. As I said before, I'm not ashamed or embarrassed. I did it to make you happy. I fell asleep hoping you wouldn't feel any different about me."

"I could never feel any different about you, Hon. You're the first one I think about when I wake up and the last one I think about when I fall asleep at night. How can I feel differently about you."

"I'm glad you feel that way," Molly said with a twinkle in her eye. "I might want to do it again."

"Anytime," I answered. "Now I think it's time to go. I wanna get home and take a nice hot shower."

"Will I see you later?" Molly asked, looking at me hopefully.

"You couldn't keep me away," I smiled.

Getting up from the bench, I took her hand, and we started walking to the car.

As I went to open the car door, Molly said quietly, "Jesse."

Turning, I said, "What?"

She came into my arms and buried her head against my chest, saying, "Let's not do this anymore."

We stood there for a while, thinking, "Why do I always do that." The last thing I wanted was to upset her, and now I could feel her trying to choke back the sobs.

"I've never cried for anyone as much as I have for you."

"I know, Hon," I swear. "I don't do it on purpose. I feel

like I'm still finding my way around this. I know that I'm the luckiest guy in the world. Hon, I love you so much that sometimes it hurts."

Through tear-streaked eyes, Molly raised her head and said, "You do love me?"

"More than anything in this world," I said proudly.

"You even called me Hon a couple of times."

"I just want us to be happy," I said.

"Me too," Molly said, "so let's go cuz you are starting to smell!"

We both laughed, then we looked at each other, knowing we had formed a strong bond. We kissed with deep meaning and longing, knowing the time was getting shorter.

Chapter 17

Friday

7/21/1959

TWO WEEKS HAD PASSED. WE WERE SO BUSY HAVING FUN. WE lost track of time by horseback riding, bowling, going to the movies, window shopping on North Michigan Avenue, eating a pretzel, and looking at Buckingham Fountain.

Mike and Joyce were married now and living in a back apartment on East 106th Street. Try as I may, I couldn't get Mike into my department at work, so he was stuck on shift work. When he worked nights, Joyce's sister, Pat, would come and stay with her. Even Augie was trying to get Mike into his department, but there were no openings so far. So, for the time being, Mike and Larry were stuck. Other than that, everything was great. We had money, our own car, and even I had a girlfriend. I try not to think about it too much, but I can't help thinking that Molly would be going home in about two months, and I'd be left to try and figure out my life. Now we were sitting in Rollie's backyard after our Friday game. I felt tingling just knowing that Molly was seated next to me with her arm around my waist and her head on my shoulder. I don't want to move, afraid I'll break the spell.

I look up to see Mike and Joyce standing at my side. Mike's saying, "We gotta go. I've got to be at work by 11:30." Looking at my watch, "it's ten o'clock, and most of the guys are gone.

"Okay, Mike," I said. "Just help me dump the cooler."

"You got it, boss," he answered.

With the cooler emptied and in the shed, we walked through the gangway to the front sidewalk. Larry, Jeannie, Augie, and Barb were standing at the curb next to Augie's car.

Standing next to me, Mike whispered, "You gotta minute?"

"Sure, Mike," I said, walking towards his car.

"I know you collected the money for our little getaway," he said. "I wanna repeat thanks, and I will pay you back."

"The fuck you will," I said, smiling, "We're all family here." I just hope you had a good t time."

"A good time!" Mike said. "She can't get enough."

"Okay," I said, "I don't need to hear anymore."

"If I can't talk to you, who can I talk to? Besides, if she ever saw the 'Chorizo' you got hanging, she'd be all over you."

"That's enough, Mike," I said. "I'll see you later."

"All I'm saying is that if something happened, I'd be all right with it."

"Fuck, Mike, that's your wife you're talking about."

"Yeah, I know, and you're like my best friend."

"Do you know what that means?" I said.

"I said it didn't matter if it happened. It happens."

I went to bed that night more confused than I'd ever been. I wasn't sure what Mike meant, but I vowed I would never bring it up again.

Chapter 18

Saturday

7/22/1959

I WAS ON MY SECOND CUP OF COFFEE HALFWAY THROUGH THE *Sun-Times* when the phone rang.

"Hello," I said.

"Hi, Hon," Molly answered. "I hope I didn't wake you up."

"Naw, I'm on my second cup. What's up?"

"Were you coming over today?"

"You couldn't keep me away. Is something wrong?"

"I'll tell you when you get here."

"It's ten o'clock. I'll be there about twelve, okay?"

"Okay," Molly said, then she hung up.

When I got there, Molly was outside, standing by the front entrance. As I walked up the sidewalk, she moved inside. I stepped inside and asked, "What's wrong?"

She walked into my arms and whispered, "Just hold me," she was shaking as we embraced.

"Why are you crying? Did I do something wrong?"

"It's not you," Molly said against my chest. "It's my parents."

"What about them?" I asked.

"They'll be here in two weeks, and I'll have to go back with them."

"I thought you weren't leaving until the end of August?"

"My dad changed my return ticket. I was supposed to go back by myself."

"You didn't tell them about us? Did you?"

"No," Molly replied rather timidly. "If I did, they'd be here by now."

"Why?" I asked, getting that feeling inside again.

"Because I know my father."

"What does that mean?"

"I just know how he's going to react."

"I'm starting to get that 'Mexican' feeling," I said.

"I'm sorry, Hon, that's how he thinks."

"And you? How do you feel?"

"After all we've been through, you shouldn't have to ask me that," she replied in a rather stern voice.

"I'm sorry, Hon, I didn't mean for it to come out that way. I'm just now realizing we don't have too much time left, and then you'll be gone. These past three months have been the best and happiest of my life. I tried to put it in the back of my mind, but now that it's here, I don't know what I'll do after you're gone."

"Jesse, "before we go upstairs, I want to say, I don't care how many times I've said it, or how many times you've said it, I love you, Flacco, and some way or another, we'll work it out. Okay?"

I looked at her, smiling through the tears, and knew I would never love anyone as much as I loved her.

"Okay, boss," I said through my own tears. "Let's enjoy whatever time we have left."

We spent the next two weeks together as much as we could, not really doing anything special. Sometimes we'd go for a walk around the neighborhood. One of Molly's favorites was to sit in Grant Park and watch when they turned on the lights at Buckingham Fountain.

The week before her parents came in, we watched a Cubs game at Wrigley Field and sat with the bleacher bums. She looked so happy. It was breaking my heart, knowing that soon she'd be going. The next evening we went for a walk along the beach at Cal Park and sat on 'Our Bench,' holding each other, afraid to let go, neither one not knowing what to say. I was utterly at a loss for words. What could I say? Molly, don't go!

I could feel her shaking, letting the tears flow. I had a lump in my throat that I didn't think I could swallow. Reaching into my back pocket, I handed Molly my hankie. She took it and, looking up at me, said, "Seems like I'm always crying."

"Keep it," I said, swallowing the lump. "Something to remember me by."

"I don't need a hankie to remember you by, Hon. You're in here," she said, placing her hand over her heart. "I'll never forget you!"

"You mean that?" I asked incredulously.

"I would never lie to you," Molly answered, wiping away the tears.

We were in each other's arms again. This time the kiss was long and soul-searching. Pulling back, Molly looked into my eyes, whispering softly, "I wanted you to be the first and do everything I said before."

"Look, Hon, like I said before, I want nothing in my life more than to be there inside you. I want to make love to you the right way, to mean something, with lots of time to enjoy. Most of all, I want to fall asleep holding you and wake up with you next to me."

"It all sounds so beautiful," Molly said. "But I don't think we have the time."

"We'll have all the time in the world in February."
"Promise me you'll be there for my birthday!"
"Nothing in this world will keep me away!
"I'll never get tired of saying this. I love you, Flacco."
"I love you more," I said, choking back a sob.
"Now, let's get you home."

Chapter 19

Sunday

7/23

It was a quiet ride from Jeannie's house to Cal Park, both of us not knowing what to say. I tried to keep it out of my head, but it just hung like a dark cloud.

I had this feeling that when she left, something would happen, and I'd never see her again.

Molly noticed me looking out the windshield, took my hand, and said softly, "Aren't you going to say anything?"

Turning off the ignition, I answered, "What do you want me to say, Hon? I don't want you to leave!"

"Something like that," she said, looking at me with hopeful eyes.

"Nothing we say or do is gonna change what happens next week. I'll watch you leave Saturday, Molly, and my life will never be the same again."

"I'm only seventeen years old," she said, her eyes brimming with tears, "but I know deep in my heart that I want to spend the rest of my life with you. I hurt when I'm not with you, hear your voice, or see you. We've both said that we've only known each other for the past couple of months. I feel as if I'd known you longer than that."

So engrossed in our conversation, neither of us heard Augie until he was about twenty feet from the car. "Jesse," he yelled, "the game's gonna start. Hurry up!"

The game started on time and ended with a 16-4 in our favor. Walking back to the car, Molly took my hand, asking, "Do we have to go to Rollie's?"

"Why," I asked.

"Can we just go somewhere and talk?"

"You really want to talk about this?"

"Don't you?"

"I already told you next Saturday, you'll be gone, and I'll have to figure out my life again."

"Can we at least go sit in the car?"

"Yeah, sure," I said, picking up my spikes and starting toward the car.

After a couple of steps, Molly reached over and, taking my hand in hers, said, "Don't give up on us just yet."

Once inside the car and lighting up one of my Salems, I was about to turn the ignition on when Molly asked, "Can we just sit here for a while?"

"Okay, but what did you mean by not giving up?"

"Before I say anything, you have to promise me that you won't do anything crazy."

"Like what?" I asked.

"After tomorrow, we probably won't see each other until after I talk to my parents."

"Why is that?" I asked, getting that sinking feeling in the pit of my stomach.

"I think I know how my father's going to react."

"What'ya gonna tell them?"

"I want to stay here, get a job, maybe go to school here.

Jeannie's parents said I could stay with them until I started working. Jeannie and I even talked about getting an apartment together."

"What about your father? What's he gonna say?"

"He'll probably blow up, saying I'm too young to know what love is, that I'll go to college, and after a couple years, I'll forget all about you."

"And your mom?"

"My mom's all right. She knows that I was never crazy about college. She just wants me to be happy the way I am with you."

"Are you really that happy?" I asked, loving her more and more.

"Jesse," Molly said, looking into my eyes, "after all this time, I know that my life is here with you and all the friends that I've met."

"That's my girl," I said, taking her in my arms and holding her tightly as if she might slip away. "You'll call and let me know what happens, okay?"

"Okay," she said, with a little less conviction than I thought.

Chapter 20

Monday

7/24

OVER THE NEXT FOUR DAYS, TIME SEEMED TO SLIP INTO SLOW motion. I would get up, go to work, come home, watch a little *Band Stand*, eat dinner, then sit and wait for a phone call that didn't seem to materialize. Nights would find me sitting on the front steps, smoking, drinking beer, and wondering why the fates could be so cruel.

Chapter 21

Friday

7/28/1959

FRIDAY, IT DAWNED ON ME THAT I WOULD PROBABLY NOT EVER see Molly again. So after three Salems and literally crying in my beer, I was getting up from the steps when Larry and Jeannie pulled up to the curb. Larry was the first to reach me and, seeing me wiping my eyes, called back to Jeannie, "Hold on."

"It's all right, Lar," I said, clearing my throat. "Hi, Jeannie," I managed to croak. "I guess it's over now, you know." Turning to Larry, I spat, "Not even a fucking phone call. I'm sorry, Jeannie."

"She so much wanted to call," Jeannie soothed, "but after her father cooled off, he said she had to go back and start school and that once she was back with 'her people,' she would put this 'little summer fling' behind her and get on with her life."

"It seemed," Jeannie continued, "the more Molly argued,

the more determined her father became. That's why she didn't call. Molly didn't know what to say. She tried to come and see you, but he wouldn't let her. She's been crying every day, which doesn't seem to matter. Her mother is the only one who says that Molly isn't old enough but knows how she feels.

"What time do they leave tomorrow?" I asked, getting a little of my resolve back.

"They're gonna leave the house about four o'clock, Jeannie answered. "What'ya got on your mind?"

"All I know is that I must see her before she leaves!"

Chapter 22

Saturday

7/29/1959

As luck would have it, I had to park four houses down from Jeannie's house. I didn't mind. It was a beautiful sunny day, with not a cloud anywhere. I stopped to look at the spot under the tree where we first sat and told each other how we felt. I almost heard the Satins singing "In the Still of the Night." I had to stop and catch my breath. I didn't want to go there with tears and feeling all choked up.

Ringing the doorbell, I could feel the sweat running down from my armpits and forming on my brow. I was so happy that it was Mrs. Goodman who opened the door.

"Hi, Jesse," she smiled, stepping back.

"Hi, Mrs. G.," I replied. "How are you?"

"I'm fine," she answered. "Come in."

"If it's all right, I'd like to talk with Molly if I could."

"Of course," she replied. "I'll just go get her."

When she turned, I saw Molly standing at the dining room

table. Her eyes were still puffy, and her face was a little flushed. As I walked up to her, she turned away from me. "Don't, Molly," I said, turning her back to me.

"What are you doing here?"

"I had to see you before you left."

"I tried to call, I even wanted to write and try to explain, but I didn't know what to say."

"It's alright, Hon," I said soothingly. "I understand, and if I could, I'd like to take you to the airport."

"Molly will be coming with us to the airport." Turning, we saw her parents and Mr. Goodman come in from the kitchen. Her father's voice had a nasal twang, almost like he had a nasty head cold.

Stepping in front of me, Molly announced, "Dad, mom, this is Jesse. Jesse, I want you to meet my dad Tom and my mom Catherine."

"Nice to meet you, Mrs. Malone and Mr. Malone."

He took my hand, shook it twice, dropped it, turned his back, and walked into the front room. Tom Malone sat down on the sofa, took a slug of beer, and proceeded to turn on the TV. I walked over and stood in front of his saying, "I'd like to take Molly to the airport if it's all right with you."

"As I said, she'll be going to the airport with us. So as we'll be leaving shortly, I think it's time you left, son."

"First, I'm not your son, and you don't say when I leave."

"Have it your way," Tom replied, getting up from the couch.

I could see the red film forming around my eyes and my hands balling into fists. We were standing face to face when Mr. Goodman broke the spell.

"He's right, Tom, this is still my house, and I'll say who stays and who goes."

I walked over, took Mr. G's hand, and shook it, saying, "That's all right, Mr. G. I was just leaving."

"Look, Tom," he said, "I've known Jesse for the past three

years and never knew him to be anything but honest, polite, and respectful, and if he says he loves Molly, I believe him."

"It really doesn't matter, Irv. Molly's my daughter, and she's coming home with us."

"Dad, please stop!" Molly shouted, still standing next to the dining room table.

"Is this what you want, Molly," he said, pointing to me, "that in five years you'll have three kids and be barefoot and pregnant?"

"If they're his kids, yes."

I could barely make out his face with all the red in my eyes. I had to stop and get a hold of my temper, I didn't want it to end this way, but I knew I had to tell him how I felt.

Taking a step back, unclenching my fists, I tried to sound as even-tempered as possible, saying, "I'm sorry things turned out the way they did. I hope that someday if I ever have a daughter, I will be as concerned about her as you are about Molly. I know that you think she's too young and should go to college and have a career, and if that's what she wants, then she should. But I'll tell you what I told her that Friday night I first saw her. Something came over me. It was a feeling that I felt all through my body. I knew right then and there that I would love her for the rest of her life.

"One last thing before I go: I don't have a lot of money, I don't live in a big house, but the house I live in is full of love. I promised Molly that no matter what happens, I'll always take care of her."

I took Mrs. Malone's hand, saying, "Mrs. Malone." Turned to Tom, "Mr. Malone." On my way out of the front room, I acknowledged Mr. Goodman, then Mrs. Goodman, who took both my hands in hers, saying, "Good for you, Jesse."

Approaching Molly, I could see the tears streaming down her cheeks. Taking out my handkerchief and wiping away the tears, I said as lovingly as possible, "Don't worry, Hon, this isn't goodbye. I'll see you in February." We kissed, a kiss filled with love, hope, and a promise we have to each other.

With her face against my shoulder, Molly whispered, "Promise me again."

Holding her at arm's length, I proclaimed loud enough for all to hear, "I don't know how many times I've said it, and I don't care. I love you, Mary Catherine Malone, and I will be there!"

I had to let go because I could feel my own tears on my cheeks. I swiftly made my way out the front door and was halfway down when I heard my name.

Turning, I faced Mrs. Malone at the top step. She looked at me as only a mother could have for her daughter.

"If you can be honest with me," she said, "I'd like to ask you something that could change Molly's life."

"Okay," I said, still a little choked up.

"Do you really love her?"

"More than my life," I honestly answered.

"Then go back in there and fight for her. My husband is very determined and controlling, but tell him what you told me, so he'll know how you feel."

"I can't right now, but I feel good knowing that both you and Molly know. I want you to know that I understand that we're both young, and I don't have what it takes to give Molly the life she deserves, but someday I will. Goodbye, Mrs. Malone, and tell Molly I will be there in February."

I don't know how I got there, but I ended up on our bench at Cal Park.

After five months of putting in all the overtime I could get in the mill and all the hours that Rollie would give me, 1960 came in on an ill wind. We were all laid off in the second week of January without knowing when we would be called back. The money I had put away was soon gone. My unemployment check and the pool hall money were just enough to get us by.

Molly talked through all the phone calls and letters as if she understood why I couldn't be there in February. I later learned from Jeannie that she knew I wasn't as serious as I said. I felt hollow, as if everything inside me had crumbled into nothing; all the hours and work I put in were for nothing. She also said that now away from home and on her own, she had started a new life.

At Temple University, she found her niche with new friends and the whole college thing. I, too, had found my niche. I vowed to never let any woman get that close to me. I would never be hurt like that again.

Everyone told me I was too young to feel that way. That sooner or later, the pain would fade. Part of what they said was correct. I was young, and the pain would eventually fade, but I also knew I would never love any woman the way I loved Molly.

I sent her a birthday card, knowing things were ending, when I got no answer. The phone calls were shorter. The letters were more minor. All she talked about was what she was doing at Temple, the football, and basketball games, going out with her girlfriends, and nothing about us.

I tried to find a reason for it but couldn't. It seemed the fates were against us. That it wasn't meant to work for us. Maybe we were too young.

Chapter 23

Friday

4/16/1960

ON A FRIDAY NIGHT IN THE MIDDLE OF APRIL, I WAS SITTING behind the counter at Rollie's, smoking my third Salem and trying in vain to not think about Molly.

Stubbing out my cigarette in the ashtray and walking to the front door, I was met there by Mike and Joyce. Unlocking and opening the door, I ushered them inside.

"Hey, guys, what's up?"

"Nothing much," Mike replied. "We were out for a walk and noticed you sitting in the dark."

"Who's watching the baby," I inquired.

"Patty and Buddy are there," Joyce smiled.

"Got time for a beer?"

"Sure," Mike answered, looking at Joyce and getting a nod.

"Let's go in the back," I said, quickly walking towards the back room. I had to be careful around Joyce. Ever since I had that conversation with Mike, I could picture myself in bed with her whenever I saw her. Trying to break that train of thought, I got three beers from the fridge, set them down on the table, and sat opposite Mike.

We each took a slug and a puff, then settled back in our chairs. Mike was the first to break the silence, "So, how's it going, boss?"

"Still with the boss, huh, Mike."

"Always," he answered solemnly.

"Have you heard from Molly?" Joyce asked, setting her bottle on the table.

"I'd rather not talk about that, if you don't mind."

"I'm sorry," Joyce said, smiling and rubbing her foot against my thigh.

Not being in the mood for conversation or 'footsies,' I said, "I think I'm gonna go get some sleep, okay."

After Joyce walked out, Mike turned and said, "If you ever want to talk, you know where I'm at."

"Thanks, Mike," I said.

"Oh, and by the way," he said rather somberly, "I'll always have your back." With that, he walked out and joined Joyce on the sidewalk. I locked the door, turned, and walked home.

Turning west on 109th Street, I couldn't help thinking I would make it with Joyce sooner or later. The overtures and sly looks were enough. But I got a full-mouth kiss whenever I expected a peck on the cheek. After our conversation, I didn't know if Mike was sincere or thought it better that it was me and not someone else.

In bed that night, I thought, "What the fuck? He's your best friend. I've got to watch myself when I'm around her."

Chapter 24

Friday

8/12/1960

WE ENDED THE SOFTBALL SEASON ON A HIGH NOTE, GIVING
Rollie a couple of trophies to put behind the counter. Pete,
Little Joe, Bobby, and Butch joined the Mexican Bowling
League on Sundays. I wanted to, but closing the pool hall on
weekends was a priority I couldn't give up. We had gone back
to carpooling for the last weeks of the season. Both Larry and
I had given our cars back to the credit union. Having been
laid off since January, I couldn't afford the car payments and
insurance.

It really wasn't that bad. I walked to the pool hall, and if I
needed a ride, both Augie and Mike would loan me their car.
While playing ball, I tried to ride with Augie as much as possible, trying to stay far away from Joyce.

I talked to Jeannie almost every Friday and Sunday while
playing ball. I think she understood what I'd gone through,
trying to go there, giving everything I could to make it

happen. In the end, we both realized that it just wasn't meant to be.

I remember the Friday night after our last game, the pool hall was closed, and everybody had left except Jeannie, Larry, and me. We were sitting in front of Rollie's. I reached in, got my pack of Salems, and offered one to Larry. Lighting up and taking a deep drag, I turned to Jeannie, who gave me a look of deep understanding.

"Jesse," she said, "again, I am sorry it ended this way."

"It's okay," I said. "I'm all right."

"When was the last time you talked to her?"

"Shit, Jeannie," Larry almost shouted. "He doesn't want to talk about it. | ."

"It's all right, Lar. If I can't talk to Jeannie, who can I talk to? Right?"

"Jeannie," I said, "the last time we talked, neither of us had much to say. So we just left it there."

Getting to his feet, Larry looked at Jeannie, then at me, saying with a smile, "I think it's time we get going, okay, boss?"

"You with that boss thing too."

"Just stating the facts, boss."

I helped Jeannie to her feet and walked her to her car. Once she was behind the wheel, she motioned for me to lean in. After giving me a peck on the cheek, she whispered, "If you ever want to talk, you know where I'm at."

"You know, I get that a lot," I said with a smile

Later, lying in bed, I kept thinking of the saying, "Time Heals All Wounds." The more I thought about it, the more I realized it was a bunch of bullshit.

Chapter 25

Wednesday

9/24/1960

THERE WAS A BITE IN THE AIR THAT THIRD WEEK OF September. Definitely jacket weather. Still out of work, with no relief in sight. The guys were still bowling on Sunday. I was still at Rollie's on the weekends. Two weeks ago, Joyce's sister Pat and I baptized Michael Jesse Kowalski. Joyce wanted me to come over more now that I'm the godfather (no way). With that thought in mind, I turned, entered the alley, and went to the pool hall.

Growing up in the Rogers Park neighborhood, I was known simply as "Cisco" and, by my fifteenth birthday, had grown into a 5 foot 9 inches, 160 pounds of wiry muscle.

Now, out of grammar school and not looking at high school, I decided to join the workforce and help at home.

With my parent's approval, I got my first job as a grocery store clerk, then a delivery boy, and eventually as a truck driver. With Salvatore "Peanuts" Finelli and Frank "Cappy" Cappello, I made a rapid ascent up the crime ladder on the north side, adding car theft and burglary to our resume.

It was spring 1926, and our reputations were well known in and around the Rogers Park area. We had a lot of connections, especially with the numerous fences who bought our merchandise. This brought us to the attention of Augustus "Rags" Ragonese. A high-ranking "Chicago Outfit" member and the Boss of the North Side.

Everything involving money had to have his stamp of approval, which included gambling, prostitution, numbers, and loan sharking. You name it. If it was illegal, he had his hand in it.

We finally met with one of his lieutenants at the Union Hall on LaSalle Street. We were told there would be no more burglaries or car thefts without his permission, or we could join what he called "The Family."

Seeing no upside, we decided on the latter, thinking we'd be much better off.

After the meeting was consummated, we left without knowing if what we had decided was good or bad.

Meeting us at the front door was "the Ragman" himself, shaking hands and welcoming us into the ranks of his "soldiers."

Our primary function was compelling the franchised "Bar Owners" and "Loan Shark Debtors" to pay up on time or face the consequences. The collections were carried out on the first of every month.

With all that we were doing, time seemed to just fly by. After ten years of running numbers, making collections, and occasionally breaking an arm or a leg, I was given my own crew. And was to oversee all of the "Family's" interests in the Rogers Park area.

I first put "Peanuts" in charge of the numbers and "Chappy" in collecting money. Most days were spent in the backroom of my father's tailor shop.

I had a lot of time on my hands after continually hearing my parents ask, "When are you gonna settle down?" I decided that maybe it was time.

I'd been dating Carla Diposso on and off for about two years, and after I proposed and she accepted, we were married. Cappy and his wife, Rose, were the Maid of Honor and Best Man. Peanuts was one of our ushers.

Now I'm sitting here in my car, with a bullet in my side in an alley on the south side, and I don't remember exactly how I got here. The pain in my side hurts like hell, my shirt is blood-soaked, and my jacket has a bullet hole. I touch my side, and I almost pass out.

The bullet must have hit a bone 'cause there's no blood in the back. I can barely keep my eyes open, and it's getting worse.

Now my hands are shaking, I'm sweating, and I can feel my eyes closing, and I can't seem to stop them. Suddenly, I hear a tapping on the window. I turn my head and come face to face with a young kid with a concerned look.

———

I first noticed a car parked in the alley behind the pool hall. I usually take a shortcut and come in through the back door. As I got nearer, I could hear the motor running, so I moved over to the driver's side and tapped on the window. He turned, and with a frightened look, he slowly rolled the window down. His face was flushed, and he was sweating profusely.

"You all right, Buddy?" I asked tentatively.

"I'm hit," he said.

"Whataya mean?"

"I've been shot," he said, slightly slurred.

"Whataya need?"

"Right now, I need something to stop the bleeding, a towel, or something, then I need a phone."

"Okay, I'll be right back."

Stepping into Rollie's apartment, I noticed all was quiet in the pool hall. Looking through the peephole, I could see two guys with guns in their hands. The taller of the two was standing by the counter, and the other was by the front door.

I grabbed a couple of towels from the bathroom and ran back outside.

"Here," I said, handing him the towels.

He immediately put one over his blood-soaked shirt and began pressing down.

"Thanks," he said. "Now, can I get to a phone?"

"We can't go inside,"

"Why not?"

"There are two guys with guns in the pool hall."

"Fuck, I thought I lost them. Look, kid, I need to get to a phone, believe me, I'll make it worth your while."

I looked at his side. The towel was completely soaked with blood.

"Can you walk?" I asked

"Maybe, with a little help."

"Let's get you inside first. I think I've got an idea."

Once he was settled in Rollie's bedroom, I got the .45 automatic, checked the clip, and chambered a round. Put it in the small of my back, put my jacket over it, and walked up to the door.

Through the peephole, I could see that both of them were now standing by the counter, talking.

"I don't think they've seen anything," the taller one said.

"What do we do now?"

When he said that, I opened the door and walked into the room.

"Hey, Rollie," I said, "did you know?"

"Whoa, kid," the taller one said. "Where'd you come from?"

"Through the back door. What's going on?"

"Never mind that. What's back there?"

"It's my apartment," Rollie answered.

"Nobody asked you to talk, fatso."

"What were you doing back there?" he said to me.

"I took a shortcut from my house through the alley."

"See anything?" the big one asked.

"Yeah, there's a car parked a couple houses down with a guy sitting in the front seat."

"Come on," he said. "Show me."

As he walked past me, he said over his shoulder, "Watch them, Mikey." Inside Rollie's apartment, I pointed to the back door. "Through there," I said.

He pushed me aside and almost ran to the door. I put the muzzle of the 45 up against the base of his skull.

"Drop it," I snarled.

"What the fuck," he barked.

"A little louder, and I'll blow your fucking head off. Now drop the gun."

"You don't know what you're doing, kid."

"I won't repeat it, Mother Fucker."

He let the .22 fall silently on the carpet and, taking a deep breath, snarled again, "I'll remember you."

I took a few steps back, just in case he tried anything.

"See that door over there?"

"Yeah," he said, not snarling anymore.

"Walk over there and go inside."

Before he turned, he glanced down at the .22 lying on the floor.

"Don't even think about it," I said.

"You ever kill anybody, punk?"

"You ever been dead before, asshole? Now move!"

Once inside Rollie's bedroom, I saw the guy with the suit standing in the corner, holding the towels to his side.

"You all right?" I asked, keeping the .45 trained on the guy in front of me.

"The towels are helping."

"You think you can watch him?" I asked, handing him the .45.

"I think I can."

"Go over and sit in that chair, and don't even blink if he does shoot him."

He managed a weak smile, then nodded.

I turned, picked up the .22, shoved it in the small of my back, then proceeded into the pool hall. When the one called Mikey saw me, he immediately pointed his gun at me.

"Where's my brother?" he asked.

"He's in the alley," I said. "He wants you to finish the hit."

When Mikey was about two steps past the counter, in one swift motion, Rollie was off the stool and had the .38 pressed behind his head.

"Drop it slowly on the floor, Mother Fucker."

With a look of great surprise and a little shock, he laid it gently on the floor.

After Augie picked up the .22, I gave him a shove, then we walked him to the back, stopping at the doorway. I turned.

"Anybody who doesn't want to be here should leave now."

The only ones who stayed were Bobby, Butch, Larry, and Mike.

"Okay then," I said. "Bobby, lock the door and turn off the sign. Butch, turn off the big lights, then wait for us out here."

Five of us were cramped in Rollie's bedroom, but we managed.

"Lar," I said, "make sure that the back door is locked."

"You got it," he answered, walking away.

Turning to the suit, I asked, "You know these guys?"

"Never seen um before."

Once we had them duct-taped and sitting on the floor, Mikey's brother looked up at the suit and stated, "You were lucky this time, Cisco. It won't happen again."

"Looks to me," the suit growled. "There won't be a next time for you."

I reached over, took the .45, then helped the suit to the couch in the next room. Laying down, he asked, "Can I make that phone call now?"

"Let's change those towels first," Rollie said on his way to the bathroom.

"It's not bleeding that much now, so keep putting pressure on it."

"I'm gonna give you a number, dial it, then give me the phone."

"Whoa, hold on," I snapped. "We just saved your ass. We still don't know who you are or why those two tried to kill you, and here you are, giving orders."

"Okay," he answered. "If you let me make this call, I'll tell you all you need to know."

The phone was on the wall, next to the fridge. I walked over, dialed the number, then handed it to the suit next to me. After a couple of rings, he said, "Sal, it's me. Yeah, I'm okay, but I've been hit. I want you to bring a couple of boys and the doc. I'm in South Chicago, in the back of a pool hall. I don't know, Sal, but this kid will tell you how to get here."

He handed me the phone and said, "He'll be coming from the north side."

"Sal," I asked.

"Yeah," he replied, "go ahead."

"Get on the Dan Ryan anyway you can, take it south to 103th Street, go east on 103 until you come to Torrence Avenue, make a right and go to 108th. In the middle of the block, you'll see the sign."

"Okay," he said. "We'll be there in about half an hour."

With Rollie behind the counter, most of the guys were back in the pool hall, and Mike was in the bedroom with the two shooters.

"I noticed that all of your friends follow your lead, and I even heard the word *boss*."

"It's just a nickname. Most of us have one. Now, what's your name, and why did they want to kill you?"

"After what you did, I guess I owe you that much."

"How's your side," I asked.

He was sitting on the couch, his left hand holding the towel to his side.

"It hurts, but I'll be all right. Listen, kid, what—"

"I'm no kid!" I snapped.

"Okay, okay," the suit responded. "I want to tell you what you did tonight. I'll never forget it. Oh, and by the way, I'm Frank Antignani. With that, he held out his right hand."

"I'm Jesse Cruz."

"Do you have a piece of paper?"

"Yeah, sure," I said.

"Write this number down, and if you ever need anything, gimmie a call. Okay."

I was lighting up a Salem when there was a knock on the back door. Mike instinctively got up from his chair and stood at the bedroom doorway.

"I got it, Mike. Stay where you're at." Holding the .45, I walked to the door and inquired, "Yeah, who's there?"

"It's me, Larry," came the muffled reply.

"I thought," he replied, "it would be better if they parked in the alley."

As he walked past me, I patted him on the back, saying, "You're not such a dumb Pollock, are you?" We smiled at each other, then Larry sat down next to Mike.

I stood at the doorway until four men of various ages approached from the alley. The two younger men led the way, then the two older men. One was carrying a black leather "doctor's bag." The second one walked past me and stopped in front of the suit.

"You all right, Frank?"

"Yeah, Sal. I'll be alright. Just let the doctor take a look at my side, okay."

Stepping back and turning to me, Sal asked, "What the fuck happened?

"It's all right, Sal. I'll explain on the way home."

"I'll take that piece now," he said, reaching for the .45.

"The hell you will," I growled, stepping back.

"Easy, Sal," Frank ordered from the couch. "He's the one who helped me. Besides, it's his piece. How's it look, Doc?"

"Most of the bleeding has stopped. I think you'll make it to my office, then we'll get that slug out."

"Sonny," he said, "You and Jimmy take those two guys with the tape and put them in my car."

"Okay, Frank," he said, moving off.

On the way out, the tall one quipped. "See you around, punk!"

"Anytime," I answered. "We can shoot some 8 ball!"

Getting up from the couch, Frank stepped up to me, extending his hand again.

As I took his hand, I could see he was back in his element again.

Shaking his, he said, "You're pretty cocky. I like that."

"He doesn't scare me," I said, standing slightly taller.

"I can see that," Frank said, letting go of my hand. "That's good to know."

"We should be going, Frank," Sal said, moving toward the door.

"Maybe I can come by one day and shoot some 8 ball. What ya think?"

"Anytime, Frank," I answered.

I walked him to the door, where he turned and said, "You

don't have to worry about those two again." He walked out. I closed and locked the door.

Later, after everyone had left, Rollie and I were sitting at the kitchen table, me with a beer and Salem, Rollie with the ever-present unlit cigar. I asked him, "What did we do tonight?"

"I'm not sure, but I know one thing, and that's who the boss is."

"You really think so?"

"I don't know about all of them, but I'm sure of Mike, Larry, and Augie. They'd do just about anything for you. You can be sure they'll always have your back."

"What about you?" I asked.

"You know me, Flacco. I'm here if you ever need anything, now go home and get some sleep."

Chapter 26

Tuesday

12/24/1960

As I made my way to Hoxie Avenue, a light coating of snow was on the ground. So far, it's been a very mild winter with little snow. After our Christmas dinner with my sister, Mary, and her family, my mother was back upstairs. I was going to Mike and Joyce's apartment for a little holiday get-together.

Augie, Larry, and I were still out of work. Mike worked nights at the Interlake Coke Plant at 112th and Torrence Avenue. I was glad that Larry, Jeannine, Barb, and Augie would be there. I didn't know what would happen with Joyce. I hadn't seen or talked to her since the baptism.

"It's been thirteen months since Molly left, and I realized that 'Time Heals All Wounds.'"

It still hurts when I think about her, only it's not the sharp pain it was before, more like a dull ache, with no more tears.

Sometimes I wonder what she's doing or if she even thinks of me.

Crossing Hoxie Avenue at 106th Street, I headed back to Mike's apartment. Rang the doorbell and took a step back. The door opened, and there stood Augie with two beers and a big grin.

"Merry Christmas, boss!" he shouted, giving me a beer and a hug.

"Merry Christmas, Aug," I said, stepping away and making my way to the kitchen table.

After all the hugs and kisses, we settled for beer and pizza. Mike didn't want us smoking with the baby there, so after the pizza was gone, we put our coats on, went out on the porch, and lit up.

"So, how's the night shift, Mike?" I asked.

"It sucks, but it pays the rent. How are you doing?"

"I'm hanging in there, but it's getting tight."

"Jesse, Augie," Mike said. "If either of you needs my car, all you have to do is ask. You know that, don't you?"

"Thanks, Mike," we both answered, then took a slug of beer.

We were about to go back inside when I stopped them with a question. "Now that we're all here, I want to ask, is anybody uncomfortable with what went down a couple of months ago? I know we don't talk about it. I don't know how it happened; it just happened. It was my fault for getting us involved."

"What the fuck is that!" Larry snapped.

"Yeah," Augie echoed.

Mike took another drag, turned to me, and said, "Sometimes you act so fuckin stupid. We all know the 'boss' is, guys." Almost in unison, they all nodded, then burst out laughing. We clicked bottles, took one more slug, then went back inside.

At about eleven o'clock, we decided to call it a night. Mike had to be at work in an hour. As I put on my coat, Mike whispered, "How's it going?"

"I'm all right for now, but thanks for asking."

"If you need anything, we're here for you."

"I know that," I answered. "The same goes for me."

"Okay, boss," Mike said. "See you for New Year's."

As I was putting my coat on, thinking I was making a clean getaway, Joyce's voice stopped me in my tracks. "Come say goodnight to your godson." I walked into the bedroom, over to the crib where little Mike was standing, holding on to the rail. "Hey, big guy," I said, giving him a peck on the forehead and tossing his hair. "Merry Christmas," I said, straightening up and turning to face Joyce.

"You know," she said, "sooner or later, you're gonna have to fuck me."

"Are you fuckin' crazy? Mike's my best friend."

"Oh, I'm pretty sure he's okay with it."

"And I don't have any say about it?"

"Mike knows how I am, and he'd rather it was you than somebody else. Besides, I've wanted to bed you for over a year now."

"Why?" I asked.

"I really don't know. It's something I can't stop thinking about. I look at you, and my heart is beating like crazy."

Feeling cornered, I saw my only avenue of escape, so brushing past Joyce, I exclaimed over my shoulder, "I gotta go!" I was in the hallway when I heard her reply, "Don't take too long."

Mike was standing on the enclosed back porch when I shakily walked up. "Mike," I said, "we gotta talk about this."

"I know, Jesse. What am I gonna do? She's got this thing about you that I don't understand."

"Mike," I said, lighting up another Salem. "I don't want to stop coming here, but it's getting a little uncomfortable."

"I know," he said. "Listen, you're my best friend, right?"

"Always," I replied.

"Then, anything that happens won't come between us."

"What are you saying, Mike?" I asked, not believing what he was saying.

"All I'm saying is that if it happens, it happens. I just don't want it to affect our friendship."

"If I can help, you don't have anything to worry about."

The porch door opened, and Joyce's sister Patty walked in and began ascending the stairs. "Hi, Patty," I said.

"Hi, Jesse," she responded.

"I guess you can go to work now, Mike. We'll talk later."

Walking out of the gangway, I noticed Larry, Jeannie, Augie, and Barb standing on the sidewalk.

"What's up?" I asked, walking up.

"Jesse," Augie spoke, "the three of us have been talking. We think it's time we had a little sit-down."

"It's okay with me," I answered. "Let's go back to Rollie's."

Barb got a ride home from Jeannie. The three of us walked back to the pool hall, entering through the back door. We each got a beer and sat at the table.

"Okay," I said, trying to sound serious. "What's on your mind?"

"It's been over a year, Mike's got a job, I'm at home with my mom and dad, our compo has run out, and we don't know if the mill is ever gonna call us back. You and Larry have got to be hurting!"

"Jesse," Larry jumped in, "we thought maybe you could call that guy Frank. Maybe he might know somebody hiring or a place we could look into."

I took a slug of beer, a drag on my Salem, put the bottle down, and looked at two of my best friends with a smile.

"You guys," I said, now laughing, "why didn't I think of that myself."

"You think he'll remember us?" Augie said, now smiling.

"Only one way to find out. You know, I think I've got his number at home. I'll give him a call Monday morning."

"That's why you're the boss, boss."

"Cut the shit, Aug. You know, I don't like that."

"It's the truth," Larry said.

"Okay," I answered, "but try not to say it too much."

"You got it, boss," Augie threw it back at me.

"Fuck you two!"

We laughed, finished our beer and smokes, walked out the back door, hugged each other, and came out of the gangway onto Torrence Avenue. They turned left, I turned right, and the three of us walked into the night.

Chapter 27

Monday

12/28/1960

"Good morning, operating engineers. How may I help you?"

"Wow," I thought. "What a sexy voice."

"Hello?" the sexy voice said again.

"Oh, I said, feeling stupid. I'm sorry. I'd like to talk to Mr. Frank Antignani."

"Mr. Antignani is in a meeting right now. Is there something I can help you with?"

"Could you just tell him that Jesse Cruz called and would like to talk to him? My number is 221-8794. Thank you."

Sitting back on the couch, I thought, "He ain't gonna call back." I took a sip of coffee, a drag on my cigarette. I began wondering about everything that had happened in the last year and a half. I met my first true love, had the best summer of my life, went through my first broken heart, learned that "time does heal all wounds," and accepted that I would probably never see Molly again.

Now, I had three guys who were my best friends. I knew they would accept my decision and were looking to me for direction. It was not an easy thing to do for a twenty-year-old kid, who now had the task of making decisions that would affect all of our lives.

I was stubbing out my Salem when the phone rang. Picking up the receiver, thinking it was one of the guys, growled, "Yeah."

"Hello Jesse, it's me, Frank!"

"Oh, Mr. Antignani, I'm sorry."

"It's all right, call me Frank. Listen, it's good to hear from you. How've you been."

"I'm all right, still shooting pool and drinking beer. How've you been?"

"Other than the little pucker scar on my side, I'm doing fine. Now tell me, Jesse, what can I do for you?"

"I thought, Frank, maybe I could come in and talk to you."

"What about?" he asked.

"I'd rather not say on the phone, okay?"

"Okay," Frank replied. "How about Friday morning?"

"Thanks a lot, Frank. I'll see you Friday."

Hanging up and turning to his Vice President, sitting across the desk, "I wonder what he wants?"

"I hope," Peanuts Finelli said rather sharply. "It doesn't have anything to do with the Pedretti Brothers." Looking down at the phone, Cisco was thinking the same thing. "I hope he's not." He said quietly to himself.

After hanging up, I called Augie and Larry, telling them the news. I didn't call Mike because I knew he'd be sleeping after working last night. I called later in the afternoon.

"Hi, Joyce," I said. "Is Mike still sleeping?"

"No, he's eating lunch right now."
"Tell him to call me when he's done."
Then I hung up before she could say anything.

Chapter 28

Tuesday

1/2/1961

I PARKED MIKE'S CAR IN THE MONROE STREET UNDERGROUND parking garage and made my way to LaSalle Street and the Union Hall. Standing in the lobby, I kept saying, "What the fuck am I doing here. There's nothing for us here. These are all engineers."

Pushing the door open, I was about to step outside when I heard my name. Turning, I saw Sal standing next to the receptionist's desk. "Come on in," he said. "Frank's waiting to see you."

He walked toward me, extending his hand, and grasping it, I asked, "How are you, Sal?"

"I'm fine," he answered, leading me to Frank's office. Once inside, as we approached, Frank stood up and moved around the desk, holding out his hand.

"Good to see you, Jesse!"

After shaking hands, he motioned me to a chair next to his

desk. Returning to his, he asked, "What can I do for you?"

In the room were two men in expensive suits. I knew I was out of my league and was looking for a way out. "I'm sorry, Frank, for taking up your time. I don't think there's anything here for us."

"Who's us?" Peanuts inquired.

"Augie, Larry, Mike, and me."

"Why do you think that?" Frank asked.

"Look, Frank," I said, standing up. "Before I called, I didn't know who you were or what you did. If I did, I wouldn't have called. When we met, you were just somebody who needed some help. I don't know why I did what I did. It was something that happened in the spur of the moment. Now I have to keep looking over my shoulder. Hoping that I don't see those two guys. Getting back to your question, I said, there's nothing here for us because we work in the steel mill. We're not engineers. I was hoping that you might know of any places that might be hiring. We've been laid off for over a year, and our compensation has run out. So I won't take up any more of your time, but if you hear anything, I'd appreciate a call."

Extending my hand, I said, "Good to see you again, Frank." Then walked over and said the same to Sal at the door. I turned to Frank and said, "You still owe me a game of 8 ball."

Pausing at the receptionist's desk, I said in a low tone, "You have a very sexy voice."

"Excuse me!" the beautiful lady almost hollered. I was smiling broadly on my way out.

"What'ya think, Frank?" Sal asked.

"I like him," Frank replied. "He's got a way about him. I think he's telling the truth about looking for work, and he has those three friends who I think will do just about anything he says. See if we have any demolition in any of our buildings. Let me know by this afternoon."

Chapter 29

Wednesday

1/3/1961

"Mijo," my mother announced from the bedroom doorway, "it's for you, somebody named Sal."

"Hello," I said groggily.

"Jesse," he said, "it's Sal Finelli. How are you?"

"I'm okay," I replied, sitting on the edge of my bed.

"Frank asked me to call you. He wants you and your three friends to come in and see him tomorrow at about eleven in the morning, okay?"

"Okay," I said, "See you then."

Chapter 30

Thursday

1/4/1961

THE MAN NEXT TO THE RECEPTIONIST'S DESK WAS SOMEONE we'd never seen before. As we approached, he met us halfway, saying to me, "You must be Jesse."

"I'm Cappello. Frank's waiting to see you in his office.

Once we were gathered around his desk, Frank came around and shook our hands. "I want you to know, I'll never forget what the four of you did that night. If not for that, I wouldn't be standing here now, but let's get to why all of you are here. I've asked Mr. Cappello to be here; he's in charge of our apprentice program for stationary engineers."

"I thought this was only for operating engineers," I said.

"We're all under the same umbrella," Frank answered. "Stationary engineers learn to operate and maintain boilers, cold water chillers, and air conditioners. We're doing demolition work in a few buildings; if you want, you can start tomorrow morning."

"What's the pay?" Mike asked.

"Ten dollars an hour," Frank answered. "The job should last for about four months. During that time, if there are any openings, you can join the Union and start the apprentice program."

"Count me in," I said, looking at my three best friends. Not surprisingly, they all nodded in assent.

"Okay, then," Frank announced. "John will tell you which building you will report to in the morning. Good luck." He ushered us out, then told the other Frank to hang back for a minute.

"Frank," he said, "I want you to keep an eye on the four. If I'm not mistaken, I might have plans for them."

"You got it, Cisco."

Waiting for Frank to return, I walked over to the receptionist's desk, noticed her name, and said, "Excuse me."

She looked at me with a questioning look and replied, "Yes?"

"I'd like to apologize for how I acted the other day."

"Thank you for that," she said with the most amazing smile I'd seen since Molly was—I thought. *What the fuck.* It was the first time I'd thought about Molly in over a year.

"Are you all right?" the sexy voice asked.

"Oh, I'm sorry," I said. "Something popped up in my mind that I forgot to ask Frank."

"Okay, fellas," Frank Capello announced, coming out of his office.

"Let's go to my office, and you can fill out some forms, and we'll find out where you'll go to work."

The next four months were about knocking down walls, putting everything in dumpsters, and cleaning up. During that time, there were three openings, so Mike, Augie, and Larry got to join the Union and started their apprentices. It took me another month.

Chapter 31

Wednesday

6/15/1962

I LOVED WALKING AROUND DOWNTOWN CHICAGO, ALL THE TALL buildings, the traffic, the people, and, most of all, the women. We've been working now for over a year. We like the job, and the pay is good. We each have a car, so we no longer have to carpool.

Larry and Augie are married now, and I think Barb is pregnant. We don't see each other much anymore, except on the weekends. Sunday is our only day to play ball and have a couple of beers together. I've sat on our bench several times, but it doesn't feel the same. (I wonder what she's doing now.) I've talked to Jeannie a couple of times. She says the last time they spoke was when Molly was in her first year at college. Since then, nothing. All the time they talked, Molly never mentioned me. I never expected she would.

I turned left onto LaSalle Street and continued on my way to the Union Hall. Upon arriving, I noticed a man standing in front, looking both ways up and down LaSalle Street. He looked to be in his late 50s or early 60s, about 5 feet 10 inches tall, with thinning brown hair and rimless glasses. He wore brown slacks, a sport coat, and an open-necked shirt.

Reaching for the door, I casually said, "How you doing?"

He didn't answer but just nodded, continuing in. I stopped at the reception desk and noticed that "sexy voice" had her nameplate on the desk – "Sondra Keene" – even that sounded sexy.

"Hi, Jesse," she said. "Frank's expecting you."

Wow, I thought, she remembered my name. When I walked in, Frank stood up and came around his desk.

"Sit down, Sit down!" He motioned me to one of his chairs. "I called you here because I've got some good news. The chief engineer in your building is leaving in two weeks for a newer and bigger building. I've talked to him and Cappy, and they both say you're ready to move up. Whatya think?"

To say I was shocked would be an understatement. I didn't know what to say. I felt tongue-tied.

"The building is 100% occupied," Frank continued. "That means you can have your pick up any three engineers you want."

"What about someone who has more seniority," I asked.

"You let me worry about that, okay? And if anybody asks, tell em to come to see me."

I was about to ask, "Why me?" when there was a commotion at the door. Before Frank or I could get up, the door opened, and the man I'd seen outside walked in. He began walking toward Frank, and I noticed his right hand had a small-caliber automatic. I motioned for Sondra to back out, which she did, closing the door.

He was standing in front of Frank's desk, with his back to me. "Just sit there, kid. This won't take long." Before I had time to think it through, I was on my feet, the .45 pressing against his spine.

"Drop it in the chair, real slow," I growled.

"What the fuck!" he exclaimed. "Do you know who he is?"

"I know who you used to be. I won't repeat it," pulling back the hammer.

With a sob, he dropped the gun in the seat, turned to me and said, "I know it was him. My two boys went looking for him about two years ago. They never came back."

"I don't know what the fuck you're talking about, but you should've never come in here waving a gun at me." With that, Frank reached for the phone,

"What are you doing?" I asked, getting a little nervous.

"I'm calling Sal and Cappy," he said.

"Wait a minute, Frank, I can handle this."

"What?" he answered.

"I said, I can handle this."

"You sure?" Frank asked, now with a little smile.

"Yeah, I'm sure."

"Okay then, just get him the fuck out of my office."

"Let's go for a walk," I said, pushing him toward the door.

Walking down LaSalle, I had my arm around his shoulder like we were two good friends. Still, I was whispering, "Don't ever come back here again, 'cause if you do, I'll put a bullet in the back of your fucking head, understand?

"But you don't know what he did."

"I don't give a fuck. Just remember what I said."

I stopped and watched him walk down LaSalle Street, his head bowed, and I felt a little sorry for him. Walking back to the hall, I suddenly realized what Frank meant that night and that I wouldn't have to worry about them anymore. They were probably buried somewhere up in Wisconsin. The thought of what I might become involved in made me a little excited but more nervous.

Chapter 32

Wednesday

6/15/1962

I stopped at Sondra's desk on my way back in, and I could see she was visibly shaken.

"You all right?" I asked.

She didn't say anything, just nodded her head.

"Okay," I said. "Do me a favor. Lock the front door."

Frank was sitting behind his desk when I walked in. "Now, that's the second time you saved my ass," he said with a smile.

"I'm just glad I was here," I answered.

"Do you have a permit to carry that?"

"No," I said.

"Then why do you carry it?"

"Every time I go somewhere, I think I'll run into those two brothers."

"I told you not to worry about them anymore, and by the way, did you take care of the old man?"

"He won't be coming around here anymore."

"Are you sure?"

"I said I'd take care of it!" I said a little forcefully.

"Okay then," Frank said, coming around his desk and walking to the door. After locking it, he turned to me, saying, "This is between you and me. You don't tell anyone, not even your three buddies."

"What about Sal and Frank?" I asked.

"You let me worry about them, okay?"

"Okay," I said a little nervously.

He went behind his desk, opened the top drawer, withdrew a small penknife, and stood before me.

"Hold out your hand," he ordered.

I didn't know why, but I felt compelled to do what he wanted. He took my hand, pricked my thumb, then his, and meshed them together, saying, "Blood In, Blood Out."

My legs were actually shaking. I kept thinking, *They only do this in the movies.* When that was done, Frank held me at arm's length and looked into my eyes, saying, "My blood is yours, and yours is mine."

I stood there as if nailed to the spot; finally, we hugged. He patted me on the back, saying, "I hope you understand what this means."

"I think I do," I answered rather shakily.

"You're part of the family now," he said. "I'll always take care of you the best I can, and I have to know that you'll always have my back."

"Anything, I promise, Frank, Will include my three partners."

"Good enough," Frank replied with a smile. "Just not about the blood, okay?"

"Okay," I answered.

"Now, get the fuck outa my office," he said, laughing. At the door, he stopped me. "Jesse," he said, "outside of business, you can call me Cisco."

"And you can call me Flacco," I said with a smile and stepped out into the lobby.

Sondra was still at her desk when I stepped out.

"You still here?" I asked.

She nodded her head, still looking at the front door.

"Are you all right, Sondra?"

She turned her head, saying, "I think so."

"Don't worry. That guy won't be back."

"I'm so glad you were here," she said, a little color coming back into her face.

"So am I," I answered.

She looked up at me, rather demurely asking, "Jesse, I'd like to ask for a favor."

"Sure," I said. "Anything."

"Would you walk me to the train station?"

"Right now?"

"If you don't mind."

"No, I was just leaving."

Right then, Frank exited his office and looked over at us. Then asked, "Sondra, I thought you'd be gone by now."

"I'm still a little shaken, so Jesse agreed to walk me to the train station."

"Well, you two have a good night. Sandy, I'll see you in the morning."

Walking south on LaSalle Street, I glanced over at Sondra. She looked about 5 feet 7 inches tall without the bouffant hairdo. Grey-green eyes, slightly arched eyebrows, full lips that looked ready to kiss at any time. Her light blue cashmere sweater let all of the contours of her breasts show. She was well endowed.

The gray A-line skirt was cut right above the knee, and the gray jacket made for a great combination. Topping it off was the black patent leather, low heel pumps.

Sooner rather than later, we were standing at the entrance on North Michigan Avenue.

"You take the train every day?" I asked. "Why not drive?"

"I don't like the traffic."

"Where do you come in from?"

"I live in Wheeling."

"And your car is parked in the parking lot?"

"It's about a half-hour to my place, Jesse. Would it be alright if I bought you a drink someday after work?"

"What about your husband?" I asked, hopefully.

"I've been divorced five years now."

"Sorry about that," I replied.

"Don't be," Sondra said. "He was a real asshole if you'll excuse the language."

"Well then, I guess I'll say yes. How about Friday?"

"Friday's fine. Will you come by the hall?"

"I'll be there about 5:30, goodnight Sondra. See you Friday."

"Good night, Jesse," she said, brushing my lips with hers. With that, she turned and descended the stairs.

Chapter 33

Thursday

6/16/1962

THE THREE OF US SAT IN ROLLIE'S BACKYARD, WAITING FOR Mike to show up. At 8:30, he walked in from the alley, grabbed a beer from the cooler, and sat down next to Augie.

"What's up, Aug?"

"I don't know, Mike."

"Did we get laid off again?" Larry wanted to know.

"Well, I gotta tell you guys, you won't be returning to the same buildings in two weeks," I said, trying to keep a straight face.

"What's that mean?" Mike wanted to know.

"The chief engineer at my building is going to a new and larger facility in two weeks, and guess who the new chief is?

"No shit," they all exclaimed almost in unison.

"Yeah, and I get to pick my three engineers."

"That calls for another beer," Mike said, standing up.

"So, what ya say?" I proclaimed, holding up my beer.
"Yeah," we all shouted, tapping our bottles in a toast.

Chapter 34

Friday

6/17/1962

Walking down LaSalle Street, I was as nervous as a long-tailed cat in a room full of rocking chairs. I'd talked to Frank before I left work. He told me Sondra was thirty-six years old, divorced for five years, with no kids, and she wasn't seeing anyone now. I asked him if it was all right to have a drink with her. He said what she did on her time was none of his business; this he said with a wink and a smile.

Choices was a bar located next to the building where we worked. It reminded me of the TV show *Cheers*. One of the bartenders looked a little like Ted Danson. No sooner did we walk in than Sondra turned and said, "We could have taken a cab."

"It's only three blocks, and my car is parked down on Lower Wacker.

The bartender had just walked away with our orders when

I felt a hand on my shoulder. Turning, I saw it was Russ Bachman, my boss.

"I heard you'll be getting my job in two weeks. Think you can handle it?"

"Yeah, I think so. Russ, you know, Sondra?"

"From the Union Hall, right? How ya doing?"

"I'm fine," she said in reply.

With that, he moved to the other side of her and began making conversation. After a while, Sondra turned her back and talked to Russ as if I wasn't there. That went on for a good twenty minutes.

Finishing my beer, I stood up and said, "Well, I gotta go. Thanks for the beer." I was halfway to the door when Sondra caught up to me. "Where you going?"

"Home," I said. "Thanks for the beer."

"You're just gonna leave me here?"

"I'm sure Russ will walk you to the train station."

"Why are you doing this?"

"Look, Sondra, you bought me a drink, then you spent the last half hour with your back to me, talking to him."

"Well, you don't talk much."

"I told you I wasn't big on small talk, and you seem to be doing all right with Russ."

"You sound like your jealous," she said, now smiling.

"I don't know you well enough for that."

"Oh, come on, quit acting like a kid."

"Fuck you," I said, then turned around and walked away.

I stopped at the corner of Wacker and Wabash, lit up a Salem, and took the opportunity to turn and look back. I didn't know if she was still there or had gone home. Either way, I didn't give a shit. Rounding the corner, I walked down to Lower Wacker, got my car, and drove home.

Chapter 35

Tuesday

9/7/1962

I GOT A PHONE CALL THAT FRANK WANTED TO SEE ME AT THE hall at about three that afternoon. I called back, asking if I could stop by after work. "No," he said. I needed to be there at that time.

I hadn't seen Sondra since that night a couple of months ago. I didn't know what to expect. I was hoping that there wouldn't be any kind of confrontation. As I walked across the foyer, headed for Frank's office, she looked up, smiled and said, "Hello, Jesse."

I didn't stop. I just answered, "Hi."

Frank was seated behind his desk, Sal and John on either side.

"Jesse, come in, take a seat." Frank motioned to a chair. "Thanks, Sondra, and no more phone calls, okay? You can light up if you want?"

"Thanks, Frank," I said, lighting up a Salem. "What's up?"

"It's after hours, Flacco, so just call me Cisco. That's Peanuts, and he's Cappy."

"Again, Cisco, what's up?"

"How would you like to make some extra money?"

"I don't need a second job, Frank."

"It's not exactly another job; it's more like a favor."

"What kind of favor?" I asked, looking around the room.

"All right, let me talk to Jesse," Frank answered, nodding to the door. Once they were gone, we sat next to each other in front of Frank's desk.

"Before we get started, there's something I have to tell you."

"Okay," he said. "What is it?"

"Well, I gotta tell ya, I'm not comfortable calling you Cisco. It would be different if we were the same age. So if it's alright, I'll just stick with Frank."

"That's fine with me, Jesse. I never liked Flacco anyway. What I wanted to talk to you about has nothing to do with our relationship. As far as I'm concerned, you are now part of the family. No one will ever know unless it becomes essential. I like you, Jesse, 'cause you reminded me of me when I was younger."

"Thanks a lot, Frank, for—" The door opened. Sondra stuck her head in, saying, "Everybody's gone now, Frank. I'll lock up."

"Thanks, Sondra," Frank said, looking at me. "Whatever happened between you two?"

"It was just a drink," I said. "Besides, I'm not into older women."

"Are you fucking nuts? She's only thirty-six years old."

"And I'm just twenty-two. Okay, now let's get back to why I'm here."

"You remember what we talked about the last time you were here?"

"Yeah," I said, "something about being part of your family."

"Not part of my family, I meant, 'The Family.'"

"What's that mean?"

"People say different names, but to us, it's 'The Family.'"

"Are you saying what I think you're saying?"

"What ya thinking?"

"I'm thinking, why me? I'm not even Italian!"

"That's why we have to keep it between us."

"Are you sure you know what you're doing, Frank? What if someone finds out? Then what?"

"I like you, Jesse. As I said before, I saw myself thirty years ago when I looked at you. You have your three friends, who I think are loyal to you and will always follow your lead. They must never know what we have between us. All they need to know is that they are doing this on the side for me to make some extra cash."

"What exactly are we doing for this extra cash?"

"We have a few taverns and restaurants around the Rogers Park area where people come in and bet on sports and borrow money. All you have to do is make a monthly collection, bring it here at the Union meeting, and give it to Sal or John."

"What do we get?" I asked.

"You get ten percent, which you can split between the four of you."

Chapter 36

Tuesday

9/7/1962

"I'll have to talk it over with my guys."

"Okay, but I have to know sometime next week."

"One last thing, Frank, if we're going to do this, I want a permit for my piece."

"I'll see what I can do. Now get the fuck out of my office," again with the same smile.

Chapter 37

Friday

9/10/1962

Bobby was now filling in for Rollie on the weekends. I called at about 6:30pm. I asked him if there was any beer in the fridge. When he replied there was, I said, "We would be using the backroom about eight o'clock."

The meeting was short and sweet. The guys all agreed excitedly, almost as if it were an adventure. Still, once I explained the circumstances, they grew somber and questioned me about everything. I told them about the money and how we would divide it up. How we would do the collections and where to turn them in. I emphasized one final thing very strongly: do not tell anyone what we are doing, especially the wives. We shook hands, finished our beers and cigarettes, went into the front, and shot some 8 ball.

Chapter 38

The Split

9/13/1962

THE FOLLOWING TWO WEEKS WERE SPENT MAKING collections. Sal went with us to make introductions; everything went smoothly with no problems. When we got our ten percent, we couldn't be happier. Then and there, we made a vow not to do anything to rock the boat.

Chapter 39

Friday

9/17/1962

IT WAS AROUND THIS TIME THAT I RAN INTO SONDRA. WE were on our way to Choices for our Friday night beer. She was standing beside the door. She stepped forward, saying, "Could I talk to you for a minute?"

Walking past me, Larry said, "We'll be inside."

"This won't take long," she said. "You'll never know how sorry I am about what happened between us. It was all my fault. I tried to make you jealous, but I made a mistake. Since we divorced, I've never been attracted to someone like I am to you. I know I'm older, and I hope I'm not making a fool of myself, but if you want, maybe we can start over again."

With that, she handed a slip of paper. "That's my home phone," then she put her head down and started to walk away.

"Sondra, wait!" I said.

When she turned, I could see she was crying.

"How about I buy you a drink?"

"Are you sure?" she asked, her face lighting up.

"Come on," I said, holding out my hand.

She took it, holding on tightly till we got to the door. "Do you have a hankie?"

"Yeah, I think so," I said, reaching into my back pocket.

"Okay," Sondra said, handing back the hankie and again taking my hand in hers. We both smiled and walked inside.

We sat in my car on Lower Wacker Drive at the night's end. We both knew what was coming, so we just let it happen. We kissed, first soft and barely touching, then deep and exploring. I felt something explode inside me, like there was electricity on her lips. Her tongue was a lightning rod hitting me from the tip of my tongue to the pit of my stomach.

When we pulled apart, she opened her eyes, saying, "Wow! Where did you learn to kiss like that?"

"You didn't do too bad yourself."

"Do you want to take me home?" she asked excitedly.

"Right now, there's nothing I'd rather do."

"What time is it?" she wanted to know.

"8:35," I said, looking at my watch.

"Are you hungry?"

"Yeah, I could eat something."

"How about a pizza and beer?"

"Great," I said. "Where do you want to stop?"

"There's a Pizza Hut near my place. We can order from there."

"I thought I was giving you a ride to your car."

"Oh," she said, sounding a little disappointed. "If that's what you want."

"No, no," I replied. "That's not what I meant. I'd love to have pizza and a beer at your place."

Half an hour later, I was in the driveway of Sondra's

townhouse on Ginger Woods Court. She was standing beside her car in the garage. "Come on," she waved me inside.

I follow her without saying a word. First, through the laundry room, into the kitchen, putting her purse on the table and next to the stairs. I handed her my jacket, which she hung along with her coat in the hall closet.

"There's beer in the fridge," Sondra announced, walking back into the kitchen. "What do you like on your pizza?"

"Sausage, pepperoni, and cheese," I answered. "Do you mind if I smoke?"

"It's all right. I'll get you an ashtray."

Walking into the den, beer and cigarette in hand, I settled on the couch, facing the TV.

"Would you like to watch something?"

"No, I think I'll just relax until the pizza gets here."

"That should be in about a quarter of an hour," Sondra said, sitting on the other end of the couch.

Putting my beer on the end table and my arm on the back of the couch, I softly said, "Come here." She slid in easily, putting her head on my chest. I slid my hand down and caressed the cool skin of her arm.

"Jesse," she said softly.

"Yeah," I replied.

"Can you stay the night?"

Tilting her face up, I looked directly into her eyes, saying, "Are you sure?"

"Oh yes," Sondra answered. "I want to sleep next to you and wake up the same way."

"Really," I said.

"But mostly," she said, "I wanna fuck you all night." She said that without even blinking her eyes or looking away.

"Wow," was all I could say. "I've never had anyone say that —" Then the doorbell chimed.

"I'll get it," I said, getting up and walking to the front door.

After our little snack, Sondra stood at the counter, wrapping the pizza in tin foil. I walked up and put my arms around her, and kissed the nape of her neck. With a moan, she sagged against me. I put my arms around her more tightly. "We can clean up later," I said against her ear. Dropping my arms, I let her lead me upstairs.

Chapter 40

Saturday

9/18/1962

I WOKE UP WITH THE FEELING THAT SOMEBODY WAS WATCHING me. Rolling over, it was Sondra looking down at me with a smile. "Good morning, sleepyhead. I thought I'd let you sleep in today."

"Thanks," I said, sitting up against the headboard. "What time is it?"

"10:30," she replied. "I tried not to make any noise."

"How long have you been up?"

"Since about eight o'clock, I've been waiting so I could take my shower."

"You look pretty fresh to me."

"Yeah, I'll bet. As you can see, this is what I wear around the house."

"I like the Bears jersey," I said.

"There's coffee and some sweet rolls downstairs. I'm gonna jump in the shower, okay?"

Watching Sondra walk into the bathroom, I couldn't help but think about what we'd done last night. I waited until I heard the water come on.

"Come on in. The water's fine!"

Later, as I was putting on my shoes, Sondra came down the stairs, entered the kitchen, poured a cup of coffee, and sat at the counter.

"Are you leaving already?"

"Yeah, I gotta go check on my mom," I answered, getting up and heading for the closet.

"Not even a cup of coffee?" Sondra asked, looking at her cup.

"I guess a coffee's all right," I said, sitting beside her.

"Last night," she said, "was great. This morning was really unbelievable."

"Yeah, I know. That's the first time I ever took a shower with anyone."

"I want to say something before you go, so don't say anything until I finish, okay? Jesse, I never thought I would say something like this, especially since we don't know each other well."

"One thing," I said, "If you're going to talk to me, you could at least look at me."

"I'm sorry," she replied, "it's a little embarrassing."

"After last night and this morning, you can feel embarrassed?"

"It's not that. I've never asked anyone to move in with me."

"What?" I said, almost spilling my coffee. "Are you really serious?"

"I shouldn't have said that. You better go and check on your mom. I'm sorry."

"Wait," I said. "Are you saying this because of last night and this morning?"

"I think I'm in love with you."

"I'm, I'm, I'm," I stammered.

"It's all right," Sondra whispered, "you don't have to say anything. Just go."

When I got to the closet, she stood at the foot of the stairs. Putting my jacket on, I turned to her, saying, "All right, I'm going, but you better make some room in your closet."

With almost disbelief, Sondra sagged against the railing, saying, "Oh, Jesse, yes, yes." In a flash, she was in my arms. We kissed, and I could taste the salt in her tears.

"If you don't stop, I'm gonna have to take you upstairs again."

"Promises, Promises."

Stepping back, I said, "I gotta go. I'll call you Sunday."

"Tomorrow?" she questioned, looking a little disappointed.

"Yeah, I want to spend some time with my mom and get together with my partners."

"What time will you call?"

"Probably in the afternoon. Now I've gotta go."

Chapter 41

Sunday

9/19/1962

I HUNG UP MY LAST SHIRT AT ABOUT 2PM. SONDRA WAS
waiting for me in the shower, where we had another go-round.
It seemed she couldn't get enough. Later sitting at the kitchen
counter, we celebrated with a couple glasses of champagne.
On the way upstairs, I told Sondra to ask Frank if I could stop
by after work and to call and let me know. She agreed and said
she had set the alarm for 6:30am.

Chapter 42

Monday

9/20/1962

Sondra looked up when I walked in the front door and stopped at the desk, "Is he still here?" I asked.

"Yes," she answered, "Sal and Frank just left."

"What?" I intoned.

"You're undressing me again."

"That's 'cause I like what I see."

"Think you can wait till tonight?"

"I guess I'll have to," I answered, walking up and knocking on the door.

Frank was already on his feet when I walked in. "Jesse," he said, "sit down. What can I do for you?"

"How are you, Frank?"

"I'm fine, just getting older. How are things on the street?"

"The streets are good, a couple of incidents, nothing we couldn't handle."

"That's what I wanted to talk about. Do you think you could handle a couple more pickups?"

"Sure, Frank, no problem. How many more?"

"There's four more, but they're on the west side."

"Just tell me where, and we'll take care of it."

"Sal will tell you at the next meeting. Now tell me what happened."

"We'd just walked out of the Corner Club when three guys walked up to us, pushing us into the alley, and were about to shake us down. They didn't know that Larry and Augie were sitting in the car. The outcome was the one with the knife took a shot to the knee, no big deal,"

"You still carry the .45?" he asked.

"Only when we're working the streets."

"How about the other three?"

"The same," I answered.

"Just remember, no hits unless I say so. You got it?"

\"I know, Frank, not till you give the word."

"Okay, now what did you want to talk about?"

"I just wanted to tell you that I moved."

"What the fuck is that? Ask Cassie to come in here."

"Who's Cassie?"

"You don't know, do you?"

"Know what?"

"Cassie is Cassondra. Now, would you please ask her to come in? Before Jesse leaves, get his new address and phone number."

"I know his address and phone number already."

"You do?" Frank asked.

"Yes," she said, "the address is 9401 Ginger Woods Court, Unit #3.

"Isn't that where you—wait a minute, are you saying what I think?"

"Yeah," Cassie replied, taking hold of my hand.

Looking at Cassie in a low voice, Frank asked, "Is this what you want?"

"Very much so," Cassie replied.

"What about you?" he asked, turning to me.

"I care for her very strongly," I said in reply.

"Okay then," Frank smiled at us. "Now get the hell out of my office.!"

Standing at her desk, I asked, "Cassondra, really?"

"I never liked that name. Now, let's go home and fuck."

To say that Cassie had a healthy sexual appetite would be a colossal understatement. Maybe that's why I slept so well.

Chapter 43

Wednesday

3/10/1963

SPRING CAME EARLY THIS YEAR. AFTER SIX MONTHS OF CLOUDY and frigid weather. It was a welcome sight to see the sun again. My mom lives downstairs with my sister, so I don't return to the neighborhood as often as I would like. Our time on the streets has grown as we have four more stops on the west side. Augie, Larry, and Mike have been excellent at not asking any questions about what we do. As far as they're concerned, Frank is the President of our Union, who does loan sharking and booking sports bets. Frank and I agree that someday, they will be told who he really is and what he represents. I think they'll be okay with it.

My life with Cassie has been great so far. I'm living a life that too few twenty-three-year-olds could imagine. A life with a beautiful older woman, who I now know is entirely in love with this tall, skinny Mexican. As for me, I care for her a lot, although, after Molly, it's hard for me to say the love word. I don't think I'll ever love anyone the way I loved her. She completely dominated my heart, soul, and every thought and action. I wanted to be with her every second that I was awake.

Everything we did together was out of love and all the other deep feelings we had for each other. She was not like some teenage crush. She's a part of who I am now.

All those years of self-pity and low opinion of myself, Cassie showed me that a beautiful girl could love someone like me, and I'll always treasure that.

Chapter 44

Sunday

5/14/1963

THE PHONE WOKE ME UP THAT SUNDAY MORNING. CASSIE picked it up on the second ring and, after saying, "Hello," listened for a minute, then handed it to me. "It's your sister Mary."

"Hi, Mar," I said a little groggily.

"Good morning, sleepyhead," she replied.

"How's Ma?"

"She's fine right now. She's having her coffee with Ralph in the kitchen. The reason I called is that you've got a letter here from the Government."

As soon as she said, "Government," I knew what it was. I'd been expecting it for some time. I sat in bed, lit up a Salem, and tried to collect my thoughts. Cassie didn't help much, kneeling behind me, putting her head against my neck, and saying softly, "Is it your mom?"

"Naw," I said. "It's a letter I got that I've been waiting for a while now."

"What is it?" she asked, sliding around and sitting beside me.

"If it is what I think it is, I have to go for my physical."

"Physical, for what?"

"I might be on my way to being drafted."

Standing up, Cassie declared, "I'll put on some coffee, and we can talk about it."

"Wait," I said, turning her slightly to face me, "You are so beautiful when you're naked."

"Thank you, sir. You always say the nicest things."

After breakfast, I was on my second cup of coffee, checking the sports section of the *Sun-Times*. Cassie was clearing the dishes and putting them in the dishwasher. She looked so happy. Every time she caught me looking at her, she would smile and blow me a kiss. I decided right then to go to the next level of our relationship.

"You wanna take a ride?" I asked.

"Sure, where to?" she replied.

"South Deering," I replied.

"You sure you want me to go?"

"I asked you, didn't I?"

"Give me a couple of minutes to change."

"You look great just like that. Come on, let's go."

"Cassie, this is my sister Mary, her husband Ralph, and my niece Margaret, and here is the one and only my mom, Ramona. Everybody calls her Ma."

Watching Cassie walk up to my mom with her hand held out, I thought they would shake hands, except my mom would have none of that. With an "Ay, Dios Mio," she took Cassie in a big hug. At first, Cassie looked bewildered, but then she smiled and hugged back.

"Que Bonita," my mom exclaimed, stepping back, smiling

at her, and with that, Cassie turned and hurried out the door. When I got to her, she was leaning against the house, sobbing. "What's the matter?" I asked, stepping in front of her.

"I know I shouldn't have come," she said between sobs. "They don't like me, do they?"

"What are you talking about?"

"Your mom. What did she say about me?"

Taking her by the shoulders, tilting her head up, I said with a smile, "My mom said, 'Oh my god, how beautiful!'"

"Really?" Cassie replied, her face beginning to brighten up.

"Really," I replied, using my handkerchief to wipe away the tears. "I'm getting pretty good at this."

"At what?" she replied.

"Just something I was thinking about, no big deal."

Walking back inside, Cassie let go of my hand. She started walking towards my mom, who was still standing in the same place, only now with a confused look and expression like "What did I do"?

Taking both of my mom's hands, she said, "I'm sorry, Ma!"

My mom replied, "Maybe I should have said it in English."

"It sounded just fine in Spanish," Cassie said, putting her arms around her.

No sooner were we in the car than Cassie was snuggled up against me, with her face buried in my chest. She did that little shake and shiver, letting me know she was crying again.

"What now?" I asked.

"I've never been so happy in all my life."

"Why's that?" I asked, not turning the ignition on.

"You love me, your sister likes me, but your mom likes me most.

"Well, my mom has good taste."

We looked at each other and knew we had committed to each other. We kissed then, nothing lustful, just a sweet, loving kiss.

Chapter 45

Friday

6/25/1963

THE FOLLOWING FIVE WEEKS FLEW BY IN A FLASH. I MET WITH Frank. He promised that both of my jobs would be here when I got back and that he had plans for the four of us. With the last shot and beer gone, we were saying goodbye for a while. I told Augie that he was responsible for making the collections and delivering the money. I had told Cassie I would be back Saturday afternoon. So now, I was on my way to the south side.

Chapter 46

Saturday

6/26/1963

AFTER MY FAVORITE BREAKFAST, CARNE CON CHILE, TWO EGGS, beans, corn tortillas, and two cups of coffee, we said our goodbyes. My mom cried. Mary and Ralph promised to look after her. With that, I drove back to Wheeling. I felt like it was my lucky day. My favorite breakfast, and now Cassie was making breaded pork chops, au gratin potatoes, and green beans. Later we watched TV, took a nice warm shower, then went to bed.

Chapter 47

Sunday

6/27/1963

WE SPENT A LAZY SUNDAY SLEEPING IN UNTIL TEN O'CLOCK. Having breakfast, spending the rest of the day reading the *Sun-Times*, then watching the Cubs lose another game. Later we went to Alexander's, had a nice dinner and a few drinks, and arrived back at about 11:30pm. We took a nice hot shower together, went to bed, and made slow magical love, finally falling asleep in each other's arms.

Chapter 48

Monday

6/28/1963

IT'S 2:30PM, AND WE'RE SITTING IN THE PARKING LOT OF THE Army Induction Center. Neither has spoken in the last half-hour, not knowing what to say or how to say it.

Finally, Cassie broke the silence almost mournfully, "I miss you already."

"It's only two years," I said.

"Two years could seem like a lifetime," she replied.

"Are you trying to say something?" I asked, hoping she wouldn't say what I thought she was trying to get to.

"It's just that I've waited so long to find someone who loved me as much as I love him, who makes me feel like a woman more than anyone I've ever met. Someone who makes me happy, sometimes so happy I have to cry. Jesse, I love you for all that and much more, like how I feel safe and comfortable together. Your sense of humor and how you're not afraid to laugh at yourself. I just want you to know that I'll always love you, and if you want, I'll be here when you get back."

"Cassie," I said, "everything you said goes double for me. You know, what I thought was going to be just a fling, for me, has turned into something that I don't want to let go of, so when I come home, if you want, we can talk about starting a family."

"Oh Jesse," she exclaimed, coming into my arms, "I want to so badly."

"Okay then, I'll see you when I get out."

We kissed one last time, putting all the love and longing of the next two years into it. I got out of the car and saw her crying again. It took a lot, but I turned and walked into the Induction Center.

PART II

1965 – 1969

IN DREAMS
By Roy Orbison

Chapter 49

Friday

5/26/1965

WALKING OUT OF THE UNION STATION ON SOUTH CANAL Street, I couldn't wait to get to the Union Hall and see Cassie again. I was a nervous wreck, shaking so bad I had to light up a Salem and try to calm down. I hadn't finished my cigarette when a yellow cab stopped in the middle of the street. With the window down, the driver yelled, "Where to soldier?" After throwing my duffel bag in the back seat, I jumped upfront with him, saying, "Operating Engineers Union Hall."

"Thanks for serving," he said, putting the taxi in gear. "This one's on me."

"Thanks, Buddy," I said.

"No problem," he answered. I sat back and enjoyed the short ride.

When he pulled up to the curb, I grabbed the duffel bag and climbed out. "Thanks again," I said.

"See you around," he replied and pulled into traffic.

Standing there on the sidewalk, it finally dawned on me that no one knew where I'd been or when I was coming home, not even Frank. I was selfish, but I didn't want any letters or phone calls from Cassie or my mom.

Getting up the courage, I opened the door and walked in. Almost immediately, I noticed something wasn't right. It wasn't Cassie sitting behind the desk, but a much younger girl. She had curly black hair and wore glasses.

Dropping my bag, I walked up to the desk. The receptionist looked at me, saying, "Can I help you?"

"Yes," I replied. "Is Cassie here?"

"I'm afraid Cassie doesn't work here anymore."

"How long?" I said, getting a sinking feeling inside.

"She left last year. Are you a friend of hers?"

"You can say that," I answered. "Is Frank here?"

"Yes, but he's a little busy right now."

"Could you please tell him Flacco's out here?"

"Frank," she said over the intercom. "There's someone here to see you. I told him that, but he said to tell you Flacco's out here."

I was halfway through the doorway when I heard her announce, "You can go in now." As I entered, Frank rose, walked around the desk, approached, and extended his hand.

"Jesse, so good to see you're back."

"It's good to be back."

"I guess we can forget about Flacco, right, Jesse?"

"How are you, Sal?" I asked as he stood up.

\"You know, same ole, same ole. You put on some weight."

"Yeah, it was that great Army food, potatoes in every meal."

"Jesse," Frank interrupted. "This is Henry Cisneros. He's our new Secretary in Charge of Education and Apprenticeships."

"Where's Frank?" I asked, shaking Henry's hand.

"He retired last year. He's down in sunny Florida now."

"Good to meet you, Henry."

"Just call me Hank, okay?"

"Okay, Sal, Hank, I wanna talk to Jesse alone now."

As Sal and Hank made their way out, Frank called to Sal, "Sal tell Nancy no more calls today."

Turning from the closed door and looking directly at Frank, I was about to ask when he said, "She went home."

"When is she coming back?"

"She doesn't know," Frank answered. "Her father had a bad stroke. Cassie went home to take care of him."

"What about her mother?" I asked.

"She passed away three years ago," he said solemnly. "Cancer."

"Jesse, she also made me promise not to tell you where she lives or her phone number."

"Why not?" I responded, getting angry.

"Because she knows that if you go there, she'll come back with you, and right now, she can't do that."

"Frank," I pleaded. "Just let me call her."

"Only if you promise not to go there."

"Okay," I said, "I promise."

"It has to be a blood promise, nothing else."

"You've got it," boss.

"Okay," Frank said, sitting back down in his chair. "Let's get down to business." With that, he got Nancy on the intercom, telling her to call Larry, Augie and Mike and tell them he wanted to see them in his office after work. Looking back at me, he said, "There have been some changes while you were gone."

"What kind of changes?"

"Well, first of all, I've been thinking about this, and after talking to Sal and Frank, before he retired, we agreed that I should take this before the Council."

"Take what before the Council?"

"Well," he said, "as of last year, Mike, Larry, and Augie are now part of the family, not the blood part like you. Right now, you're the only one at 75 East Wacker. Mike is at the Prudential, Larry's at Standard Oil, and Augie's at the Art Institute."

"I thought we were doing a good job there."

"There was never any problem there."

"Then, why?"

Frank motioned me to one of the chairs and, after lighting up one of his cigars, said, "Are you in a hurry to get home?"

"I guess not, but I'd like to know where all my stuff is."

"All your stuff is back at your mother's house; Cassie's stuff was stored. I asked because I want to talk to the four of you, They won't be here until after 5, so if you want to call Cassie, I'll give you the phone number."

After the 6th ring, I hung up and turned to Frank, saying, "I guess she's not home. I'll try later."

"Well," Frank said, "now that you promised not to go there, I can tell you where she lives. It's a little town in Tennessee called Cleveland if you can believe it."

"Really," I smiled, "Cleveland, Tennessee."

"Yeah," Frank laughed. "Who would've thought. Now, how about a beer? The fridge is in the closet."

After a big pull on his beer and put his cigar in the ashtray, Frank smiled and said, "Okay, now tell me, where have you been in the last two years."

I didn't finish my summation because, at that moment, the door opened, and three of the best friends any man could ever have walked in. We all looked at each other for what seemed an hour or more.

Finally, Mike broke the spell, walking up and giving me a big bear hug saying, "It's about time, Mother Fucker!"

"Fuck you, Mike!" I replied.

"Anytime, honey," he mimicked. We both laughed.

"Good to see you back, boss," Augie chimed in with a hug.

"Me too, boss," Larry exclaimed, "but I ain't gonna hug you unless you kiss me first."

"Fuck you too, Larry," I said with a smile.

"Okay," Frank said, puffing on his cigar. "Now that we got all that pussy shit out of the way, you three get a beer and let's talk. By now, you all know who I am and what I do; you've all agreed to join the family and work mainly for me. Right now, I can't name the other members of the "Council," but they've all agreed to what I'm telling you. Okay, any questions?"

With no questions, I looked at my three best friends and wondered what they were thinking. Frank and I had discussed this before, and he knew where I stood. "First of all," he said, "you answer to me first, then the Council. Nothing is done without our approval. If you go on your own, you're on your own. If anything happens, I'll always have your back as much as possible. Now, I want you to go home, think hard about this, and let me know by Monday."

Looking at the three of them, I wasn't surprised to see they all nodded in agreement. Turning to Frank, I said, "We're all in."

"Good, I'm glad to hear that, so starting Monday, none of you will be working in any building. You will be working as Union Security!"

"What's that mean?" Larry wanted to know.

"That means," Frank answered, "that you will be spending your time here at the hall, ensuring nothing goes wrong. In about two weeks, you'll have a gun permit. You'll have to get your own piece and ensure it's clean. Two of you will be here at all times. How you work that out is up to you. I expect you to be there if I have to attend a meeting, dinner, or any function. Okay, so far?" we all nodded again.

"One thing, Frank," I asked, taking a drag on my Salem, "do we still make the collections?"

"Only if you want."

"What do you guys think?"

"Anything to get away from the 'old lady' for a while," Augie laughed.

"One last question, Frank," Mike asked, looking at me for approval. "What does all this stuff mean? If the time comes, we might have to take somebody out?"

"Hopefully, that time won't ever come, but if it does, do you have a problem with that? If you do, tell me now."

"No problem, just want to ensure we're all on the same page."

"Okay then," Frank announced. "I'll see you three Monday bright and early. Jesse, you go home, take a couple of weeks off, then come and see me. If you need anything at that time, call me."

"I'll be ready in a week," I replied.

"We're all good then, right?"

"Right!" we all answered.

"Then get the fuck out of my office," he laughed.

Standing outside, I looked at my three best friends, knowing that what we had agreed would affect us for the rest of our lives. "If anyone wants to back out, now's the time," I said.

"What the fuck's that all about?" Larry asked, glancing at Mike and Augie, who turned back at me.

"Take it easy, Lar," I said. "We should understand that if we go along with this, it's not like TV or the movies. This is for real, and there's no backing out later."

"We made a pact a couple of years ago," Mike said rather calmly, "that you spoke for the four of us, and I think it still stands.

"I think we go home, you guys talk it over with the girls, and we meet at Rollie's Saturday night, okay? Now, which one of you is giving me a ride home?"

"I'm still in the neighborhood, so I'll take you."

"Thanks, Mike," I said, and after hefting my duffel bag, we walked around the corner and into the parking lot.

Traffic was light on the southbound Outer Drive. We exited on 22nd Street, going west until we connected with the Dan Ryan Expressway.

Lighting a Salem while passing Comiskey Park, I turned and asked Mike, "Still living at home?"

"Yeah," he answered, "I've got the whole basement to myself."

"How about Joyce?"

"She's still at the same place on 106th. About six months ago, she started working at General Mills."

"Who watches Li'l Mikey?"

"She takes him by her mother's house and picks him up after work."

About a half-hour later, we were parked in front of my house. I was a little anxious to see my mom and was about to open the door when Mike put his hand on my arm.

"You got a minute?" he asked.

"Anytime for you, Mike. What's up?"

"First of all, I'm so glad you're back. There's something I have to talk to you about. You know we have always been able to talk to each other about anything. I've tried with Augie and Larry, but I'm not as comfortable as I am with you."

"You know you can always talk to me, Mike. I'll listen, never take lightly what we talk about, and one last thing: It'll always stay between us, okay?"

"Thanks, Jesse, that means a lot to me."

"Now, what's the problem?" I asked.

With one big pull on his cigarette, Mike finally opened up to me with something I wasn't prepared for.

"It's about Joyce," he said, suddenly not looking at me. "I think she's fucking this guy at work. He's from the east side. His name is Ray Kosich, and he's there every time I go over to see Li'l Mike or pick him up for my weekend. Last Saturday morning, I went to pick him up. Joyce had on a light duster and was sitting on the couch in his underwear. It's almost like she's flaunting it in front of me."

"I feel like I should beat the shit out of him, but if I do, she'll just make it harder to see my son."

"Give me a week to get back in, Mike, then I'll have to see my godson."

"You won't do anything to hurt my chances with Li'l Mikey, right, promise!" he pleaded.

"Don't worry, I got your back. Now, I've got to see my mom, and I'll see you tomorrow at Rollie's."

"It feels terrific to have you back, boss!"

"Still with the boss, huh?"

"Always," he said, putting the car in gear, and pulling away from the curb.

Chapter 50

Saturday

5/27/1965

THE MEETING AT ROLLIE'S WAS A SOMBER AFFAIR, WITH NONE of the usual bull shit. We made a pact to always stick together, have each other's back, and make all significant decisions. It was good to see the guys again in the pool hall. Most were married now with one or two kids. It was good to see Rollie there on the weekends again. He retired after thirty-two years in the steel mill. I told Larry, Mike, and Augie I would spend the next week at home with my mom and that I'd be ready to go the following week.

Chapter 51

Thursday

6/2/1963

ON THE THIRD TRY, I WAS FINALLY ABLE TO TALK WITH CASSIE. We talked for about an hour. She told me how sorry she was she had to leave, but she didn't know where I was or how to get in touch with me. I said it was my fault for not trusting her and asked when she was coming back. Her father needed long-term care, and right now, there was no timetable for when he would improve enough to be on his own.

I asked if I could come down there to see her and try to rekindle what we had. "I don't think that would be a good idea right now," Cassie intoned.

"Why not?" I asked, almost seeing another man standing next to her.

"Well, actually," she said, "I'm seeing someone now. He's the physical thera—"

Looking down at the receiver, I'd just hung up. I decided that "real love" would never be for me.

Chapter 52

Saturday

6/14/1965

SATURDAY MORNING, I CALLED MIKE, TELLING HIM I WAS going to see my godson and that I'd stop by. After breakfast, two cups of coffee with the *Sun-Times*, I took a shower, got dressed, then drove over to Joyce's. Walking down the gangway, I stopped at the front door and rang the doorbell. The guy who opened the door stood about 5 feet, 10 inches tall, about 180 pounds, with black wavy hair, a pencil-thin mustache, and a somewhat swarthy complexion. I thought that he could have been Italian.

"Can I help you?" he asked, eyeing me up and down.

"Is Joyce home?"

"Who wants to know?"

"Little Mike's godfather."

"Who was at the door, Ray?" Joyce asked, coming down the stairs.

"Says he's Mike's godfather."

"Well, I heard you were back," she smiled.

"Hello, Joyce. I just stopped by to see Mikey. I hope you don't mind."

"Sure," Joyce said. "He's upstairs in his room."

Reaching behind my back and feeling the butt of my .45, I turned to Ray. "You think maybe you could get a beer and come back in about an hour?"

"You think maybe you could go fuck yourself," Ray hissed through clenched teeth as he moved toward me. The .45 appeared in my hand almost before I knew it. Cocking the hammer, I said rather calmly, "You can walk out or be carried out." Ray decided to walk.

Hearing Ray walking in the gangway, I turned to find Joyce walking into the kitchen and sitting at the table. As I walked over, I asked, "Got any beer?"

"Old style?" she asked, getting up.

"That's good," I answered, really noticing Joyce now. She was wearing short tan shorts pale yellow sleeveless blouse, and open-toed sandals. Looking at her tanned, firm legs, I felt a stirring in my crotch.

We both lit up and talked for about half an hour. After a pause and a sip of beer, I stated, "There's something different about you."

"Thanks for noticing," she smiled.

"Well, you don't have glasses, and your hair is a little longer."

"How about you? It's been two years, you know," she said, still with that sly little smile. "The only thing is I've put on a couple of pounds," I said. "Now, let's go see Little Mikey."

Tiptoeing into the room, I stood and looked down at my godson. Even sleeping, I could see both Joyce and Mike in their son. Back in the kitchen, I finished my beer, lit up another Salem, and turned to Joyce. "I want you to do me a favor."

"And what's that?" she answered, almost as if searching for

something.

"Whenever Mike comes over to see or pick him up for his weekend, it would be better if your boyfriend wasn't here."

"Whatever," she replied. With that, she sat back and lit another cigarette at the table.

"Thanks for the beer, and now I've gotta go."

"Jesse," she said in a pleading way. "Why don't you like me?"

"I like you, Joyce. We've known each other for almost ten years, you married my best friend, and Little Mike is my godson."

"That's not what I mean," she replied. "You say you like me, but you won't screw me. Why?"

"We've been through this before," I said. "If it was anyone else, Mike is my best friend."

"I know," she half-whispered. "But we're not married anymore."

"He's still my best friend. How could I face him?" I answered, feeling my resolve slipping away.

Joyce took a drag on her cigarette, stood up, took four steps, and stood within inches of me, "Don't you want to me?" she asked coyly.

"I'd be stupid to say yes."

"Wait for a second," she said, walking towards the front door. Taking a key ring off the hook, she handed me a key, saying, "That's the front door."

Mike was sitting on the front porch when I pulled up next to the curb. He got up as I climbed the stairs and stood next to me.

"Hey, Mike," I smiled.

"Hey," he said back. "How did it go?"

"Well," I said. "Whenever you go see Mikey, or ask him for your weekend, he won't be there. All you have to do is call."

"How'd you do that?" Mike inquired.

"After I convinced him to take a walk, I spent a couple of minutes with Mikey, then sat and had a beer with Joyce.

"What'd you tell her?" he asked eagerly.

"I told her that if it happened again, you would take her to court and fight for full custody."

"And," Mike asked.

"She said she'd take care of it."

Wrapping his arms around me, Mike exclaimed, "I knew you'd take care of it. That's why you're the boss."

"You know, I'll always have your back, Mike."

"And I'll always have yours, no matter what."

"I know that, but now I gotta go home and eat."

"How about one beer for the road."

"Okay, but then I gotta go."

When Mike came back outside, he had a beer in each hand. We sat on the top stair, opened the beer, and lit a smoke. After a long pause, he said, looking down at his beer, "You know, you're more than my best friend, you're like a brother to me, so there's something I have to ask you."

"Okay, Mike," I said, already knowing where this was going.

"Did you fuck her?!"

"What the hell, Mike? We've already been here before."

"Did you fuck her?" This time a little more empathy.

"No, I didn't!" I answered, getting a little heated.

"It's not like she didn't want to, right? She's been wanting to fuck you since before we got married."

Saying that, we both looked at each other, starting with a grin, then a smile, and lastly, a substantial relaxing laugh. As I turned to go, Mike put his hand on my shoulder.

"One promise, not in the house with your godson there." We looked at each other, knowing nothing else needed to be said.

"I'll see you later at Rollie's," I said, getting in my car ad pulling away from the curb.

Chapter 53

Sunday

6/18/1965

IT'S BEEN THREE WEEKS SINCE MIKE AND I HAD OUR TALK. We're at Cal Park and about to start our third game. So far, we're 2 – 0. Although we don't talk about it, Mike seems to be his old self again. I hope we never do, cause how can I tell him I couldn't keep the "one promise."

How could I tell him that I couldn't wait to get to Joyce's apartment, even knowing that Li'l Mikey was there? I was so "hard up" that I couldn't think about anything else. I tried to tell myself that it was clouding my reasoning because I hadn't been laid before I left Germany.

It was paramount to me to keep my friendship with Mike. I thought it was the most important thing to me at that moment. I tried to steel myself to that thought. As I walked into the apartment. I thought my resolve was back in full force. I thought I could pull this off. That's how much Mike's friendship meant to me. Joyce was sitting at the end of the couch, with only the lamp, taking a drag on her cigarette. She said matter-of-factly, "I didn't think you'd come."

"I almost didn't, but I knew I had to tell you I can't do this. Mike is my best friend, and even if I could, I couldn't do anything with Li'l Mikey in the house."

"Well," she said, taking another drag, "you won't have to worry about that tonight."

"Why's that?" I asked.

"He's at Pat's house. I told her I got called in for an extra shift at work."

With my resolve slipping away, I turned and walked toward the refrigerator. "Got any beer?"

"Yeah, I think there's a couple."

"You want one?"

"No," she answered, "I've got a drink."

"What're you drinking?"

"Rum and Coke, you want one?"

"Why not?" I said, feeling a stirring in my crotch.

"I'll make you one," Joyce said, walking to the kitchen counter.

Seeing her standing there with her back to me was all I could do to just rush up and grab her. Her hair was down around her shoulders, the sleeveless top was not tucked in, her beautiful legs were lightly tanned, and she was barefoot. Busy mixing my drink, Joyce didn't hear me come up behind her. I kissed the nape of her neck while putting my arms around her and cupping her breasts.

Joyce sagged slightly against me with a soft sign while holding my hands to her breasts.

"I don't remember them being so big and full," I said. Turning her around so we stood face to face, I kissed her softly."

"Why don't we go upstairs," She stepped into my arms, and we engaged in a deep, longing, hungry kiss.

Taking my hand, she hiked me upstairs, where I paused in

front of Li'l Mikey's bedroom. Joyce continued to her bedroom as I opened the door, looked inside, and found the room empty. As I entered her bedroom, Joyce rose and stood beside the bed.

"Satisfied?" she asked.

"Just wanted to make sure," I answered, approaching within two feet of her.

I started unbuttoning my shirt when Joyce put out her hand, saying, "Wait, I want to undress you." Once my shirt, shoes, and socks were discarded, she went to unbuckle my belt. "Look at me," she said, "I'm shaking."

Later, I'm standing here watching Mike fly out to the center field for the final out in our 16 – 10 loss to the J.M Corner Club team. As the guys were getting their things together, for some reason, I started walking toward the "old beach." To this day, I still don't know why. So long in my reverie, I didn't hear Jeannie come up and stop behind me.

"When I saw your car still parked at the curb, I knew you'd be here," she said, sitting next to me.

"It's better when there's nobody swimming," I answered, seeing the look of concern on her face.

"You still think about her?"

"Almost every day. Mostly I think about the day she left. I promised her I would be there for her birthday, and I didn't keep it. I wonder what's she doing now. Is she working, is she married? Are there any kids?"

"I wish I could talk to her, tell her how hard I tried to be there. Maybe if we hadn't gotten laid off, things would have been different, but I had to take care of my mom, and it wasn't easy when you're collecting compo."

"Why don't you call her?"

"I wouldn't know what to say. Besides, she'd probably hang up, and I wouldn't blame her if she did."

"I don't think she would," Jeannie said with a smile.

"I think she's forgotten all about me by now."

"I wouldn't be so sure about that. Look, Jesse, there's something I have to tell you, but not here. Do you think you can come over later?"

"Sure," I answered, curiosity starting to get the best of me.

"How about six o'clock," she said, looking down at her watch.

"By the way, where's Larry?"

"He's parked there by the curb. Come on, we'll take you back to your car."

Walking in the front door, I gave Jeannie a peck on the cheek, then followed her into the kitchen. "Where's Larry?" I asked, sitting down at the table.

"He's in the garage with his baby," was her reply. "They don't call him 'wheels' for nothing."

I laughed before sitting. Jeannie got us each a beer. I lit a cigarette as she looked me straight in the face.

"First, we know what the four of you are doing at work, making the collections, working as security bodyguards and whatever else Frank wants you to do. Barb and I both agree that as long as they don't bring the work home, it's fine. I don't think Joyce knows anything unless you talk in your sleep."

"Who told you about work?" I said, getting angry.

"Don't worry, Jesse, we would never do anything to jeopardize any one of you."

"I hope that's true, Jeannie because if it ever got out, we'd be dead meat."

"We know how serious it is, Jesse, we've talked it over a few times, and we both came to the same conclusion."

"As for Joyce, we've known each other for a long time, and I can see the change in you. The way you look at Mike, the way he looks at you, you're not as close as you once were, and it's eating him up inside."

"I didn't know that," I said a little sadly.

"Really," Jeannie answered. "He's your best friend, and you didn't notice anything." She continued, "Look, Joyce can fuck whoever she wants, and she must be a great fuck 'cause this tension between you and Mike, and you're going to have to decide between a fuck and your best friend."

The back door opened, and Larry came in, wiping his hands on a garage towel. "Hey guys," he said, taking three beers from the fridge, then sitting next to Jeannie. "Am I in time?" he asked, looking at her, then at me.

"I've something to tell you," she said, lighting her second cigarette. "I thought it would be better here than at the beach."

"Okay," I said, taking a slug of beer and lighting up one of my Salems.

"You know when I told you not to be so sure that Molly had forgotten you? Well, she hasn't."

"Whatya mean?" I asked.

"She was here."

"When?" I almost shouted.

"About a month after you went into the Army, she didn't tell anybody. She wanted to surprise you. She was coming to live here." Taking another drag, Jeannie continued, "She didn't know that I was married or where I lived. She went to my parent's house, and they gave her my phone number. On the way home, I told her what had happened and that no one knew where you were stationed. She was disappointed but determined to get a job and wait for you to come home."

"What happened then?" I asked, thinking maybe she was still here.

"I'm getting there," Jeannie replied, nervously looking at Larry. "The next two weeks were spent going to interviews and putting out resumes. We told her she could stay with us until she found a job and her own place. During the third week, she went for an interview. She was accepted at Kahler

Elementary School in Dyer, Indiana, teaching 7th-grade history."

I turned and looked at Larry, then Jeannie. Neither one looked happy. "But she's not here anymore, right?" I asked, getting that sinking feeling I hadn't felt since Cassie had left.

"It all started the last week of August, and as luck would have it, we were playing Tommy Stetich's team."

"Shit," Larry declared. "He spent more time on our side of the field than his. Every time he tried to talk, Molly would just move away. Finally, Molly asked me to take her home by the fourth inning. She never went to another game."

"For the next couple of weeks, everything was fine. Molly started teaching. She used my car. I drove Larry's, and he pooled with Augie and Mike. It was the middle of September, Augie

was bowling on Sundays, Larry spent a lot of time in the garage, and Mike was with his son as much as he could. Tommy started calling, asking if he could talk to Molly. She kept saying no, but he wouldn't give up."

I asked how he got the number. "He lied, saying he got it from the phone book. We're not listed," Larry said through a cloud of smoke.

"I think he got it from Joyce," Jeannie interjected. "Anyway, one day, while Larry and I weren't home, he called and convinced Molly to see him, saying he just wanted to talk. Larry didn't want him in our house, but between the three of us, we knew it would be better if Molly wasn't alone. He showed up Friday at about 7:30, and after the hellos and handshakes, we settled in the front room. Tommy apologized for what happened in Rollie's backyard. He said he didn't mean to fight with Jesse. Jesse used to be his best friend. Said he knew what he did that night to Molly? It was wrong, and he was sorry."

"With all that said, Larry and I went downstairs. We know that Tommy wanted to talk to Molly alone."

"Did you believe him?" I asked, looking at both Jeannie and Larry.

"He seemed genuinely sorry," Larry chimed in. "He didn't even have his usual smirk."

"I guess Molly believed him," Jeannie said, "'cause they started dating the following week. It started slow, but by Thanksgiving, they were pretty steady."

"Was Molly happy?" I asked, not really wanting to know.

"She seemed happy enough," Jeannie answered. "She said that she liked Tommy, and they had a lot of fun together."

"It was like that for a while," Larry interjected. "Molly was excited about teaching and had her name on a waiting list at the BarBarry apartments in Dyer."

"I gotta use the bathroom," I said, standing up.

"Anybody wants another beer?"

"Yeah, I'll have another one."

Larry smiled as soon as I closed the door. Jeannie turned to Larry, saying, "Should we tell him the whole story?"

"I think he has the right to know," was his reply.

With a fresh beer and another Salem, I looked across at Jeannie and knew there was something she didn't want to tell me. So I asked, "That's it?"

"No," Jeannie answered, "but before I tell you, you have to promise you won't do anything stupid."

Giving her a questioning look, I asked, "What happened? Why did she leave?"

Jeannie looked at Larry and, getting a nod, continued, "It all fell apart, Christmas Eve. We were sitting at the bar in Augie and Barb's basement, waiting for Mike. We had just made a toast when Tommy stood up, walked in front of Molly, and blurted out, 'Molly, will you marry me?'

"Everything stopped then and there: the Christmas music, the blinking lights around the bar, and even the TV picture froze. We all turned and looked at both of them. We knew something was wrong because Tommy had his smirk back on. Molly put her drink on the bar, saying, 'Are you serious?'

Real serious, Tommy answered her. He stepped closer to Molly. Molly was like, 'Wow.' Where'd that come from?

"So Tommy said, 'Look, I know it's sudden, but we've been together the last four months. I thought we were ready.' But he looked like he knew something was wrong. Molly finally got over the shock and told him, 'Tommy, I like you a lot. We've had some good times. You're fun to be with, but I could never marry you.'

"Tommy was pretty angry and asked why not. Molly said she just didn't love him. Tommy stood there, staring at Molly for an eternity, finally almost shouting, 'It's that fuckin Mexican again, right?' Augie came around the corner of the bar and said, 'Fuck you, Tommy!' Tommy threatened to break him in half. We were so engrossed in what was happening that we didn't see Mike standing at the bottom of the stairs. Tommy took a couple of steps back, turned and faced Mike. Then he and Mike got into threatening to kick each other's assess. The rest of us were frozen, waiting to see what would happen next.

"Tommy was on the stairs when he turned and looked at Molly with a pure evil stare and told her, 'I should have fucked you the first time?' Mike took a step toward him, but Molly grabbed him by the arm, telling Mike to let him go. Tommy seemed to have taken the holiday season with him when he left. The whole atmosphere was quiet and somber. We all knew that something was missing, and it was you."

Jeannie said, "That night, I sat with Molly most of the night, listening to her cry, and telling me how much she still loved you. She thought the strength of her love would help her get through the two years, but in the end, she realized it was a long time. The hardest part Molly told me was, what if you didn't feel the same anymore? And with that, in two weeks, she quit her job, took her name off the waiting list and was gone."

"Did you ever talk to her again?" I asked, trying to swallow the lump growing in my throat.

"I called once. Molly's mother told me she was living somewhere in Philly and promised Molly not to give anyone her phone number."

Standing beside me, Larry put his hand on my shoulder, saying, "We're both really sorry, but we thought you should know the whole story."

I felt my worst fear had come true. I wasn't getting a second chance. That's all I had hoped and prayed for.

"I gotta go," I said, standing up and walking toward the front door.

"Are you gonna be alright, boss?" Larry asked.

"Yeah, I just gotta get some air."

Finally, sitting in my car, the dam burst and the tears came in big gushers before I could light up. I don't know how long it lasted, but I felt a sense of relief when I was through. I knew now that love would never have any meaning for me. Ultimately, any relationship I had with women would never be permanent. With that on my mind, I stopped at the Step-Hi bar and got drunk.

Chapter 54

7/19/1966

The saying was, "Time Flies When You're Having Fun." It was hard to believe that it was over a year ago that Larry, Jeanie and I had our talk in their kitchen. I don't know if we were having fun, but time passed. We were fully entrenched in the "Family" and were considered good loyal soldiers. Our duties had increased. Besides the collections, we were now into loan sharking, which brought in more money for us. Everything was going right except for some broken arms and busted kneecaps.

Regarding security, we spent the whole day in the hall, talking to Frank or Sal. Sometimes we would go with Frank to a meeting or if he was having dinner away from the Hall. Last year in April, we accompanied him to Las Vegas for the annual Operating and Stationary Engineer convention. Mike and I were with Frank, Augie, and Larry, with Frank's wife Carla and his daughter Anabella.

Our personal lives hadn't changed much; we still played ball on Sundays. Augie was bowling Sunday nights. Jeannie was pregnant with their first. Larry, as usual, was in the garage a lot. Mike lived in the projects with a woman he met at Cal Park. Her name was Lori Gaudry. She had a little girl and was originally from the east side. But soon after her divorce, she moved to the projects.

We tried to get together at Roillie's as often as possible, sometimes drinking in the back room while playing cards or shooting pool. I was still at home with my mom, who was still the best cook on the south side.

With all the stops we made on the west side, many people knew us, especially in the Pilsen neighborhood. Every once in a while, we'd stop for a couple of drinks while making our collections. Everything was great. Even Larry and Mike were now speaking a little Spanish.

Chapter 55

Monday

7/26/1966

WE WERE JUST FINISHING OUR COFFEE DOWNSTAIRS WHEN WE were called to Frank's office. It was a Monday morning. Frank was unpacking his briefcase when we walked in. "Sit down, guys. Sal will be here soon." He said that without a smile. "It's okay if you want to light up."

A couple of minutes later, Sal sat beside Frank's desk. "Okay, gather around," Frank announced, relighting his cigar. "What is said now stays in the room, okay?" We all nodded, not really sure what was coming next.

"A couple of weeks ago, I got a phone call from a friend. His name is Mateo Tortello. He's the President of the Local in Philadelphia. It seems," he said, "at the end of the second quarter, the books came up a short. His nephew, who is in charge of the Pension Fund, was seen at the race track and in Atlantic City casinos.

"But to make a long story short, they found he was skimming off the top. Mateo doesn't want to use anyone from the local because his nephew has a lot of friends, and the word might slip out. He asked me for a favor, and I said I'd send some of my people out there. Okay, so far?" Frank asked, looking directly at me.

"So far, so good," I answered.

"Okay. Now, if you drive, rent a car with Philadelphia plates, don't go or call the local. Just catch him one day at home. Explain that they know what he's doing, that it has to stop, rough him up a little if you have to, but no broken bones, and I mean that! And one last thing, no names or where you're from! Are we all on the same page?"

We all looked at each other, nodding.

"Good," Frank said. "If anything, you can call Sal or me. Just let me know when you're leaving," He rose from his chair, smiling. "Now get the fuck out of my office."

Walking towards the door, I felt a hand grab my arm. Frank, standing next to me, asked, "A minute?"

Motioning for Sal to leave, he pointed to a chair, and I sat down. Frank intoned, sitting on the edge of his desk and puffing on his cigar, "I think I know what to expect from you. I'm sure you'll do the right thing, but I'm nervous about sending you so close to Upper Darby and Molly."

"How do you know about her?" I asked, shocked.

"I know everything about you, Flacco," he laughed. "Don't forget you're in the Family. All I'm saying is be careful and don't fuck up!"

"I won't," I said, getting up.

We hugged each other, Frank whispering in my ear, "You know where you stand with me," and with a peck on the cheek, sent me on my way.

We were sitting, having our second cup of coffee when I turned to Larry and Augie. "You two okay for this trip?"

"I am," answered Augie.

"Good to go, boss," Larry intoned.

"Think it's best if we take Larry's car, it's probably in the best shape. We have all the time we need, so we don't have to be in any hurry."

"We'd like to catch him at home on the weekend and stay away from the locals," I said. "Mike, you've got all the information from Sal, right?"

"Yeah, boss, his name is Anthony Tortello. He's married and lives in Lansdowne. It's just west of Philly."

"You got the address?" Larry inquired.

"Whatya think?" Mike laughed.

"What do we do about names?" Augie said. "Just in case."

"I'm gonna go talk to Cisco." Turning to leave, I was stopped in mid-stride by Larry's voice.

"One last thing, Jesse."

"What," I answered, turning once more, facing them.

"You know what." Now it was Augie's turn.

"Yeah," Mike put in. "What about her?"

She doesn't have anything to do with this!" I hissed. "This might be my only chance to see her again."

"We all know what Cisco said: Go in, do the job, and come home. You willing to go against that?" Augie continued.

"I already talked to Cisco about it," I answered.

"But you don't even know where she lives," Larry said.

"I know, but her parents do."

"We're not supposed to be riding around Philly looking for an address," Augie, always the serious one, said.

"Look," I said, "you guys can stay in the motel if you want, but I'm gonna go."

Suddenly, Mike rose up from his chair, put out his cigarette, walked up to me, and with the most severe look I'd ever seen, said, "How the fuck can you say that to us. We made a pact. We're all in this together."

"So you go talk to Cisco, and we'll figure out how we'll get there."

I told Cisco we'd be leaving early Friday morning and

would let him know when we arrived. He told me to take care of my personal shit and not to fuck up the job. When I returned, we all shook hands, finished our coffee, and went upstairs to work.

We were standing next to my car in the parking lot after walking Cisco to his car and watching him drive away. Augie was the first to jump in. "I think we should take two cars with our gear under the spare tire."

"Why two cars?" I asked.

"Less suspicious with just two guys in the car, okay?"

"Good idea, Aug," Larry said. "I'll take my car."

"And I'll take mine. Mike, I'll pick you up Friday at about 5am, and we'll meet at Larry's."

Chapter 56

Friday

7/28/1966

MIKE WAS STANDING ON HIS MOTHER'S FRONT PORCH WHEN I drove up Friday morning. His car was in the garage. He left it there because he didn't trust Lori driving it. We went to Calumet Bakery, picked up some sweet rolls, then moved to Larry's house. Augie was there, having a cup of coffee when we walked in. Nobody said much in between the sweet rolls and coffee. Finally, I had to say something on my mind since last Monday.

"We all good to go? Anybody got anything to say? Now would be a good time."

"We're all good to go. I'm just a little nervous about 'roughing this guy up.' What exactly does that mean?" Augie pointed out.

"I know what you mean, Aug. I'm a little anxious. We must show him that 'The Bosses' know what he's doing and that it has to stop, or we'll be back. Treat it like we're making a collection, and remember, no broken bones." We all laughed, finished our coffee, went outside, stowed our gear under the spare tire, and left on a trip we knew would either make or break us.

We spent Friday night at a Comfort Inn outside Cleveland, Ohio.

"Cleveland, home of the Rock and Roll Hall of Fame. Whoa. What the fuck," I said out loud.

"You want me to pull over," Mike asked anxiously.

"It's alright, Mike," I said. "Just thinking out loud."

"What about?"

"Thinking it might be some kinda sign: Cleveland, Ohio, and Cleveland, Tennessee. I haven't thought about Cassie in a long time."

"I don't believe in any of that shit," Mike chuckled.

"Just a thought," I said, settling back in my seat.

Chapter 57

Saturday

7/29/1966

At about 3:30pm, we exited Highway 76 at the Chestnut Street exit, found a Holiday Inn, and settled in for the night. I sent Larry and Augie to find a car rental company. Mike and I took turns with the shower and waited for their return. They showed up a little later with a 65 Buick four-door sedan with Pennsylvania plates. After Larry and Augie had showered and changed clothes, we met up at the bar, next to the front desk, for a drink.

It didn't take long to find Walnut Street, Upper Darby, not being a vast city. It was dusk when we pulled up in front of 7240 Walnut Street. We all looked at the white, shingled home on well-tended grass and a flower bed on both sides of the front of the house. On a raised slab were two black posts holding a patio cover over the front door.

My mouth was so dry that I took a stick of gum, hoping to produce some saliva. Finally swallowing, I motioned to Larry.

"You're with me. Augie, take the wheel." Walking up to the front door, I paused and swallowed again, looking at Larry, who smiled, saying, "Just be yourself."

Two or three seconds after ringing the doorbell, I was tempted to run back to the car. What stopped me was the beautiful woman who opened the door and, with a look of complete surprise, stood there with her hand over her mouth. Opening the storm door and stepping inside, I extended my hand, saying, "Hello, Mrs. Malone. How are you?"

Getting her composure, she asked, "Jesse, Larry, what are you doing here?"

"We're just passing through on our way to New York. A friend of mine from the Army invited us down to Atlantic City."

"Well, come in, come in," she beckoned to the couch. "Have a seat."

"Only for a minute," I answered, sitting beside Larry.

"Tell me, Larry, how's Jeannie?"

"We've been married three years now, and she's expecting our first baby."

Watching Catherine, I couldn't help but notice how she hadn't changed much, the same hairdo, with not one hair out of place, very little makeup, and a couple of small crow's feet, but no laugh lines yet. A salmon-colored blouse, opened at the neck, with a single strand of pearls tucked into a pair of charcoal gray slacks, topped off with a couple of gray pumps.

"Look, Mrs. Malone."

"Call me Catherine," she said.

"I'm sorry, but that's not how I was raised."

"Well, good for you."

"I know Molly doesn't live here anymore, but if you could give me her phone number, I'd like to say hello," I implored.

"As much as I want to, it wouldn't be a good idea."

"Why is that?"

"Because she's been married for the last two years."

Hearing the word married must've transported me to an alternate world because I didn't hear anything she said after that. I was brought back by Larry kicking my foot and nodding to Catherine.

"I'm sorry," I said meekly. "Just a little brain freeze. Two years, you say. Is Molly happy?"

"As far as we can tell," Tom Malone answered, descending the stairs.

"Tom," Catherine said, rising from her seat. "Look who's here."

Larry and I rose and walked to the center of the room, extending our hands. "Larry, Jesse, good to see you both again."

"Thank you, Mr. Malone," I said. "We were just passing through, thought we'd stop and say hello."

"That's really nice of you. Please sit."

"I'm afraid we can't. Two more of us are waiting outside, so we gotta get going."

After the handshakes, smiles, and hugs, we turned to leave. At the front door, I turned, hearing Tom say, "Jesse, a minute?" I motioned to Larry, who walked out the door as I turned to face Catherine and Tom.

"Jesse," he said, "I'd like to apologize for my actions back in Chicago. I said things that I had no business saying. I was only thinking of Molly and what I thought was best for her. I never thought that Molly, only seventeen years old, could know anything about what it is to love someone. Ultimately, I should have listened to my wife, who knows a little more about women's feelings. Look, Jesse, like a lot of parents, I—"

"Excuse me, one second," I said, opening the front door and motioning to Larry. I said, "Give me a couple of minutes, okay." Closing the door and turning again, I said, "I'm sorry. Mr. Malone, you were saying."

"I was saying that, like many parents, I thought I knew what was best for Molly. You know, go to school, get her degree to have a career, maybe get married, and if it didn't work out for any reason, she'd have her degree to fall back on. But in the end, I was wrong. The one thing I didn't count on was her love for you, so I knew when she returned to Chicago."

"So far," Catherine said, joining, "she hasn't opened up to either of us. Something happened in Chicago that changed her. She's not the same Molly we knew before."

"And you still don't know?" I said, lying.

"No," Tom replied, "And now that she's married, she's put it in the past."

"I'm sorry to hear that, but tell her I wish her nothing but happiness and a good life."

"Is that all?" Catherine asked, stepping closer.

"What do you want me to say? I fell in love the first time I saw Molly. Out of all my friends, she chose me, the tall skinny Mexican, who never had a girlfriend, held a girl's hand, and never really kissed a girl. Someone so nervous, he'd start shaking just sitting next to her.

"There are so many other reasons I could say, but they would pale in the light of knowing that she saw something in me that I didn't know I had. Whatever it was, it made me feel like I was just like most of my friends who had girlfriends."

Looking at Catherine, who was visibly touched, Tom just cast his eyes down at his hands. I didn't think that, after all this time, I would still be moved to talk about Molly. I could feel my eyes starting to mist up. So I had to end it. "One last thing that really made me love her, she made me believe in who I was and not have such a low opinion of myself. When you talk to her, tell her she was my first and last love, and I thank her for giving me that wonderful and magical summer."

Shaking my hand, Tom looked me straight in the eyes and, with a smile, said, "You're always welcome here."

"Thank you," I said, walking to the door.

"I'll walk you out," Catherine said, joining me at the door.

Standing on the sidewalk, Catherine turned to me. "Jesse, there's so much more I wish I could tell you, but just know this: Molly has never stopped loving you. She still talks about that summer and how it felt to be in love. I'm so sorry it didn't work out."

Taking both her hands, I whispered, "Goodbye, Catherine."

Stopping at the curb, Larry looked somewhat anxious. "You alright, boss?"

"Yeah," I answered, relieved. "Let's go eat. I could go for a nice big steak. What about you?"

After four T-bone steaks, baked potatoes, and salads at Ruth Chris Steak House, we were back at the motel's bar. Over beer and cigarettes, we nervously tried to devise a plan. Not that easy. Never having done anything like this before. After a lot of back and forth, we played it by ear, hoping everything would go right.

Chapter 58

Sunday

7/30/1966

IT TOOK AN HOUR AND A HALF TO GET TO LANDSDOWNE AND another half-hour to find 31 East Plumstead Avenue. The one-story bungalow sat on a three-foot-high cinder block founda-tion, with three concrete steps leading to the front door, fronted by a glass-enclosed storm door. A bay window took up most of the right side. The rest of the house was gray vinyl siding and a black shingle roof.

"Let's go for a ride," I said to no one.

"Where to?" Larry asked, putting the car in gear.

"I need a public phone."

"What for?" Augie asked, lighting a cigarette.

"If he's home, we must find a way into the house. If he's not, we don't want him coming home before we are ready."

We found one inside a gas station about six blocks away. After dialing and taking a drag on my Salem, I was about to hang up when after the third ring, a frantic voice on the other end said, "Hello," rather softly.

"Hi," I said, "I'd like to speak to Anthony Tortello."

"What is this about?" she answered.

"Is this his wife?"

"Yes, it is."

"I'm calling from Franklin Cadillac. He came in last Sunday looking at a new Cadillac, and I was just wondering if he'd decide about coming back".

"I'm afraid I don't know anything about that."

"Well," I said, "could I talk to him?"

"He's not here now. He's out of town on business."

"Thank you, I'll try back later."

Now parked three houses down on the opposite side of the street, I kept thinking, *I've gotta make sure he's not there.* "Larry," I said, "you and Mike, make sure we're good to go. Do what you have to get in the house."

Watching Larry and Mike cross the street, Augie turned, saying, "You said he wasn't home."

"Just wanna make sure. We don't need surprises, right?"

"Then why is Mike coming back, and where is Larry?"

I met Mike in the middle of the street. "What happened," I asked. "And where's Larry?"

"He told me to come and get you, then he went inside."

Stopping in the front room and looking around, I observed a neat and well-kept house.

Tony's wife stood at the sliding door, looking out at the backyard. Larry was by the kitchen sink with a grin as big as the Cheshire Cat. Turning back to her, I started with, "I'm sorry, Mrs. Tor—!"

"Hello, Flacco!" she said, still looking outside.

"What!" I thought, *Did I just hear, right? I must be hearing things. It couldn't be, could it?* The voice was a little deeper but sounded like her.

Looking at her back, I was dumbstruck. My feet were

stuck in wet cement. I couldn't move; my arms were too heavy. Finally, with all my strength, I grasped the back of a nearby chair. When I got my voice back, all I could utter was, "Molly?"

When she turned, I wasn't there anymore. I was sitting on our beer cooler in Rollie's backyard, looking up at the most beautiful girl I'd ever seen in my life. It was a Friday night that I'll remember for the rest of my life. I don't know how long I was gone. I only knew I didn't want to come back. I wanted to stay in that time when I came to know the one true love of my life.

As I looked up and handed her a beer somewhere in the distance, I heard her voice, "Say something! Please, Jesse, say something!" When I blinked, I was back in Molly's kitchen, swallowing the lump in my throat and afraid to move. "It's you!"

"It's me," she answered, moving around the table and coming into my arms.

"I'm glad you did that," I moaned, squeezing her so hard. I felt her sharp intake. "If I'd moved, I might have fallen."

We were both sobbing openly. " I'm sorry, Molly," was all I could say.

"You always could make me cry," she sobbed.

"I never meant to," I said, taking out my handkerchief.

"I know that," Molly answered, wiping my face, then hers.

"You're more beautiful than I remember, Mary Catherine Malone! I've missed you so much, I thought I'd never see you again."

"I've never stopped loving you," Molly said, choking on the words.

Easing her away from me but holding her at arm's length, I whispered, "Do you remember what I said back then?"

"Do you still mean it?"

"More than ever!" I answered.

Pushing away from the counter, Larry announced, "We'll be outside, boss."

With a questioning look, Molly asked, "Why, boss?"

"It's just a nickname," I answered.

"I like it better than Flacco," she said with a smile.

Once again, we were holding each other. Molly still fit perfectly in my arms. "Jesse," she whispered against my chest, "please kiss me." It started tenderly, as if it was the first time, eventually building into one of longing and remembrance.

"I needed that," Molly said breathlessly, "to ensure you were actually here."

"I'm here," I said, wiping away more of her tears. "Whatever I said or did, Molly, I never meant to hurt you. I was a young guy who met this beautiful girl who, for whatever reason, liked me, and, not having any experience with women, I didn't know how to handle it. I made many mistakes, but I never stopped loving you and Molly. I wish more than anything in the world I could've been here for your eighteenth birthday. When you went away to school, I thought there was still a chance for us, but after the letters and phone calls stopped, I realized that you had moved on with your life."

She was crying again, only this time it was big sobs wracked her body. I handed her my hankie. Standing her ground and choking back sobs, she answered, "I didn't tell anyone I was moving to Chicago, not even Jeannie. I wanted to surprise everyone. When I got there, you were already in the Army, and nobody knew where you were. I learned from Larry that you would be gone for two years, so I decided to wait for you, not even sure if you still felt the same. I was staying with Jeannie and Larry. I had a job teaching 7th grade at Kahler Elementary School in Dyer, Indiana. Everything was fine. I was happy and sure I could wait out the two years. It all changed when I started believing Tommy Stetich had somehow grown up."

"You don't have to say anymore, Molly," I said. "I know all

about what happened. Taking her in my arms again, I whispered, "One day, I'll have to put a bullet in his head."

"Is that why you carry a gun?" she asked, feeling the .45 in the shoulder rig.

"It's part of my job," I answered, holding her away from me again. "I'm in charge of security at our Union Hall."

With a questioning expression, she asked, "Then why do you have to talk to my husband?"

"Molly," I said, trying to sound sincere, "maybe you should sit down."

"Can't you just tell me?"

"Okay," I said, "I guess you'll find out in the end. We were sent here to give your husband a couple of options."

Suddenly there was an almost palpable change in the atmosphere. Molly was once again standing at the sliding doors, looking outside. I knew I would have to choose my words as I tried to explain why we were there.

"Molly," I said, "I'm so sorry. If I'd known it was you, I would never have come. You have to believe me."

"And here I thought you came looking for me."

"Look, I broke a promise to those who sent us. We were to tell no one who or why we were here, but I couldn't help myself. I had to try and see you. I found out you were married when I stopped at your parent's house, and although I pleaded with them, they wouldn't tell me where you lived or your phone number. We all knew his name was Anthony Torrtello, his address and phone number, and he was married. That's all, not even his wife's name or if there were any kids."

With her back still turned to me, Molly said matter-of-factly, "Tony doesn't want a family."

"What about you?"

"Not with him."

"Do you love him?" I asked, hoping to get the correct answer.

"Not like I thought I did."

"Why's that?"

"I don't really know," Molly stated. "He's not the same guy I married. He spends more time with his friends at the track or in Atlantic City.

"I'm sorry to hear that, Molly."

"Are you really?"

"I always wanted you to be happy."

"I'm happy now," Molly declared, looking at me hopefully.

"Molly," I answered, "don't say that. You're only making things harder."

"I don't care," she said, "I don't care." Tears were running down her cheeks now. "If you ask me, I'll leave right now and go back to Chicago with you."

"If only it was that easy."

"Don't you want me to," she asked, almost pleadingly.

"Right now, Molly," I said, looking at her, my heart aching with my love for her, "it's the only thing I want the most in my life. Since I found you, I have been given a second chance."

"Then what's stopping us?" she asked. "You said you still loved me."

"That's just it, Molly. I love you too much to give you that kind of life, always looking over our shoulder, worrying he might be there."

"As long as I'm with you, I won't be afraid. I can face anything as long as we're together."

"You don't understand, Molly. I fucked up once already by going to your parent's house. Remember, I told you we weren't to see or talk to anyone while we were here. Your husband mustn't know who sent us or where we came in. Can't you see Molly? He'll know where you're at if you ever file for divorce."

"Are you afraid of him?" Molly asked, walking back around to my side of the table.

"I've never been afraid of anyone. I'm just following orders. Molly, more than anything, I want us to be together, but if you went back with me, they would know that I had fucked up."

"Who's they, Jesse? Who are your people?"

"I can't tell you that, Molly, besides you're better off not knowing."

"Look, Hon," Molly replied, "I think you know by now. As long as we are together, I don't care what you do."

"Wow," I said, taking hold of her hands. "That's the first time I've heard that in a long time."

We stood there looking at each other for what seemed like hours, then she was in my arms again with a slight pull. With her head against my chest, Molly whispered, "Oh, Jesse."

Feeling her body against mine gave me a feeling I had not felt before. I knew right then and there that we would one day be together no matter what.

Barely above a whisper, I said meaningfully, "I've never stopped loving you, Molly."

"I know," she answered. "And I never knew I could still love someone as much as I love you."

We kissed again, this time out of pure love and knowledge that now the fates were on our side.

"What do we do now?" I asked.

"You must make one promise to me, and it has to be above all else."

"Anything," I answered.

"Promise me," Molly said, "that you'll wait for me, and when I'm free, I'll come to you."

"Molly," I said, looking deep into her eyes, "I've been waiting for you my whole life. I'll wait as long as it takes."

The sound of the phone broke the spell. Molly looked up at me, saying, "It's probably Tony. I'd better answer it." After some back and forth, she hung up, turned and said, "They're on their way to the Union for a pizza and beer. He'll be here in a couple of hours."

"Hon," I said, "now you have to promise me that you

won't tell him or anyone else that we know each other or where we came from. Promise me more for my sake than anything else. One other thing, I don't want you here when he comes home. Is there any place you can go for a couple of hours?"

"Rock Creek Park," Molly answered. "It's about fifteen minutes from here."

"Okay," I said. "It's 4:15. I think you should leave about 5:30 and stay there until about 7 o'clock. Can you do that?"

"Come with me, Hon. We have so much more to talk about."

"I can't, Molly."

"Why not?" she implored. "I'm sure they can handle Tony, I can tell Larry how to get to the park, and they can pick you up on their way."

"You've thought of everything," I smiled. "Okay."

"Just give me a minute," she said, walking back to her bedroom.

When Molly emerged from her bedroom, I noticed the chain around her neck with the gold crucifix and my high school ring. "I always said it looked better on you." We walked hand in hand, out the front door, down to the sidewalk where Larry and Mike were leaning against the car with Augie sitting behind the wheel.

After discussing the situation, they agreed that I should go with Molly. They would handle Tony, and they would see me at the park.

Sitting on a park bench, looking out at the swimming pool, Molly mused, "It's not beautiful like Cal Park."

"Especially 'Our Place.'" I smiled.

"You think we'll ever walk along the beach again?"

"We'll do it more than once. I promise you that."

"Do you still go there?" she asked.

"After every Sunday game."

She settled in the crook of my arm. I smelled the sweet scent of her hair and kissed the top.

"Oh, Jesse," she exhaled, "I can't wait for that day."

Before we knew it, Mike stood behind us and took off the gloves. "We'll be waiting in the car."

"Everything go, alright?"

"I think he got the message."

As Mike walked away, I turned to Molly, saying, "Don't go home immediately. Give it some time."

"Walk me to my car," Molly choked out the words.

"Don't cry, Hon, it won't be long."

"I feel like it's happening all over again."

"No, it's not, Hon. When I made that promise seven years ago, I was a young kid, who was head over heels in love, who did not know if he could ever keep that promise. I'm still head over heels in love, but I know now that I can keep that promise."

Walking back to her car, holding hands, I glanced at Molly, thinking I could never love anyone the way I loved her. I still couldn't get over the fact that she could've had just about any of my friends but instead had picked me, and now she was promising her love.

We were standing beside her car. Larry had driven a few car lengths, giving us a little privacy.

"Don't forget, Hon, I have your phone number. I'll try and call whenever I know he's at work. Just promise you won't give up on us. I'll talk to my father tomorrow."

"Why?" I asked.

"Because he's a lawyer, and he might know a good divorce lawyer."

"Again, you've thought of everything."

She came into my arms, and I didn't want to let go. I couldn't let go. I wanted to stay in that moment for the rest of my life.

"I love you, Jesse," she whispered.

"I love you, Mary Catherine Malone,"

We kissed one last time, and for all it's worth, it was the kiss I'd never forget.

Watching her drive away, I walked to our car on shaky legs.

"You okay?" Augie inquired as I sat down next to him in the back seat.

"Yeah," I answered.

"Let's go home."

Chapter 59

Tuesday

8/1/1966

THE HAMBURGERS, SAUSAGE, AND HOT DOGS WERE ON THE grill, and the potato salad, baked beans, and salads were on the picnic table when we walked into Larry's backyard that Tuesday afternoon. Jeannie, working the grill, was the first to spot us, dropping the spatula and rushing over to greet us. Barb was sitting at the table, holding "little Johnnie" in her lap. Lori, also seated, was watching her daughter set the table.

After three hugs and kisses, we settled down for smokes and cold beer. Sitting next to Lori, Mike asked disbelievingly, "What are you doing here?"

"Jeannie called and invited me," she answered. "Was that alright?"

"Sure," he said, looking across the table at Jeannie, and mouthing, "Thank you."

"Okay, you guys," Larry announced at the grill. "Come and get it."

Jeannie turned as we lined up alongside the table and asked, "Jesse, you got a minute?"

"Yeah, sure," I said.

We walked a few steps away. Jeannie turned and asked, "Did you find her?""Yeah," I answered, "by accident."

"What's that mean?" she asked.

"Right now, I'll just say she's married. I'll explain the rest later, okay?"

With the food either eaten or put away, we settled back with full stomachs and a sense of well-being. As dusk appeared, everyone was starting their goodnights and see-you-laters. Taking a long swallow and clearing my throat, I looked down the table at my three best friends, smiled, and said, "You guys take the rest of the week off. Tomorrow morning, I'm going to see Frank. Okay, now let s clean off the table and go home."

Standing on the curb in front of the projects on Bensly Avenue, Lori had taken the girls inside. Mike turned and asked, "Wanna come in for a beer?"

"Thanks, Mike, but I wanna go home and see my mom."

"Okay," he answered, "then I'll see you in the morning."

"Why, Mike, you don't have to go."

"I know, but I want to."

"I'm just gonna talk to Frank."

"If that's what you want, I guess I don't have to go," he said, turning to go.

What the fuck are you doing? I thought. *You really hurt him this time.* "Mike," I said, grabbing his arm, "I could use the company."

"You sure?" Mike asked, a smile starting to emerge.

"Yeah, but you buy breakfast."

"Again," he laughed.

"I'll see you at about 10, okay?"

Chapter 60

Wednesday

8/2/1966

FRANK WAS ALREADY AROUND HIS DESK WHEN WE WALKED IN.
"Jesse, Mike," he said, shaking my hand. "Come in, come in."

"Have a seat," he added, shaking Mike's hand. Sitting on
the edge of his desk, he turned to me with a smile, saying, "I
heard you had a good trip."

"Yeah," I replied, looking sideways at Mike. "Everything
went okay."

Frank followed with a puff on his cigar, "I got a phone call
Monday that our friend had to take some time off from work,
something about personal business."

"That's too bad," Mike announced.

"Something like a 1-2 punch," Frank smiled.

"What's that mean?" I asked, turning back to Frank.

"Well, Monday morning, his wife filed for divorce and
moved back with her parents."

"No shit," I said, trying my best to act surprised. I turned once again to Mike, who nodded with a wink.

"Okay, you two," Frank smiled, sitting at his desk. "Let's cut the fuckin' bullshit."

"What?"

"You think we didn't know who Tony was married to?"

"You mean, you knew all along," I asked, not believing what I was hearing. "What the fuck, Frank."

"Easy, Jesse," Mike said, his hand on my arm.

Sitting straight up in his chair, sternly looking at me, Frank said, "First of all, watch your mouth! Don't ever forget who you're talking to."

"I'm sorry. I just want to know why."

"We wanted to know how far your loyalty would go."

"Whose we?" I asked, standing up.

"I told you before, you answer to me first. But this time, I'll let you in. It was the 'Council.' All that shit about not talking to anyone, no names or where you were from, was to see if you'd pull it off."

"How'd we do," Mike asked.

"Everybody's happy," Frank intoned, once again coming around the desk. "Mike," he said, "Give us a minute."

With the door closed and Mike in the lobby, Frank turned to me and said, "This won't take long, sit down." Once again, he was sitting on the edge of his desk. "Look, Jesse, you know how I feel about you, but you will show me the respect I deserve. Just remember, you are a part of the family. When we're alone, we can bullshit, but otherwise, it's business?"

"I gotcha, Frank," I said, getting up.

"We're good, right?" he said, now smiling. "And you'll be back Monday."

"Monday, bright and early," I smiled.

"Okay, then get the fuck outta my office!"

Pulling up to the curb on Bensely Avenue and slipping the gear into park, I turned to Mike, who was lighting up and taking a deep drag. "Mike," I said, "thanks for being there with me today. It meant a lot."

"I told you I'd always have your back," he said.

"And I almost lost that. I'm sorry."

"I hope I never do."

With a heartfelt handshake and "I'll see you at Rollie's Saturday," he departed. I crossed over to Hoxie Avenue, turned south, and drove slowly past Joyce's parent's house, hoping she'd be sitting out front, but as fate would have it, it wasn't to be. I fell asleep that night with the image of Joyce's head bobbing up and down on my crotch.

Chapter 61

Friday

8/4/1966

I DECIDED TO WAIT A COUPLE OF DAYS TO CALL MOLLY. WHEN I did, we talked for well over an hour. I tried to sound surprised when she explained how she called her father that Sunday night, telling him what she wanted. She said he seemed relieved, telling her there was a divorce lawyer in their firm. How she went to meet him Monday morning, and the papers were filed that afternoon.

He advised her that she should move out and wait to see what his lawyer had to say. With the help of her father, she told her lawyer the whole story about us. He replied that she should stay with her parents until everything was settled.

The thought was that if Tony found out about us, he might want to make problems.

"How long," I asked.

"We'll know more when we hear from his lawyer," she answered tentatively. "You think we can wait?"

"I told you before, Molly, I've been waiting for you my whole life."

"We'll make it, won't we?" she asked.

"Just keep believing, Hon," I answered. "I'll call you Sunday, okay?"

"I love you, Jesse," she whispered.

"I love you more, I replied, hanging up the phone.

Chapter 62

Sunday

9/6/1966

I TOOK MY MOTHER FOR BREAKFAST AT THE PURPLE STEER ON the East Side and got back just in time to change clothes and leave for Cal Park. We won our game with Eddie and Cooney's tap on a pair of two-run homers by Mike. Augie left after the game. He had to be at Bryn Mawr Lanes at five o'clock.

Walking in from the parking lot and spots where Augie was bowling, we walked over. I sent Larry and Mike to get a round of beer for the crew. Turned and walked into the lounge, ordered three beers, and waited for Mike and Larry to join me at the bar. We were enjoying our cigarettes and beer when, for some unexplained reason, I felt a presence standing behind me. I turned slowly, with my hand inside my jacket on the handle.45, I came face to face with a dark-haired woman who seemed familiar.

"Jesse," she said, trying to talk over the jukebox. "Don't you remember me?"

"You do look familiar." I smiled.

"I lived across the street from you on Burley Avenue."

Just the mention of Burley Avenue was all I needed to hear. "Camille Ortega," I almost shouted. She nodded, and we embraced in a hug of familiarity.

"It's been a long time," I said, trying not to look too conspicuous while taking all of her in.

"You haven't changed much," she said, giving me a knowing look. "Except you've put on some weight."

"Army food," I replied. "Potatoes with every meal."

"Are you with someone?" Mila asked.

"Just my two buddies here, Larry and Mike. How about you?"

"I'm with my sister, Rose, and her husband. He bowls here on Sundays."

"Do you have to get back right away?"

"Not right away." She smiled.

"Can I buy you a drink?" I asked, hopefully.

"Okay," was her reply. "But do you think we could get a booth?"

Once we were settled in the booth with our drinks, I lit up a Salem, then we got slowly into the old neighborhood, our friends, our parents, and what we'd been doing for the past thirteen years. Somewhere between the "whatever happened to," the subject of marriage came up.

Mila told me she'd been married for five years but was now divorced and surprised I'd never married. That serious break was broken when she appeared to look over my shoulder as if someone was approaching. Before turning, he was standing at our table, looking down at Mila. He looked about 6 feet tall, black hair slicked back, a prominent widow's peak, long sideburns, a mustache, and a goatee. "I wanna talk to you," he almost snarled.

"Not now, Oscar," she replied.

I sat back in the booth, putting both hands inside my jacket. He wore a black button-down shirt, gray slacks, and roach-killer shoes with a black leather coat.

"Why not?" he snarled again.

"We don't have anything to talk about anymore," Mila said with a rough timbre.

"Don't make me drag you out of there," he said, reaching for her arm.

"Excuse me," I announced.

"Yeah!" he growled, turning to me, "Who the fuck are you?"

"I'm a friend of Mila's."

"How good of a friend?" he hissed with a sneer.

"Grammar school," I answered.

"Okay, Mila's friend, I think you should sit there and mind your own fucking business," he said while leaning on the table.

I brought both hands from inside my jacket, the .45 cocked and pointed directly at his crotch.

"Listen, asshole," I said, showing him the .45, "don't move because I've got two choices for you, either you straighten up very slowly, turn and walk out, or I blow your balls off."

He looked from me to the .45, his eyes as big as saucers, licked his lips and said with a cocky voice, "You wouldn't do that here!"

"Try me," I answered in a slow whisper.

This time he looked from me, then to Mila, who seemed to be in total shock, slowly straightened up, glanced at me, saying, "This ain't over yet." He turned and made his way out. I nodded to Larry and Mike, and they moved to follow Oscar. With the .45 back in its rig, I glanced down at Mila, who looked at me as if I were a total stranger. Sliding out of the booth, she looked past me, saying, "I have to get back," and almost ran out of the lounge.

Everyone settled back in their seats as I walked into the

bowling alley. Mike and Larry walked up to me, saying, "He's gone. What was that all about?"

"I'll tell you about it later, okay? Just give me a minute."

I walked up behind Mila, watching her sister's husband bowl. She knew I was there but continued to look straight ahead.

"I'm sorry you had to see that," I said solemnly. "That's not what I wanted."

She turned and, still frightened, asked, "Who are you?"

"I'm sorry," I repeated. "Say hi to Rosie." Turning, I met up with Larry and Mike and walked out to the car together.

Little by little, and with the consent of the "Council," we began taking control of all the illegal activity in Rogers Park and surrounding neighborhoods. We knew Frank had talked to the "Council" on our behalf. They were all right getting their cut off the top. Frank tried to talk us into moving to the north side, but we convinced him we were "Southsiders." Besides, Augie said, "Everything would be better if no one knew where we lived."

Chapter 63

Sunday

9/20/1966

Life was good then. We all had money. Larry and Augie were out in the suburbs. Mike and Lori bought a house in Hegewisch with a mortgage. (Still keeping up appearances.) I was still at home with my mom and paying rent.

That Sunday, Larry, Mike, Fat Rollie, and I were in the backroom. We were in the middle of a game of Pinochle when Bobby came in, announcing, "There's someone to see you out front, Jesse."

"What'd he want?" I answered.

"It's a she," Bobby smiled.

Walking to the door and looking out, I saw her standing by the counter, nervous. She wore a pair of jeans, white tennis shoes, and a light blue windbreaker.

"Mila!" I exclaimed, walking up and taking both her hands in mine. "What are you doing here?"

"I came to talk to you. Do you have a couple of minutes?"

"Sure," I said, motioning to the back room. "Come in."

Immediately, Mike announced, "Let's take a break." After they had walked into the pool hall, I closed the door, then turned to Mila, saying, "Here, sit down." I half-turned to face her, asking, "How'd you find me?"

"I asked your friend Augie, and he told me you would probably be here."

"Well," I said, "what can I do for you?."

"I don't know if I'm good at this, but I want to apologize."

"For what?" I inquired.

"For the way, I acted at the bowling alley."

"You don't have to. I'm just sorry it turned out that way."

"My brother-in-law told me all about you. How you're well known on the west side. They all know the name 'Flacco.'"

"Look, Mila, I don't make excuses for who I am or what I do. I never have and never will."

"I've heard stories about Flacco, but I never thought it could be you in a million years."

"Well, now you know," I said, standing up and extending my hand.

She stood up, said, "I won't take up any more of your time," and started for the door.

"Mila," I said.

She turned, saying, "Yes,"

"Are you hungry?"

"I could eat something," she smiled. "What's on your mind?"

"How about some seafood?" I inquired, smiling.

"Sounds good." She smiled back.

"Where's your car?" I asked as we stepped outside.

"Across the street." She gestured to a dark blue Mustang.

"Is it locked?" I asked.

"Yeah, it's locked."

"Good, we'll take mine."

After the U-turn, we were headed north on Torrence Avenue; ten minutes later, we were parked in front of Heinie's Shrimp House on 92nd and Mackinaw Avenue.

We pulled into the front of the house with one whole chicken, two pounds of shrimp, and a lot of french fries.

"We've got company for dinner, Ma," I announced, stepping into the living room.

"Who is it?" she answered from the kitchen." Larry, Mike, or Augie?"

"Naw, Ma, she's better looking," I said as we walked into the kitchen. "You remember Mila, right?"

"Hay Dios Mio!" my mother exclaimed.

Once the hugs were done, we settled in for some shrimp, chicken, and fries. Mila had a healthy appetite, consuming her fair share of shrimp. A little later, we were sitting in the front room, each with a beer and cigarette, talking about old times when my mother announced she was going to bed. We were so engrossed in the old days that we forgot it was 10:30pm.

"Come on," I said, "I'll walk you back to your car."

Once outside, we walked towards Torrence Avenue when Mila took hold of my arm. Turning to me, she said, "I'm really sorry about what—"

"I told you, you don't have anything to be sorry about."

"Yes, I do," she pleaded, "because I can see now that you haven't changed, you've just grown up."

"Thank you," I smiled, "and so have you."

"I had a great time, especially seeing your mom again."

"She did too."

"Maybe one day, I can have you over for dinner."

We crossed the street and stood next to her car. She took my hand and looked at me, saying, "I'd really like to see you again."

"Sure," I said. "Give me your number, and I'll call you."

"No, that's alright," Mila answered, opening the car door.

"Wait," I argued. "What's wrong."

"Nothing," she said. "It's just that I've heard that before."

"Hold on, Mila. I meant what I said. I'm sorry you took it that way."

"Are you sure?" she implored.

"I said it, didn't I?"

"Okay, then," she said with a smile, handing me a piece of paper. We both stood there, looking at each other. She had a look that I took to mean she was expecting something.

Feeling that, I reached and pulled her into a tight embrace and followed with a deep meshing of our lips. Pulling away and looking at her (she still had her eyes closed), I whispered, "I had a great time too."

"Where'd you learn how to kiss like that?" she expanded.

"I watch a lot of movies."

With the motor running, Mila rolled down the window, saying, "I hope you call," and then drove away.

Chapter 64

Thursday

9/25/1966

I CAUGHT HELL ALL WEEK, ESPECIALLY FROM LARRY AND Augie.

"What's her name? How do you know her? Does she have any sisters? Boy, she's hot. When are you gonna see her again? Did you notice her chest?" The only one not asking was Mike, who sat there with his coffee, shaking his head.

I was about to confront him when Frank came into the hall and motioned us to sit. "Listen up," he said. "I need a favor."

"Sure, Frank," I replied. "What do you need?"

"They're having a problem at the Prudential, and I need a couple of you to go over there, talk to them and let me know what's up, okay?"

"Okay, Frank," I answered, standing up. "Larry, you and Augie take a ride, find out what's going on, then come back, okay?"

As Larry and Augie went up the stairs, Frank turned to me, saying, "Come up to my office in a little while." Once Frank was gone, I sat next to Mike, lit up a Salem, blew out a plume of smoke, and asked, "What's up, Mike?"

"Nothing," was his answer. He kept his face averted and wouldn't face me.

"Come on, Mike," I said," We've known each other a long time. I think I know when something's bothering you."

Mike took a long pull on his cigarette and looked at me with a hurt expression.

"What's the matter?" I pleaded.

"You're right, Jesse," he said. "We've been friends a long time. Shit, man," he said, getting heated, "I've always thought of you as a brother, not just a friend."

"I know, Mike. I've always felt—"

"Let me finish," he demanded. "You were best man at my wedding, you baptized my son, and even after I got divorced and I knew you were banging Joyce, I thought, better you than someone else. I know how crazy that sounds, but that's how much I cared about our friendship."

"What's all that got to do with now, Mike."

"I remember what happened when Molly left. You went into a dark place. You weren't the Jesse we all knew. You lost that twinkle in your eyes, that crooked smile with the one dimple. The knack you had for laughing at yourself. Then you met Cassie, and you came back a little. It wasn't the same, and we knew that you cared for her. For a while, things were good. It was like old times. Soon you were drafted and gone for two years. Nobody knew where you went or when you were coming home."

"Fuck this, Mike. I don't need the history lesson."

"Shut up and just listen for once." His face had a look I'd never seen before. "When you found Molly again, we all thought you'd been given a second chance. We could see the love between the two of you was just as strong as ever. We could see that the old Jesse had been in there somewhere and was now back and smiling.

"Look, Jesse, I wouldn't be telling you this if I didn't care. I don't know what happened at the park that day, but since we've been back, you haven't mentioned Molly once, and now you're chasing this cunt around."

"Watch it, Mike!" I answered angrily, standing up.

"Or what?" he said. "You gonna take me on?"

"If I have to!" I taunted, clenching my fist.

"Hey, what the fuck's going on here?" Frank yelled from the doorway.

"Just a little difference of opinion," I answered, still staring at Mike.

"Listen, you two," Frank added sternly while striding up next to us, "there's only one opinion that matters, and it's mine, right."

"Right, Frank," I answered.

"Mike?" he said.

"Okay, Frank."

"I thought I asked you to come upstairs." He looked at me, annoyed.

"I was on my way," was all I could say.

"Before we go," Frank said, looking at both of us, "whatever it is between you two, get over it."

With the okay from Frank, Mike went home early. After he left, Frank asked, "I thought you two were best friends? Like brothers?"

"We are," I said, "but sometimes he's more like a mother. Don't worry, I'll straighten it out."

It was after 6pm when I pulled up to the curb across from Mann Park on Exchange Avenue. I'd never been to Mike's house before. Still, I had no problem finding 13022. After Lori ushered me in and pointed to the basement, I found Mike watching the Cubs and Pirates playing a night game in Pittsburgh.

As I walked up behind him, I noticed the score, Pirates 3, Cubs 2. "Same ole Cubbies, Mike."

He got up and said, "I'm sorry about today. I spoke out of turn."

"Just stop right there," I said. "First of all, you got any beer?"

"Behind the bar," he said, walking behind me, then sitting at the bar.

After a long pull on my beer, I lit up a Salem, walked around the bar, and sat down next to him.

"I didn't think I had to explain myself to anyone. Then I realized you were doing it because of our friendship and what that means to me.

"You know, I'll always have your back."

"I know that, Mike, but bear with me, okay? I met Molly, who fell in love with me.

"I remember that night," Mike said with a smile.

"When I saw her with Tommy, I thought I didn't have a chance, but in the end, it worked out. Although I screwed up a few times, she always stood by me. How did you say it? Get my head out of my ass! Mostly, I didn't understand why a beautiful girl would want to be with me."

"I could never understand that, either!" Mike laughed.

"Fuck you, Mike," I said, and we laughed. The hurt feelings faded away.

"I don't think I would or could love anyone as much as I love Molly. I know now that she's part of my life. I want to spend the rest of my life with her. We talked about how we had so much time to make up for at the park that day. She couldn't wait to return to Chicago and see everyone again, but first, she had to file for divorce. She was sure her father would know a good lawyer. I had her parents' phone number, mine, and Rollie's, which we've talked about twice a week.

"I didn't know that. I'm sorry," Mike apologized.

"That's alright, Mike, nobody knew. The last time we

talked, Molly told me Tony was giving her a hard time. He wouldn't sign the papers. His lawyer said Tony wants to get back together. And that if Molly wants to start a family, he's all for it. He even quit his job with the Pension fund. Now he's just an engineer at one of the buildings downtown."

"What did Molly say?"

"She wants no part of it, Mike. She'd be here right now, except her lawyer thinks it would be better if she stayed there until it's final. Especially if Tony found out she was here with me. He could cause problems."

You didn't have to tell me all that, Jesse."

"Yes, I did, Mike, you're my best friend, and I'll always need you by my side."

After we both lit up another cigarette and opened another beer, we talked about different things; finally, Mike touched on the other part. "What about what's her name:"

"I've known Mila since we were kids."

"You're not kids anymore," he intoned.

"I know, Mike, and I won't lie. If I fuck her, that's all. It will be okay."

"Okay," Mike said, standing up and taking my hand.

"Fuck the handshake," I said, standing up. I grabbed him in a bear hug, "We good?"

"We'll always be good," he answered.

"So, I'll see you tomorrow."

"You got it, boss."

"Fuck you, Mike!"

"Right here!" he said, laughing.

After another hug, I left, with the final score Cubs 5, Pirates 3.

Chapter 65

Sunday

10/5/1966

We arrived at the bowling alley near the end of the third game, so we decided to stay and watch the last three frames. Augie changed his shoes when they finished, and Larry and Mike made their way to the bar. I turned to follow and met with Mila's sister Rose. "Hi, Rose," I said, extending my hand. "How are you?"

"Fine," she answered. "Jesse, this is my husband, John."

"Good to meet you, John. No late-night bowling?" I asked.

"Not tonight," Mila had a dinner date with a friend from work."

As he made his way to the bar, Augie tapped me on the back and said, "You've got the first round."

"Okay," I said, turning back to Rose. "Tell her I said hi."

She looked at me as if expecting me to say something else. "What?" I asked.

"If you weren't going to call her, why didn't—"

"Wait a minute, hold on," I answered, getting angry. "That's none of your business."

John made a move to come around Rose.

"That's enough, John." I glared, stopping him in his tracts. "I meant to call but thought it better if I surprised her coming here. Look, Rose, don't even tell her I was here," and with that, I turned and walked into the lounge.

Chapter 66

Thursday

10/20/1966

In the almost four months since I left Molly, I thought about nothing except the idea that someday she would be here with me and all the beautiful things we would do together. The phone calls that were once exciting and hopeful are now filled with apologies and silence. Molly kept saying how sorry she was that things weren't moving faster. Tony was adamant about not signing the divorce papers. Saying if they would only have a sit-down, he could convince her to give him another chance.

I kept telling her I'd wait for as long as it took. Her lawyer said it could be settled before the year was over. (I'm hopeful.) Meanwhile, I'm trying to stay firm in my commitment to her, but I feel I'm at a crossroads. This thing with Mila was confusing. I had feelings for her, and although it's not loving, I could use a little fun. (And if I'm lucky, a little sex.) So I decided to try and see Mila again.

Chapter 67

Sunday

10/23/1966

AFTER THE SECOND ATTEMPT AT TALKING TO MILA ON THE phone (she wouldn't speak to me), I decided to go see her sister Rose. As luck would have it, when we pulled into the parking lot, Rose and her husband walked out through the side door.

"Keep the motor running," I told Larry as I exited the car.

Stopping in mid-strike about ten feet in front of our car, Rose asked, "What do you want, Jesse?"

"I think we got off on the wrong foot."

"That's too bad," she answered, walking away.

"Rose," I said, "just give me a minute, okay?"

"I'll warm up the car," John intoned, walking away.

"Now what?" she asked.

"I made a mistake, and I'm sorry. I should have called. I thought it would've been a pleasant surprise if I showed up here."

"Nice idea," Rose smirked. "It didn't work."

"I know," I answered. "She won't even talk to me."

"You called?"

"Twice, both times, she hung up. I just want to talk to her."

"All I can say is that we're having Thanksgiving dinner at our parent's house, and we usually leave about 10 o'clock.

"Thanks, Rose," I said. "Thanks a lot!"

Chapter 68

Thursday

11/27/1966

ANOTHER TYPICAL THANKSGIVING IN CHICAGO, COLD, WITH overcast skies but no snow. I'm sitting in my car with the motor running and the heat on high. I'd just lit up my third Salem when Mila finally walked out of the front door.

I left the car running and was halfway across the street when she noticed me, stopped, and asked, "What are you doing here?"

"Trying to apologize!"

"Don't do that," she said, turning away.

"Just give me a minute," I pleaded. "Then I won't bother you again."

"It's nice and warm in my car," I said. "I promise I won't try anything."

I took her hand, we crossed the street and settled in my car. We sat in silence for what seemed minutes. Mila kept her face averted, staring straight ahead. Finally, I had to say something.

"Okay," I said, "I fucked up. I should have called. I really wanted to see you, but I had this stupid idea; instead of calling, I went to see you at the bowling alley, except when I got there, I found out that you had a dinner date."

"How long were you sitting out here?'

"Not long," I answered, lying through my teeth.

"How long?" she persisted.

"9:30."

"You sat out here all this time to tell me that."

"I just thought you should know. Now I'll walk you back to your car, and I won't bother you again."

"Would you have shot him?" Mila asked, finally turning to face me.

"Shoot, who?" I asked.

"My ex, Oscar."

"Depends on what he did. Is he always like that?"

"Most of the time. How about your friends? Are they like you? Do they carry guns?"

"Yes, they do."

"Why?" Mila asked, looking for a reason.

"We work Security at the Union Hall, and we're licensed to carry them."

"That's not the word on the west side."

"You shouldn't believe everything you hear," I answered, getting angry and frustrated. "Look, Mila, I don't think this will work out, so I'll just be on my way."

"Just like that," was her reply.

"You ask too many questions, and I've already told you more than I've ever told anyone."

"I'm sorry, Jesse," she said. "I just wanted to know a little more about you."

"That would have come in time," I said, lighting up another Salem.

"I still owe you dinner," she said rather meekly.

"Don't worry about it," I answered.

"You don't have to."

"I want to. After all, it's just dinner."

"Well, if you put it that way, okay."

"What do you like?"

"Surprise me." I suddenly started laughing.

"What's so funny? I'm a good cook?"

"It's not that," I said, trying to compose myself. "I don't even know where you live."

"Of course you don't," Mila said with a laugh. "I live in Lansing."

"Really," I exclaimed. "Where in Lansing?"

"Wentworth Terrace, it's on 174th."

"I've been by there a few times. My buddy Larry lives not too far from there."

"Okay," Mila said haltingly. "How about Saturday, six o'clock.?"

"I'll be there," I said as Mila exited the car.

Chapter 69

Saturday

11/29/1966

WHEN MILA OPENED HER APARTMENT DOOR, SHE WORE A light gray cashmere sweater, black slacks, and black patent leather pumps. She looked radiant.

"Hi," she smiled. "Dinner's almost ready."

"I guess I'm just in time."

"There," she said. "Let me take your coat."

After handing my coat, we walked into the dining area. The kitchen was next to it, with a small counter separating the closet and the kitchen. There were sliding glass doors with a small balcony. On the other side was an alcove with a television in an entertainment center, a couch, and an armchair.

"Would you like something to drink?" Mila inquired.

"What're you having?"

"Just a glass of wine," she answered, walking towards the counter.

"That sounds good," I said, never having a drop of wine in my life.

"Make yourself comfortable." Mila placed the glass of wine next to me on the end table. "You want me to put the TV on?"

"Not right now," I said, taking a sip of wine.

Returning with her glass, Mila sat on the couch, smiled and said, "I hope you like lasagna!"

"I'm sure I will," I replied, trying to remain calm

"Is something wrong, Jesse? You look nervous?"

"Can I have my coat?"

"What," she exclaimed.

"My coat," I said again.

"Why, did I do something wrong?"

"No," I said, "it's nothing like that. I just need it to be out on your balcony and have a cigarette."

"Oh," she said, "you don't have to go outside. Let me get you an ashtray."

Placing the ashtray, Mila kept her eyes cast down at the floor, but I noticed what appeared to be a single tear drop at the corner of her eye. Taking her hands in mine, I asked, "What's wrong?"

"I thought you were going to leave," she said in a tiny voice, finally looking up at me.

"I would never do that," I said as gently as possible, "no matter how bad your lasagna is."

She looked up at me, saw that I was smiling, then buried her head against my chest, saying, "Oh, Jesse." I tilted her face up, and we kissed, a kiss so tender that I could taste the salt of her tears. While soothing her, I whispered, "Maybe you should check on the lasagna."

With half-closed eyes, Mila replied, "Okay, but just one more." This time, the kiss was more intimate and soulful, with both of us finally able to catch our breath. We stood there looking at each other, knowing there had to be more before the night was over. The whole meal was excellent. The salad, the lasagna with sausage and the garlic bread all went down with no problem.

"That was great, Mila. I don't think I can eat another bite."

"How about some coffee with your cigarette?"

"Fine," I said. "Let me help you with the dishes."

"You don't have to," she replied.

"I know," I joked, "but I have to do something to earn that dinner."

After the coffee and cigarette, we sat in awkward silence, each waiting for the other to say something. Looking down at my watch and noting that it was 10:40 pm gave me an excellent reason to make my move. Standing up, I said, "Thanks, Mila, I had a great evening, and even the food wasn't bad," she noticed I was smiling.

Standing up, she also replied with a smile, "I'm glad you enjoyed my dinner, and by the way, thanks for not bringing your gun."

"It's downstairs in my car."

"Well, thanks anyway."

At the hall closet, Mila stopped with her hand on the doorknob and turned. We both looked at each for what seemed a long minute. Finally, she smiled and said, "Yes," in a throaty voice, took my hand and led me to her bedroom.

Standing next to her queen-size bed, Mila attempted to walk away toward the bathroom, saying, "Just give me a minute, okay?" When I didn't let go, she looked at me in surprise with a "What?"

Sitting on the edge of her bed, I gently pulled her back. "I want to undress you," I whispered.

Later, lying in bed, our legs intertwined, and her head in the crook of my shoulder, Mila whispered, "Can I tell you something?"

"Sure," I said, "go ahead."

"Before I fall asleep, I want to tell you that I've never been made love to like that ever."

I was about to answer her, but she was already breathing softly.

Chapter 70

Sunday

11/30/1966

After a slow and fun-filled shower with Mila. (She's insatiable.) I made it home in time to take my mom to 8 o'clock mass at St. Kevin's Church. When mass ended, we went to the Purple Steak for our traditional ham and cheese omelet. We were finishing our second cup of coffee when my mom asked, "How come we don't look for a place on the east side?"

"What's the matter," I asked. "You don't like South Deering anymore?"

"It's not the neighborhood. I just think maybe we should be looking for a nicer place." She looked at me with a sad smile, "You think I like people to come up those stairs with the peeling plaster walls, the one light bulb on a string!"

"You really feel that way about it?"

"I thought," she said, "now that there's just the two of us, we could find someplace a little smaller."

"You know, Mijo, I never ask you what you do, what kind of job you have, but I know you're making good money, and I thought that maybe we could find a nicer place."

I could see that she was having a hard time trying to keep it together.

"Weren't you a little embarrassed when you brought Mila to the house?"

"Tell you the truth, Ma, I never thought about it. You don't think about it when you don't have a girlfriend. I forgot that when Cassie was here, we were downstairs, If it means that much to you, we can start looking around, but I'd like to stay in South Deering, okay?"

"You mean it?" she said, taking both my hands in hers. "For real?" she almost shouted.

"Yeah, Mom. For real."

Later that day, I called Molly but got nothing after five rings. I fell asleep on the couch, waking up at about three o'clock. My mom was downstairs with my sister, so I ordered a quick shower. After drying off, I walked back into the front room, sat on the couch in my underwear, and redialed Molly's number.

"Hello."

"Hi, Hon," I said.

"Oh, Jesse," she replied, "I'm so glad you called."

"What's the matter?" I said. "I don't like the sound of your voice."

"I don't know how much longer I can stay here. Tony won't sign the papers. He's a real asshole."

"He still thinks we can get together again. A couple of times, he's come to the house when my dad and I are at work, trying to talk to my mom. He's been waiting for me after work, so now my dad waits for me, and we come home together."

"My lawyer thinks it's a good idea to get a restraining order, so he'll stay away until this is all over. My lawyer also said that if he doesn't sign by the end of the year, I should leave if I still want to."

After a slight pause and being unable to think of anything to say, I just blurted out, "Molly, Hon, I'm so sorry that I've put you through this. I really am."

"What's that even mean?" she retorted.

"It means that if I hadn't gone to talk to your husband, you'd still be married, and I wouldn't feel like shit."

"How can you say that to me?" she said through the sobs I could hear on the other end.

"I'm not saying I regret finding you again. I feel that we should have come back together. I was too busy thinking about what my boss would say, not what my heart told me. Molly, please listen to me, Okay?" (Silence on the other end.) "Molly."

"I'm here," she replied softly.

"Sometimes, it's hard for me to say *I'm sorry, but 'after all that you've been through, I promise I will make it up to you. I promise to.'*"

"Jesse," she answered somewhat meekly, "promise me that you won't ever give up on us."

"I will never give up on us," I declared. "I don't know how many times I've said it, but I'll say it as often as I have to, I love you, Mary Catherine, and I promise that nothing will ever come between us again."

"I'll always love you, Jesse."

"Molly," I asked, "do you think you can hold out until after Christmas?"

"I don't know, but I'll try."

"Good," I said, "because I'll be there sometime between Christmas and New Year."

"Really,?" she asked, her voice going up about three octaves. "That would be the best Christmas present ever."

"This time, I promise I'll be there."

"Will you be coming alone?"

"You'll have me all to yourself. Think you can handle it?"

"I can't wait," Molly said.

"I've been waiting a long time," I answered.

"Hon," she said, "there's something I want to tell you. It's something that I'm so sorry about. I hope it won't make a difference."

"What?" I asked.

"I wanted so much for you to be the first."

"That's the last thing I'm worried about, so long as I'm the last."

"I promise you will be."

"I'll call you next week, okay?"

"I'll dream about us tonight, and I'll be counting the days."

Chapter 71

Monday

12/1/1966

Frank was waiting for us in the lobby when we walked into work that Monday. "Come into my office if you want to grab a coffee downstairs." With coffee in hand, we settled around Frank's desk. A couple of minutes later, Sal and Hank walked in and settled on each side of Frank.

With a puff on his cigar, Frank looked around the room, settling on me. He spoke evenly and without a smile, saying, "I don't have to tell you that this doesn't leave the room." We all nodded, then looked at each other. I had the feeling that there was another job he had for us.

"There's a place on the west side called LaPaloma Cantina and Dance Hall. You guys don't do any business there because the owner is a friend of mine. His name is Vicente Robles, and I've known him for a long time. Five years ago, he added the dance hall to his tavern. We financed it, and he's been making his payments every month. About three months ago, he retired, and his son Ricky runs it, and he hasn't made a payment yet. I sent a couple of guys to see him, and they got roughed up pretty bad.

"Now, I want you to go down there and find and fix the problem. You've got the okay to do whatever it takes. Now, are there any questions?" When no one spoke up, he looked around the room, announcing, "Then we're all good."

As we filed out of the room, I stepped over to his desk, asking, "Frank, you got a minute?"

"Something on your mind about the job?"

"Naw," I answered., "We can handle it. I just need some time off."

"You mean, like a vacation." He smiled.

"Something like that."

"Any place special?"

"I thought I might fly out to Philly."

"Molly?" he asked with a twinkle in his eyes.

"Yeah," I said, "I've waited too long, and now I won't let anything come between us."

"When were you planning on leaving?"

"I thought sometime after Christmas."

"Take care of LaPaloma, then you're on your own, okay?"

"No problem, Frank."

"How much time do you need?" Frank asked, now sitting behind his desk.

"I'm not really sure."

"Take as much time as you need."

"Thanks, Frank," I said, getting up from my chair.

Coming around his desk, Frank approached, then put his arms around me, saying, "I don't have to tell you how much you mean to me, so I won't. Just don't fuck this up, okay?"

"Okay," I replied.

With a kiss on each cheek, Frank walked me to the door.

Once downstairs, we gathered around the coffee pot to

make our arrangements. Augie was the first to ask, "Did Frank say what I think he said?"

"What do you think he said, Aug?" I asked, pouring another cut for myself.

"I think he meant that all bets are off."

"Look, guys, our job is to go there, talk to Ricky, find out the problem, and fix it. But just to be on the safe side, we take the equipment. So we'll meet at Robbie's Wednesday night at 10 o'clock. Okay? So we don't talk about it anymore."

Chapter 72

Wednesday

12/3/1966

LARRY WAS THE LAST TO ARRIVE. WE WERE DRINKING AND smoking, trying to hide our nervousness. This would be our first time doing anything under these circumstances.

"Anybody got any idea how we go about this?" Augie asked.

"I think," Larry said, "We will wait till he closes and everybody is gone."

"Can you open the door?" Mike asked.

"No problem," he boasted.

"Alright," I said, "let's get ready."

The four Walther PPKs were lying in the safe, along with the box of black rubberized gloves. After putting on the shoulder rigs, we each took one and inserted a full clip of 7.65mm slugs. To say we were nervous would have been an understatement. We sat at the table, not saying much, each with his own thoughts.

We went through the back door and arrived across the street from the LaPaloma at 1:30am. 18th Street was clear, with most snow piled up against the curb. We were parked about thirty feet east of Ashland Avenue, watching the front door. There were only a few cars in the parking lot, and with all of the signs off, we figured it was the last call for alcohol. Soon they were gone except for one parked in the back, covered in shadows.

"Remember, Augie, 1966 Buick Electra, gray with a black vinyl top."

"Got it, boss," he answered, exiting the car.

We watched him cross the street, enter the parking lot, then disappear into the shadows. A couple of minutes later, he crossed over and got in the front with Larry with a big smile.

"What's so funny?" Mike asked.

"That asshole must be conceited," Augie replied, still smiling.

"Why's that?" I asked.

"Because his license plate reads, 'Guapo1.'"

"What's that mean?" Larry inquired.

"It means handsome," I said, laughing.

"He's parked next to the back door. I think Larry should have no problems, okay." I said. "Larry, go around the block and park as close as possible to the alley." While Larry was picking the lock, we took out the silencers and attached them to the Walthers. Once he was done, Larry returned to the car, keeping the motor running.

We were in a short hallway with one open doorway on the left. The lights were on, and we could hear heavy breathing, grunting, and moaning. Ricky was sitting behind his desk, which was located by the far wall. He and the woman sitting in his lap were facing the sidewall. Ricky was holding her by the waist with his eyes closed. She had her blouse open, her bra pushed up, and her breasts were bouncing so fast that I thought they might bounce off. We waited until they were done, then walked into the room. The woman was the first to see us and was about to scream. Mike put his finger to his lips and quietly shushed her. She stood up and was about to tuck herself into her bra.

"Just stop right there!" Augie said.

"What the fuck! Who are you" Ricky demanded, standing up.

"Get yourself together, Ricky, then sit down," I told him.

"Whatya want?" he asked, still a little out of breath.

"I told you to sit down. I won't repeat it."

Turning to Augie and motioning to the door, I said, "Escort her outside and don't forget her ID."

Mike sauntered over to the corner of the desk, saying, "We're just here to have a little conversation."

"About what?" he answered.

I could see the expression on his face when he saw the black gloves holding the Walthers.

"Well, Ricky, you see, it's like this. We understand that you're behind on your payments. Is there some kind of problem that Frank doesn't know about?"

"Oh, so that's what this is all about. What do you think? You can just waltz in here and threaten me. Well! Fuck you!"

The look on Ricky's face told me he had overcome the shock of us being there. He was becoming arrogant and defiant.

"No need to get testy, Rick," I said, inching closer to his desk. "Like we said, we're here to find out if there's a problem or not."

"There's no problem here," Ricky answered. "The deal he made was with my father, now I'm in charge, and you can tell that fucking wop that if he wants. He can come down here and collect."

"Listen, asshole," Mike growled. "That's not how it works."

"Chinga Tu Madre, Carbron," Ricky shouted at Mike.

"La Touya, Beche Maricon," Mike answered, moving to confront Ricky. At that precise moment, everything seemed to be moving in slow motion. As Mike rounded the desk, there was a soft *psst*. Mike was spun around by the force of the .38 slug that tore into his shoulder and exited his back. He looked at me, saying, "Jesse," before sinking to his knees while holding onto the corner of the desk

As Ricky was pivoting towards me, a hole appeared above his right eyebrow and blew off most of the back of his head, which splattered all over the back wall. I stood in a trance, seeing Ricky with blood trickling down his face, asking, "Why?"

The sound of Augie running into the room and exclaiming, "What the fuck!" brought everything back into focus. "Boss, are you all right? What happened?"

"Help Mike," I ordered. "He's been hit. I gotta call Frank." After helping Mike to a chair, Augie returned to the bar with a couple of bar towels.

"It's a through and through," Augie announced. Most of the bleeding had stopped.

Frank picked up on the third ring, and when I told him what had happened, he said the first thing was to get out of there and take Mike to the doctor's house. Make sure there were no witnesses, then come and see him in the morning.

Mike was lucky. No bones or arteries were hit, and after dropping him off at his place, Augie went home. I spent the night on the couch at Larry's house.

Chapter 73

Thursday

12/4/1966

AFTER PICKING UP MIKE'S PIECE, WE STOPPED AT ROLLIE'S and deposited our gear in the safe. We then made our way downtown and arrived shortly before Frank.

Half an hour later, we were downstairs having our coffee and sweet rolls when Frank walked into the room and approached us. He stopped in front of me, looking me straight in the eyes. I'd never seen Frank like that. He seemed very agitated. When he asked, "What the fuck happened, and someone get me a coffee."

When I explained what had happened, he seemed to relax a little. "How's Mike?" he asked.

"He's alright, it was a through and through, and the doctor patched him up pretty good."

"Next time," Frank said, "always look under the desk, okay?"

"It won't happen again, Frank," I promise.

"I hope so," he answered. "Now I know you three have no reason to lie to me because I must explain everything to the Council."

"You have my word on that, Frank," I said.

"Okay then," he said, "Jesse, come to my office.

"Have a seat," Frank said, sitting behind his desk. "Now that I know what happened, I'd like to know why?"

Lighting up a Salem, settling in the chair, I began. "He looked really scared when we first walked in, but his mood and confidence started to turn up as the conversation turned to why we were there."

"What happened then?" Frank inquired, leaning forward.

"I think that's when he had the gun in his hand because he got real cocky, saying that if the wop wanted the money, he should go there and collect it in person."

"His exact words?" Frank wanted to know.

"To the letter, boss," I smiled.

"Then what happened?"

"Mike called him an asshole, saying it didn't work that way. When Ricky told Mike to go fuck his mother in Spanish, he didn't realize that Mike understood, and when Mike told him the same thing, that's when Ricky shot him. As Mike was going down, Ricky started to swing my way. All of a sudden, a hole appeared on his forehead."

"What did it feel like?" Frank wanted to know.

"I don't remember pulling the trigger. I just remember Mike going down. Augie came in, saw Mike, and helped him into one of the chairs. That brought me back, and the first thing I thought of was to call you."

"Stay with that in case the Council wants to talk to you."

"It's the truth, Frank," I emphasized.

"I believe you, Jesse," he answered with a smile, "and in case you're worried, I sent one of our cleaning crews to make it look like a robbery."

"You really take care of everything."

"I told you I'd always have your back," Frank assured me. "Now, I want the three of you to take the rest of the week off. Also, tell Mike to take as much time as he needs."

"What about Ricky and the money?" I inquired.

"Don't worry, I'll talk to Chente. We'll get it worked out."

Chapter 74

Monday

12/8/1966

THE FOUR DAYS OFF WERE THE FIRST TIME WE DIDN'T SPEND time together. Larry and Augie wanted time with their families. I went to see Mike a couple of times. He was healing nicely, and Lori took good care of him without asking questions. I spent Saturday night at Mila's place, hoping that maybe a little sex would help me get a good night's sleep. Every time I closed my eyes, I saw Ricky sitting in his chair with a bullet hole in his forehead. Mila woke me up at about 2:30 in the morning, saying I was talking in my sleep, saying, "Mike, Mike, get up!"

"Jesse," she wanted to know. "What happened to Mike?"

I was shaking, and my pillow was soaking wet. After I calmed down a little, turning the pillow over, I said, "I can't talk about it now." Finally, lying on my side with Mila's arms holding me, I fell into a deep, dreamless sleep.

Chapter 75

Wednesday

12/24/1966

I<small>T</small> <small>WAS</small> 6:30 <small>IN THE EVENING WHEN WE WALKED OUT OF</small> M<small>ILA'S</small> parents' home. There were four inches of snow on the ground. The temperature was already down in the mid-30s, and the wind chill factor made it seem in the single digits. There was no doubt that it would be a "White Christmas." The weather report on WLS radio was three more inches by tomorrow morning.

We were bundled up pretty well, with my Corduroy pants, turtle neck under my shirt, and brown leather coat. Mila wore a Christmas sweater over her blouse, black slacks, boots, and a gray car coat.

It took a while for the heater to kick in, so we sat there hugging each other; finally, I couldn't wait to ask.

"How come your parents still live in the same place after all these years?"

"I don't know," she answered. "We've tried talking them

into someplace like Dalton, Cal City, or Lansing, but they like where they are. Maybe someday they'll change their minds."

"How about the East Side or Hegwisch?"

"We've thought about that too," she answered.

I lit up a Salem and was about to put the car in gear when Mila put her hand on my arm.

"Jesse," she asked, "do you think we can talk about it now?"

"About what?" I snapped.

"Whatever is on your mind," Mila said with a concerned look.

"It doesn't concern you," I said, beginning to feel agitated.

"What ya mean it doesn't concern me? At night when we're in bed, all you do is toss and turn and call for Mike. I wish you would talk to me and tell me what happened?"

"If the time ever comes, you'll be the first to know. Now can we just drop it and enjoy the night?" I put the car in gear and pulled away from the curb. It took a half-hour to get to Larry's and Jeannie's house in Lansing. At 173rd and Burnham Avenue, we turned left, went two blocks to Willow Street, made another left, then pulled to the curb in front of Larry and Jeannie's house. Most homes were decorated with lights on the shrubs, the windows, and the front door.

In the big bay window was a beautiful pine tree full of light bulbs, garland, tinsel, and a beautiful angel on top. We were met by Jeannie, standing behind the storm door. With a big smile, she opened it and invited us in. Larry came up from the basement, took our coats, saying, "The others are downstairs."

After the hugs and kisses, we walked towards the stairs. Jeannie took hold of my hand and pulled me aside as I was about to follow Mila and Larry downstairs.

"I'd like to talk to you for a minute, okay?"

"Sure," I said, "What's up?"

"When was the last time you were home?"

"About two weeks ago," I answered. "Why?"

"What about your mom?"

"She's in Saginaw, Michigan. What's this all about?" I asked, a little upset.

"About a month ago, I got a phone call from Molly. She didn't want you to know."

"Why?" I asked.

"I think she wanted your address to send you something for Christmas."

"I just talked to her the other day. I'm gonna be with her next week."

"You're going next week!" Jeannie almost shouted.

"Yeah," I said happily, "I've already got my ticket."

"When do you leave?" she asked anxiously.

"Next week, Monday, and Jeannie, she's coming back with me."

"To stay?" Incredulously hopeful, Jeannie smiled.

"Yeah," I said, "if I have anything to say about it."

With a big hug, Jeannie sobbed, "Oh, Jesse, I'm so happy for the both of you. Do the guys know? Are you going alone?"

"Mike's not happy, but I convinced him I'll be alright. Besides, Molly's ex doesn't even know me."

"Would you do me a favor?" Jeannie asked, tears running down both cheeks

"Anything," I said, "you know that."

"Go home tonight, check your mail, and both of you return safely."

"I'll do that. Now, let's go downstairs."

Later, watching the big, wet snowflakes accumulate on the windshield, I was lighting one of my Salems when Mila put her hand on my arm, making me turn to face her. "Jesse," she said, "I'm going to stay at my parent's house the night. Okay?"

"Yeah, sure," I said. I'd been looking forward to spending the night in her bed. We both enjoyed each other. Mila was very adventurous and willing to do everything we could think of.

Mila was all that I could handle in bed. (That's all it was on my part.) All the time we'd been together, there was never any expression of love from either of us. I don't think it was ever expected. After dropping her off, I made my way back to South Deering. It took a little longer than usual, what with the big, wet snowflakes.

Chapter 76

Friday

12/26/1966

MOST OF THE MAIN STREETS WERE CLEARED OF SNOW. THE sun was out, and the temperature was in the high 30s. After picking up the package at the post office, I returned home. Sitting on the couch, and with nervous fingers, I opened the box. Inside was an envelope with my name – it appeared to be a Christmas card – underneath was a 45 RPM record with a picture of Roy Orbison. I decided to open the card first. It contained the usual season's greetings and was signed "Love, Molly."

Written on the inside flap was, "Hon, please play the side with 'In Dreams.' I heard it about two weeks ago and couldn't stop crying. It brought back many memories of walking and talking at Cal Park beach. Walking and holding hands on 79th Street or kissing and holding each other under the Skyway Over Pass. Jesse, promise me that you'll think of us when you hear the song."

With shaking hands, I managed to light up a Salem and put the 45 RPM on the turntable. I didn't know what to expect until the first words were sung by Roy Orbison:

I close my eyes, then I drift away.
Into the magic night, I softly say,
A silent prayer, like dreamers, do
Then I fall asleep to dream, my dreams of you,
In dreams, I walk with you, In dreams, I talk to you

Molly was so right. The memories flooded back to Cal Park, 79th Street, Wrigley field, eating cheese-covered pretzels while watching the lights in the Buckingham Fountain. Spending the day at Warren Dunes, then watching the fireworks at Trumbull Park.

What those memories made me realize was how much I missed her. How I couldn't wait to see and be with her.

Chapter 77

Monday

12/29/1966

MIKE WAS IN FRONT OF MY HOUSE AT 7AM SHARP, BEEPING THE horn, until I came downstairs with my suitcase in hand. I put it in the back seat and jumped in front with Mike. "How's the shoulder?" I asked, lighting up a Salem.

"I think I can go back to work next week."

"Don't rush it, okay? Frank said to take as much time as you need."

"I know," he said. "I just gotta get out of the house. You sure you don't want me to tag along?"

"Thanks, Mike," I said, "but I'll be fine."

"Have it your way," he answered, pulling away from the curb.

Molly was waiting for me in the Baggage Claim area. Even all bundled up, her face slightly flushed, she was still the most beautiful woman I'd ever known. We stopped a few feet from each other, neither knowing what to say or do; finally, I

smiled and said, "Hello, Molly." She answered, "Hello, Jesse."
Then we were in each other's arms. It took my breath away,
knowing I was finally here and holding her in my arms.

In the car, we shared a kiss that took us to another place in
time. A place where we knew for sure that we had been given
a second chance at love. I was about to light up a Salem when
Molly held my arm, saying, "Do you have to?" If it were
anyone else, I would have done it anyway, but looking at her
face, seeing all the love I would ever need, there was no
contest.

"Tell me again," she intoned.

"Tell you what?" I asked, knowing full well what she
wanted to hear.

"You know," she answered, again with that beautiful smile.

"I love you, Mary Catherine Malone!"

"I love you, Jesse Cruz.!"

One final kiss, and we were on our way.

It was the same Holiday Inn that we stayed at on Chestnut
Street; only this time, a woman was working at the front desk.
After making a copy of my credit card, the key she handed me
was Room 110, next to the swimming pool. I was taking my
suitcase from the back seat when I noticed that Molly had
taken out a smaller trunk.

With a questioning look, she asked, "What?"

"Nothing," I answered,

"Do you know how long I've waited to sleep with you?"

"I can only guess," I smiled.

"Let's put them in the room and go. My mom's making
dinner."

We found a liquor store about four blocks down where I
picked up supplies and a pack of Salems. At 5pm, Molly rang
the doorbell, and we walked into the front room. "Mom, dad,
we're here," she announced.

Tom was the first to appear, extending his hand, saying,
"Jesse, so good to see you again."

Shaking his hand, I answered, "Good to see you too, Mr. M."

"Can we just drop the Mr? It makes me feel old. How about just Tom?"

At the sound of my name, I turned to see Catherine exit the kitchen and advance toward me with open arms. While in her embrace. I softly said, "I suppose it's Kate now."

"I suppose so," she said, giving me a tender kiss.

Molly and I were sitting on the couch. Her parents each had an armchair facing us. After all the pleasantries, the weather, and my flight, we sat for dinner. I couldn't contain my surprise when I saw the breaded port chops, scalloped potatoes, and creamed broccoli. "How did you know," I said, looking straight at Molly.

"I called Jeannie, and she asked your mom. I hope you don't mind."

"I know," Kate said from across the table, "they're not as good as your sister Angie's."

"Wow," I exclaimed, "you know everything!"

"I'll thank your mom when I see her," Molly said, taking hold of my hand.

We didn't talk much during dinner, but as Molly and her mom cleared the table, Tom and I retreated to the front room, where we each lit a smoke and settled into an armchair.

"When do you plan on leaving?" Tom wanted to know.

"Anytime after New Year's. Whenever Molly's ready."

"We thought we'd like to take you both for a nice New Year's dinner."

"That'd be nice," Tom answered.

We left about an hour later and arrived at the motel forty-five minutes later. Walking into the room, I took Molly's coat and scarf and, along with mine, hung them both in the closet. Molly was standing in front of the dresser, her hands clutched in front. I walked up, took both hands, leaned in, and brushed her lips with mine.

"Whispering, "I can't believe we're finally together." Looking into my eyes, she answered, "It's been a long time."

We embraced, and the slow, meaningful kiss told us we were at the place we were meant to be. Turning her head slightly, Molly whispered softly in my ear,

"Make love to me, Jesse."

As I drew back, I looked at her face, the face of someone I had loved for so long, who was now giving herself to me. I had promised her all those years ago that it would be something special when we did. "There's nothing I want to do more in my life," I said.

"I don't know how long I can wait."

"It'll be worth it," I promised. "Why don't you unpack while I take a quick shower."

Standing by the shower, in my skivvies, waiting for the hot water, I felt a whiff of cool air touch my back. Turning, I was confronted by the most beautiful image I'd ever seen. Molly stood in the doorway in all of her magnificent beauty, not embarrassed, unashamed, and, most of all, not hiding anything. She had a look of wonderment and all-knowing at the same time.

I was dumbstruck.

Finally, I stammered, "I...I...I was waiting for the hot water."

Molly asked mischievously, "You think there's room for both of us?"

Even when she walked, it seemed her feet never touched the floor. The only movement was the slight swaying of her full and perfectly rounded breasts.

Molly stopped before me and, looking down, smiled. "I'm so glad that you're happy to see me."

To say I was fully aroused would have been an understatement. I pulled my skivvies down, saying, "I think the water's warm enough," holding me in her hand, she led me into the shower. As I was washing her back, I had a flashback of doing the same thing with Cassie. Shaking my head to clear it, I was reminded that this was Molly, and no matter what my feelings for Cassie were, this was the woman I had loved ever since that Friday night in 1959.

Turning her around, I let the water cascade down her back. We kissed under the showerhead. The warm water washed over us. With her eyes still closed, Molly reached down and again took me in her hand and began stroking me ever so slowly.

Getting serious, Molly looked at me without a smile, saying, "Hon, I know I've told you this before. I've only been with one man, and that was Tony."

"I don't care about that; I never have."

"I know that, and I love you even more.":

After toweling off, we were again standing next to the bed. My voice was utterly useless; all I could do was stand there and breathe in the beauty lying on the bed. Molly's hair fanned out around her, and her lips were moist with no need for lipstick. Molly, her breath shallow and her chest heaving held out her hand, saying, "I wanna make a baby!"

We gave it our best shot.

At that precise moment, 750 miles away in Hegewisch, Mike Parobek was pulling into his garage after an evening of shooting pool and a few beers with the guys at Fat Rollies. Exiting his car, he was greeted by a voice from the open service door, a voice he knew only meant trouble. There was no disguising the meanness. "Hello, Mikey."

Reaching inside his coat and gripping the automatic in the shoulder holster, Mike growled, "Whataya want, Tommy?" He was about to draw the automatic when he felt the cold steel of the pistol against the back of his neck.

"Don't do it," the voice snarled.

Mike instinctively recognized the voice. "You too, Victor?"

There was no answer except for a hand going inside his coat and taking his automatic out.

Walking around the front of Mike's car, Tommy stood under the shop light with his trademark smirk, saying, "I told you one day I would have the odds on my side, remember?"

"I never needed any odds to fight you, Tommy."

"Who said anything about fighting, Mikey? We're here to fuck you up," Tommy answered with a snarl.

From the corner of his eye, Mike saw Victor move around to his right. Then a stunning blow broke most of the cartilage in his nose. Blood flowed over his mouth and down his chin. Staggered by the impact, Mike fell against the side of his car. Seeing this, Frankie Fontaine swung his baseball bat and broke Mike's right arm below his elbow. Next, Billy Boutner swung his bat and crushed Mike's kneecap. A couple of kicks to his rib cage, and he knew it wouldn't be easy to get up, but being the fighter he was, Mike knew he wouldn't go out of his way. Straining with one good arm and leg, Mike tried with all his might to make a fight of it. He was halfway up when he saw Tommy standing by his side with a baseball bat, but all he could think of was saying, "Fuck you, Tommy!"

Before swinging the bat to crush Mike's skull, Tommy answered, "See ya, Mikey!" Mike's last thoughts before slipping into oblivion were, "I'm so sorry, Lori, and please take care of our baby."

Lying now in a pool of his blood, Mike coughed up a goblet of blood. His legs twitched, and then he was still. Looking down at the unmoving form of what was once Mike Kowalski, Tommy turned to the other three and said with his usual smirk, "Let's go."

And so they did, walking out the service door, into the alley, and were gone.

Chapter 78

Tuesday

12/30/1966

THE PHONE'S SOUND WOKE ME FROM A DEEP AND DREAMLESS sleep. Glancing at my watch on the nightstand, I wondered aloud, "Who could that be at this hour?" On one elbow, Molly looked back at me with a questioning look.

"Yeah," I growled into the receiver.

"Jesse, it's me, Larry. You've got to come home fast."

"Why, what's the matter? Can't I leave you guys alone?"

"It's Mike, Jesse. He's dead."

"What!" I shouted. "How, when? This better not be some sick joke 'cause I'll beat the shit outta you when I get back."

"It's no joke, honest. Lori found him on the floor of his garage. Whoever it was, they really beat the shit outta him."

I felt a numbness come over me, like a giant cramp. I couldn't talk or move. I sat there holding the receiver to my ear but not hearing anything that Larry was saying. When I could move, I dropped the receiver on the nightstand, where Molly picked it up and began speaking to Larry.

I sat motionless, not even hearing Molly hang up the phone. When I finally could move, I looked up to see Molly naked. Despite all the sadness, I felt a stirring down between my legs. "Hon," I said, "maybe you should put something on."

"I'm sorry," she said and disappeared into the bathroom.

I lit up a Salem and tried to think of what to do. I knew I had to get back as soon as possible, hoping that Molly would understand. Emerging from the bathroom and wearing one of their bathrobes, she sat at my side. She put her arm around my shoulder and lovingly whispered, "I'm so sorry about Mike. He was like your brother."

The anguish, sadness, and bitterness I'd felt gushed out of me in big sobs and tears. Molly turned to me and held me in a loving embrace.

When I was done, and her tears had stopped, I looked at that beautiful face. The tears ran down her cheeks, "I love you, Jesse."

We looked at each other silently for a few seconds, then I had to tell her, "I've got to go back as soon as possible." With a hurt look as if I'd slapped her," she replied. "You mean we."

"I can't have you around until I find out who did this and why?"

"Listen, Jesse, Flacco, or whatever you call yourself. (She was mad now.) I don't care who or why. You are not leaving me again. I've waited too long to be this happy, and I won't let you spoil it. I won't have it. Don't you realize that you're my life now? I won't have one without you. My life is with you now. I don't care about what you have to do or why. Just know that I'll always be there with you."

"Wow!" I exclaimed. "Now I know why I love you."

"You bet your ass." Molly smiled. "Now, let's call the airport."

Chapter 79

Friday

1/2/1967

WE TOUCHED DOWN AT MIDWAY AIRPORT AROUND 2:30 IN the afternoon. Jeannie and Larry were waiting for us in the Baggage Claim area. After the hugs and kisses, I asked Larry, "What the fuck happened?"

"Wait till we get in the car," was his reply.

Inside the car, Larry told them what had happened. "Lori was on her way up from the basement to check on the girls. She passed the kitchen window and noticed the garage service door was open, and the light was on. She grabbed her coat and went to find out what Mike was doing in the cold.

"It was there that she found Mike on the floor next to his car. Her next-door neighbor, coming home after his shift at the mill, heard her scream. He came running over and found her doubled over, clutching Mike's workbench. He managed to help her inside, where he called 9ll, then Lori's parents.

Lori's sister called us, and by the time we arrived, the cops were already there."

"What about the girls?" I asked. "Are they alright?"

"They're fine," Jeannie answered. "They're with Lori's parents.

"And Lori?" I asked. "How's she doing?"

"She's okay, although she suffered a miscarriage on the way to South Chicago Hospital. She's staying with her parents for now."

"Okay," I said. "Let's go."

"Augie and Barb are waiting for us at his house, okay?" Larry intoned.

"Yeah, okay," I replied.

It was a quiet ride, and we soon pulled into Augie's driveway. As he rushed out to greet us, he looked different. Gone were the boyish uncaring good looks. He appeared older, more mature. I suppose we all did. Mike's death had changed us. I wasn't sure if it was for the better or not.

After a couple of beers and smokes, we determined that it couldn't be anyone from the north or west side, simply because no one knew where we lived. So we should concentrate here on the south side.

"We're gonna have to watch our backs now," Augie stated.

"I'll call Frank and tell him what happened when I get home," I said, getting up from the chair. "Just one more thing, Aug. I gotta make one phone call, okay?"

"Sure," he said, "it's right on the wall."

She picked up the third ring with a bright, cheery "Hello."

"Hi, Ma!" I answered, trying to sound more cheerful than I felt. "How were things in Saginaw?"

"Everybody's fine, Mijo. Snowed a lot for two days, then it got freezing. It feels good to be home. How are you? Where are you right now?"

"I'm at Augie's, just finishing a beer. I'll be home in a little while, okay?"

"Okay," she replied, "be careful driving."

Hanging up and turning to Augie, I asked, "You got my car keys?"

"They're hanging right there by the door," he motioned,

"You ready?" I asked Molly, putting on my coat.

"Whenever you are," she said, grabbing her coat.

Sitting in my car, waiting for the heater to kick in, I turned to Molly, and in a reassuring voice, I implied, "Why don't we stay at a motel for a couple of days?"

"How come?" she replied.

"Just thought we could spend a couple of days alone."

"Hon, I've already seen the peeling plaster, the worn wooden stairs, and the single light with the string."

"How, when?" I said, confused.

"When you were in the Army, I wanted to meet your mom, so I talked Jeannie into taking me to your house, only your mom wasn't home."

"Why didn't you say something before?"

"Jesse," she said, "I don't love you because you're rich and live in a big beautiful house, but because you're you! Now let's go home."

"Did I ever tell you how much I love you, Mary Catherine Malone?"

"Not for a couple of days anyway," she smiled.

At 7:05pm, we pulled up to the curb. Turning the ignition off, I told Molly, "I'll come back for the suitcases. Let's go upstairs."

Sitting in the kitchen, my mom didn't hear us as we silently climbed worn wooden stairs and entered the dining room. Motioning Molly to stay where she was, I entered the kitchen, put my arms around her, kissed her on the cheek, and whispered, "Hi, Ma."

"Aye, Mijo, you're home," she exhaled.

"Yeah, Mom, and I've got someone here who wants to meet you."

"Where?" she inquired.

Motioning Molly into the kitchen and helping my mom up from the chair, I introduced them. "Molly, this is my mom, Ramona. Everybody calls her Ma. Ma," I continued, "this is Mary Catherine Malone."

Ma walked up to her, took both hands, and said with a tear-choked voice, "So you're Molly?"

Then holding her at arm's length turned to me, saying, "Aye, Que Bonita."

Molly must have known what *Bonita* meant, dropping both my mom's hands and then encircling her in a big hug. Pulling away, my mom turned and asked, "Have you eaten anything for dinner?"

Despite our protests, she just happened to have some Carne-con-chili, rice, beans, and flour tortillas.

We were both pleasantly surprised to see Molly ask for seconds, my mom saying, "I like her already."

Later leaving them alone to get better acquainted, I took my time putting the car in the garage and bringing in the suitcases. When I walked back into the kitchen, Molly turned to me and, with a big smile, gushed, "Guess what? Your mom said she would show me how to make the Carne-con-chile, rice, and pinto beans."

"No, no, no, Mija," my mom interjected. "It's not your mom. It's Ma!" And with that, they both stood up for another hug.

That's great!" I joined in, "but right now, I've got to make a phone call." Sitting on the couch, I dialed the private number, hoping Frank was still awake. It was 10:45pm when Frank finally picked up the receiver. Starting off the conversation, he told me that Augie had called and that he had already put the word on the street.

"Thanks, Frank," I said. "But this is personal."

"We'll talk about it when you come in, just don't do anything stupid."

Before I could answer, he hung up. I put down the receiver very gently, got up, put a smile on my face, and walked back into the kitchen.

Chapter 80

Wednesday

2/13/1967

IT'S BEEN OVER A MONTH NOW SINCE MIKE'S FUNERAL. THE two-day wake at the Elmwood Funeral Home on the east side was quiet and somber. It was a closed casket; Mike's face was beaten severely, and Lori didn't want to see him that way. After the mass at St. Kevin Church in South Deering, he was buried at Holy Cross Cemetery in Calumet City, not far from his parents.

We were reminded by Frank that anything lethal would need the consent of the Council. It was personal between Augie, Larry, and myself, and we didn't need the okay.

"I told you before," Frank emphasized from behind his desk, "anything like this, and you're on your own."

"Do you trust us, Frank?" I asked.

"You know better than that," Frank stated angrily.

"Do we?" I continued

Walking around his desk, coming directly in front of me, Frank announced: "Augie, Larry, go get a coffee!"

When the door had closed, he turned to me with a saddened look, saying, "I've always had your back, Jesse."

"Until now," I said.

"All I'm saying is that I don't want to take a vote on you, Augie, or Larry."

"You have my word on that, Frank. Listen, we know how much you've done for us. We'd never bring any heat on the family.'"

"Your word?" he asked.

"Always," I answered.

"That's good enough for me."

Standing next to his desk, I waited.

Looking up, Frank asked, "What?"

"Aren't you forgetting something?"

As the smile took over his face, Frank intoned, "Okay, now get the fuck outta my office."

"That's better," I said on my way out.

―――――

It was three o'clock in the morning when Molly noticed the empty space on my side of the bed, then found me sitting on the couch in the front room.

"What's the matter?" she asked quietly.

"You shouldn't be here now."

"What does that mean?"

"Molly, I gotta find out what happened to Mike and why."

"I understand," Molly said emphatically. "But what's that got to do with me?"

"I don't know if it was just Mike, or are they coming after the three of us. I just want to make sure you're safe."

"I told you, Jesse, I'm not gonna do this anymore. If you want me to leave, I will, but I won't come back."

"Don't say that," I pleaded.

"I have to," she said. "You know, all those years that I thought I'd never see you again, then to see you standing in my kitchen, I thought maybe we'd been given a second chance."

Kneeling in front of me, with both my hands on her cheeks, she said with all the love I'd ever heard in someone's voice, "I love you so much that sometimes it hurts. Right now, I can't think of my life without you."

I told you I don't care if you ever asked me to marry you because I'm happy just being with you. I want to be a part of your life and raise your children. I want us to be a family together, to live life together, but most of all, to grow old together and see our grandchildren."

"Right now, I've never been happier in my whole life. I think I've loved you since the first time we met. Rollie's backyard will always be something special to me. My life is here with you now. In fact, you are my life. I don't care what you do or how you do it. I'll never ask about your businesses; as long as there are no children, I never will, so please don't send me away.

Gently taking her in my arms, I whispered, "You are my life too, and I meant every word. I told you I'll love you for the rest of your life."

"Oh, Hon," she cried against my shoulder. "I'll always remember that. I'll always feel the same." We both stretched out on the couch, and I got a good night's sleep for the first time in a long time.

Conclusion

1968 – 1969
THE SEARCH FOR TOMMY

Chapter 81

Friday

4/6/1968

WE'VE BEEN LIVING IN DYER, INDIANA, SINCE APRIL LAST year. It's a bi-level home a couple of blocks off North Gate Drive. My mom is so happy. It's like she's in seventh heaven. Molly is back teaching, only now it's at Protsman Elementary School. Since Mike's passing, Larry, Augie, and I have grown closer. We are far more observant of our surroundings. After putting out the word to his people, Frank has heard nothing about the incident.

The more we rationalize it, the more we think it has to be someone from the South Side. The reason is that nobody on the north or west side knows where we live, so now we have decided to make the rounds of the taverns and pool halls. So far, nothing has come of it. We're now waiting for the softball season to start to see if Tommy's playing.

Chapter 82

Friday

4/21/1968

ALMOST THREE MONTHS WENT BY, AND THERE DIDN'T SEEM TO be any changes, but we'd become more determined now to find out what happened. Molly and the girls were very supportive and not asking any questions. Lori sold the house and went back home with her parents. Somehow she blames us for what happened to Mike. I've tried to explain that we all went into this knowing there could be consequences, but not losing the baby.

Chapter 83

Sunday

4/23/1968

WE'RE SAT IN ROLLIE'S BACKYARD AFTER SUNDAY'S GAME, AND I'd just lit up one of my Salems when Bobby motioned me to the door.

"What's up, Bobby?"

"Davy Cinchler is inside. He says he got something to tell you."

I turned, nodded to Larry and Augie, and walked into the back room together. After a good slug of beer and sitting at the table, I said, "Okay, Bobby, let's have him."

While walking into the room, Davy seemed a little tentative about where he was. "Hi, Davy," I said, "come on in, have a seat."

"How about a beer?" Augie chimed in.

"Sure, okay," he answered.

After sitting down with a beer in front of him, he seemed to relax.

"Okay, Davy," I intoned, "what can we do for you?"

"Well, you know," he said, lighting up a cigarette, "Mike not only lived next door to me, but he was also a good friend of mine."

"Cut the bullshit, Davy," Larry growled. "You got something for us."

"Easy, Lar," I interrupted. "What's on your mind, Davy?"

"I stopped at the Crowbar on the East Side the other day, and Billy Boutner was there. He seemed to be pretty well sloshed. He was talking to Mitch, the bartender, and the talk turned to what happened to Mike."

"Go on," Augie urged.

"Mitch said that it was too bad. Mike was a good guy. Then Billy chimed in that it was really cool. Mitch asked him how he knew, and Billy said he was there."

I turned to Davy. "Are you sure, and who else was there?"

"He didn't say, only that there were four of them!"

"Does he still live in the projects?" I asked.

"Yeah," Davy answered, feeling more at ease, "and he works at the Rinso Factory, and get this, he cashes his paycheck every other Friday at the Crowbar."

"Okay then," I announced. "Thanks a lot, Davy. Anytime you want to shoot pool, it's on the house."

"Thanks, guys," Davy smiled. "If I hear anything else, you'll be the first to know."

"We won't forget this, Davy," Larry said, getting up and walking to the door.

Once Davy left, we sat around drinking, smoking, and contemplating our next move

"First up, Larry, see if you can catch Davy. Ask if he can find out what shift Billy works."

Larry was back in about ten minutes. "He'll let us know before Friday," Larry reported.

"I say we take him out right away," Augie stated.

"Not until we find out who else was there; I want all four of them."

"You're right, boss, no sense going off half-cocked."

"Right?" Augie stated, calming down.

"We must remember what Frank said about going off on our own," I reminded. "That means no fuck ups and no witnesses."

"Fucking A," Larry agreed, taking a slug of beer, then slamming the bottle on the table.

Chapter 84

Thursday

4/27/1968

WE'D JUST SAT DOWN FOR DINNER WHEN THE PHONE RANG. Standing and reaching for the wall phone, Molly motioned for me to take the call.

"Go ahead," I said, taking a sip of Pepsi.

"Hello," she said, sitting back down. "Yes, he is," handing me the phone, "It's Bobby."

"Hey, Bobby, what's up?"

"I got a call from Davy. He says he wants to talk to you."

"Call him back. Tell him we'll be there in an hour."

"Got it. See you then."

Forty-five minutes later, we parked in front of Rollie's, walked inside, nodded to Bobby, then walked into the back-room, shutting the door.

About ten minutes later, the electronic lock sounded, and the door opened. Butch walked in, followed by Davy. "Hey, Davy, sit down. Have a beer," I said. "Thanks, Butch."

Feeling a lot more comfortable, Davy took a slug of beer, a drag on his cigarette, then commenced to tell us what he knew. "First of all," he said, "Billy works the day shift. Monday through Friday. He gets off at 5 o'clock and is usually at the Crowbar by 5:30. He drives a tan 55 Ford four-door hard-top. He parks on 106th and Bensely, then walks into the projects to his place."

"You did all that by yourself?" Larry asked.

"I just asked around a little," Davy answered rather proudly.

"We really appreciate all you've done, Davy, and if there's anything we can do for you, all you have to do is ask, right guys?"

"Yeah, Davy," Augie stated.

"Fuckin A," Larry chimed in.

"Well," Davy said, sitting back in the chair. "I was hoping that maybe you could put in a good word at the Union for me about a job."

"Sure, we can do that. We'll talk to the Union rep first thing Monday morning."

"Okay, Jesse, thanks a lot, and I'll keep in touch."

With the door closed, we sat there for a couple of minutes in silence, then Larry spoke up,

"Well, whaddya think?"

"About what?" I answered.

"Bringing him in."

"Into what?" I answered, already knowing where this was going.

"In with us," Larry said thru a plume of smoke.

"You mean to take Mike's place," I answered grimly.

"We know he could never take Mike's place, no one can, but we are short one."

"I don't believe you guys have already forgotten Mike?"

"No, Jesse," Augie tried to assure me. "We'll never forget

Mike and what he meant to all three of us, but this is just business."

I knew what they were saying was right, but I still had difficulty believing that 'my protector' was gone.

Chapter 85

Friday

5/14/1968

WE'VE BEEN WATCHING BILLY EVERY DAY FOR THE PAST COUPLE of weeks, noting the only day he doesn't come home after work is on payday, Friday. Parking in the same area on Bensely Avenue and entering the projects through the same walkway. So here we are, standing inside the entryway, waiting for Billy to show up. If Billy decides to run, Larry's sitting in his car across the street.

At about 11:30, Larry flashed his lights, meaning Billy had just parked his car and was on his way toward us. Taking the Walther out of the shoulder rig, chambering a round, I held it down at my side. A couple of heartbeats later, Billy walked through the entrance, turned, and saw Augie, then murmured, "What the fuck."

"Hi, Billy," I cheerfully exclaimed. "How the fuck are you?"

"What a minute," he stammered, backing up and

bumping into Larry, who had his Walther aimed at the back of his head. Noticing the silencer, he began shaking, "I can explain what happened."

"That's good, Billy," I said. "You can explain on the ride."

Billy was sweating profusely inside the car and pleading for his life. "We were only supposed to rough him up a little."

"Is that why you broke his arm and leg, Mother Fucker?" Augie snarled.

"Who else was there, Billy, be honest, and it just might help you," I cajoled.

We were parked next to a small garbage dump west of Torrence Avenue at 116th Street. "Relax, Billy," I said, "light up one if you want. We're in no hurry."

His hands were shaking so badly that I had to put the cigarette in his mouth and light it up. After a deep drag, he stated that the other three were Frankie Fontaine, Victor Lazaro, and Tommy Stetich.

"Before we let you go, just a couple of things. Whose idea was it, and who finished it?" I asked.

"It was all Tommy's idea."

"Why?" I said, starting to see the red mist forming before my eyes.

"Tommy said that Mike had made him look bad in front of some girl and that he promised he would get back at him."

"Who finished it?" Augie growled.

"T-T-Tommy did," Billy stammered. "I swear we were just gonna rough him up a little. Please, Jesse, I didn't know that was gonna happen. I've got a wife and a little girl at home. I'm sorry. Please don't kill me." Billy was openly crying now, big sobs racking his body.

I felt a little sorry for him as I looked over the backrest. "I'm sorry, Billy." There was a soft *psst* as the slug entered his forehead. We left him on the white sand, hoping the rats would find him.

Chapter 86

Sunday

5/30/1968

I WAS PUTTING ON MY SPIKES WHEN LI'L JOE, BUTCH, AND Bobby walked over and, standing over me, announced through Li'l Joe, "We went to Loncar's last night for some chicken, and guess who was behind the bar?"

"You want me to guess?" I asked.

"Naw, that's alright," Bobby interjected. "It's Victor Lazaro."

"He tends bar every weekend?" I asked

"That's what he told me," Li'l Joe implied.

"Is it true what I just heard?" Augie inquired, walking up to our little gathering.

"Is Larry here yet?" I asked, standing up.

"I haven't seen him yet," Augie answered. "Is it true about Victor?"

"Let's not talk about it until Larry's here," I said, looking around at our little group.

We finished our warm-ups when Larry and Jeannie pulled up to the curb. They walked around to our side of the diamond. Jeannie walked over to where Molly, my mom, and the rest of the women were sitting. I motioned Larry to my side. "What's up, boss?" he asked, taking out a cigarette, then lighting up.

"We have to talk after the game."

"Okay," he answered, "I'll be here."

Gathered around the front of my car, the three of us had just finished our conversation when Bobby, Li'l Joe, and Butch walked up and confronted us.

"What's up, guys?" Augie stepped in front of me.

"It's okay, Aug," I said. "What's up, Butch?"

"Jesse, we know it's none of our business what you're doing, but Mike was our friend, so if you want, we can take care of Victor."

"You really mean that?" I asked incredulously.

"Yeah," Bobby said, "and that goes for the rest of the guys."

"We really appreciate that guys, but this is personal for us, but thanks anyway. Besides, we don't want you to do anything that would get you in trouble."

"But," Augie said, "if you really want to help, you can keep your eyes and ears open for anything about Frankie Fontaine or Tommy Stetich."

Chapter 87

Monday 2am

5/31/1968

WE'RE STANDING IN THE SHADOWS, NEXT TO VICTOR'S CAR, parked alongside the back door of Loncar's Bar when the light over the entry goes on. We know he's about to come out. Drawing the Walther from its rig, Larry stepped out and around the front of the car.

"Hi, Vic," he intoned, ensuring Victor could see the Walther with a suppressor attached.

"Hey, Larry," he answered shakily. "What ya doing here?"

"We came for a little talk," Augie answered from the other side.

"Hello, Victor," I said, standing at the rear of his car. "We've come to talk about Mike Kowalski. You remember him, don't you?"

"Look, Jesse, what happened was an accident. It wasn't supposed to end that way. Tommy went crazy laughing all the while he was hitting Mike. I've never seen him like that. He had this weird look, and his eyes had rolled up in his head."

"Did you try to stop him?" I asked, stepping closer.

Victor simply looked down at his shoes. "No," he said, barely above a whisper.

"You could've stopped him!" I snarled. "Get him inside," I said to Larry and Augie.

Motioning with the Walther, Larry urged, "Get in,"

"Fuck you, Pollock," Victor argued. "You ain't got the balls to pull the trigger."

"Speaking of balls," Augie said, stepping to the side and swiftly kicking Victor right between his legs. As he sagged against the car, Larry opened the driver's side door and, together with Augie, put Victor in the seat.

We gave him a couple of minutes to catch his breath, then holding him by the back of his head, I asked him one last question, "Who took Mike's piece?"

"Tommy," he choked. With that, I slammed his forehead against the steering wheel. Augie roared, "Say hi to Billy, you Mother Fucker," all the while sliding the ice pick up into Victor's brain stem. He bucked a couple of times, then went limp.

We left him like that, with the ice pick sticking out and his forehead resting against the steering wheel.

Chapter 88

Thursday

7/4/1968

"Not as good as the first time," Molly exclaimed as she climbed inside my car, ", especially the end. I don't think there were enough M80s, you know, that big bang,"

"Yeah," I said, "and the fireworks lasted longer." It was our first 4th of July in nine years, and even the crowd seemed smaller.

Molly reached over and touched my arm as we exited the I-80 onto Calumet Avenue South. "Can we park somewhere for a couple of minutes.?"

"We're almost home. Can't it wait?"

"No, it can't," Molly answered emphatically

"Okay," I said, pulling into the Burger King parking lot. "What's up?" I asked, lighting up a Salem.

She framed my face with her hands. "Jesse," she asked in a low voice, her eyes searching mine earnestly, "do you love me?"

I turned my head quickly, "'Course, I love you."

Her hands twisted my face back to hers. Her eyes were solemn," Jesse, I need you to say it like you mean it."

"Molly," I asked, "what's going on?"

"I'm pregnant," she answered just barely above a whisper.

"Are you serious?" I exclaimed wide-eyed.

"Don't be mad," Molly said.

"Mad?" I said. "Hon, you've just made me the happiest man alive."

Chapter 89

Thursday

7/4/1968

On the way home, we stopped at a liquor store and bought a bottle of Asti Spumante to celebrate. Later that night, my mom was excited but not surprised, saying she could tell by Molly's appetite and her 'glow.' Molly's parents sounded overjoyed and promised to come down soon.

Later that night, after separate showers, Molly came to me, sitting on the edge of the bed. I watched as she slowly walked toward me. Unashamed of her nakedness, proud of her beauty, making no attempt to cover herself. I sat there, watching her approach, mesmerized, still not believing this beautiful woman had given herself to me.

When she finally stopped before me, she said in a husky, sensual voice, "I want to make love to you." Pulling her closer until I caught her scent.

"Is it too full?" she asked, looking down.

"Are you kidding?" I breathed heavily. "It's beautiful."

Cupping her ass cheeks, I pressed my lips to her warm, soft parts. The muscles of her thighs were tense and trembling as she clung to me. "Jesse!" her voice husky in my ear, "I have to lay down."

Looking down at her, her hair splayed out on the pillow, her face full of love and understanding, I couldn't wait to continue. We found our rhythm and rode it to the end. Laying together with the closeness of our bodies and the satisfaction of our release, Molly opened her mouth slightly. I could feel our breaths intermingling. Her warm scent came up to my nostrils. She turned slightly, closed her eyes, and whispered, "I love you."

"I love you more!" I answered, pulling her closer.

"We're gonna make great parents, aren't we?"

"You bet!" I exclaimed.

And so, holding each other, we fell into a deep and fulfilling sleep.

Chapter 90

Tuesday

9/15/1968

With Molly three months along and (Thank God) no morning sickness, she is showing a slight bump. Things at work have become more or less regular. Frank has been great, not asking anything about what we're doing. We are still doing our stuff on the north and west side. We've talked about bringing someone in to fill in Mike's place (nobody can ever do that!). It was on a Monday that Frank came downstairs while we had our coffee.

"You know," he said, "I've never interfered or asked about what you were doing. As I said, as long as it didn't involve the 'family,' you were on your own. I also know about the guy they found in the dumpster behind the bowling alley."

"That would be Frankie Fontaine," I said.

"Yeah," Frank answered, "but broken arms and legs, plus a slug in the forehead, what was that all about?" he smiled.

"That's what happened to Mike," Larry chipped in.

"So that's it," Frank asked. "It's finished."

"Not by a long shot," I answered

"What's that mean?"

"We'll never stop until we do," I confronted him.

"Okay," Frank said, "just finish it soon."

"It'll be finished when it's finished," again confronting him.

"Again, Jesse, watch your mouth!" Frank said sternly.

Looking at me squarely in the eye, he warned, "One day, that big mouth will get you in trouble."

"We're sorry, Frank," Augie said, stepping in between us. "So far, nothing has panned out. We've got everybody on the lookout, but so far, nothing."

Looking past Augie, Frank nodded to me. "In about half an hour, come upstairs to my office."

Watching him walk up the stairs, Larry stated, "Whatever happens, we've got your back."

"I know," I said, walking over to get a refill.

Walking into Frank's office, he gestured with his ever-present cigar for me to sit. Without a smile or even mentioning my name, he snarled, "You still don't realize who has the last word around here."

"I'm sorry, Frank, I just wanted to—"

"Fuck you, Jesse." He slammed his hand on the desk. "I've covered your ass more than once because I like you, even your three friends."

"It won't happen again," I promised.

"It damn well better not."

"Is that all?" I asked, standing up.

"For now," he answered.

"One last thing," he reminded me, "if I tell you to shut this thing down with Tommy, you will shut it down?"

"Okay, Frank," I said on my way out.

"How's your ass?" Larry asked, smiling as I walked into the hall.

"Sore," I said as we all laughed.

The following two days passed with still nothing on Tommy. We were starting to think that maybe he had left the area. I called work Friday morning and told Nancy that Molly had a doctor's appointment at 11:30 that morning and that I would be in later in the afternoon. Ten minutes later, she called back, telling me it was okay with Frank for me to take the day off.

With the doctor saying everything was normal, we decided to have lunch at Red Lobster on Calumet Avenue in Munster. Molly's appetite hadn't changed, and even though she'd put on a little weight, she'd never looked more beautiful. I had never believed it before, but now I could see it on her face. (She has that glow!)

The phone rang as Molly, and my mom walked in the front door. "Hello," Molly said, picking up the receiver. "Oh, hi, Bobby. Yeah, he just walked in. Hon, it's Bobby."

"Yeah, Bobby, what's up?" I inquired after taking the phone.

"I didn't want to bother you, but Davy Cinchler is here. He wanted your phone number. I didn't give it to him, so I decided to call you."

"Thanks, Bobby, put him on."

"Jesse?" Davy asked.

"Davy, how are you?

"First of all, thank you for getting me into the Union."

"You helped us a lot, Davy, just a little thank you. Now, what's on your mind?"

"I'd rather tell you in person if it's alright with you." |

"Okay, give us half an hour. Now put Bobby back on."

"Yeah, Jesse," Bobby intoned.

"Make sure Davy is by himself, and we'll be there in about half an hour, okay?"

"You got it. Remember, if nobody's out front, it's all good."

We drove by, and the front was empty, so we parked around the corner on 109th Street. Coming through the alley and walking in through the back door, we sat at the table, and after grabbing a beer and lighting up a smoke, Larry went to fetch Davy.

"Come on in, Davy, grab a chair. I said, " Augie, get Davy a beer," motioning to an empty chair. Once we were all seated, I looked over at Davy and asked, "What's on your mind?"

After taking a long pull on his beer, he began, "Last Sunday, we were at the track, and we bumped into Tommy O'Hara and Whitey Fleming. Right out of the blue, they asked if we had seen Tommy Stetich lately. We said we hadn't seen him in quite a while. Tommy was supposed to play ball with them but never showed up. They even went to his house looking for him. His mother said he hadn't been home since the middle of January. She also said that Tommy and his girl-friend spend all their time at a campground somewhere in Indiana."

"And you waited till now to fuckin tell us, you asshole," Augie snarled, rising to his feet.

"Easy, Aug." Larry urged. "Let's hear him out."

"Thanks, Lar," Davy replied, taking a deep drag on his cigarette. "Like I said, I didn't say anything because I wanted to check out the campgrounds nearby."

"And?" I asked, suddenly feeling a surge of adrenaline.

"We found him. He's at a place called Yogi Bear Camp-ground. It's in Portage, Indiana. You can see it from the expressway."

"How do you know it's him?" I asked.

"We drove around till we spotted him. He and his girl-friend were sitting around a campfire."

"He didn't spot you?" Larry inquired.

"Not with the tinted windows," Davy smiled. "He's on the last street before the little lake. The fourth lot from the corner was a black and gray Chevy Impala in the driveway."

"And you're sure it was him?" Augie asked.

"I know Tommy when I see him," Davy replied, taking a slug of beer.

We all stood up, and I extended my hand to him. I said, "We won't ever forget this, Davy, but there's just one more question I'd like to ask."

"Sure, Jesse," he answered. "Anything."

"Why are you doing this? What's in it for you?"

He looked taken back. "Whatya mean."

"I mean, Mike wasn't your friend, yet you've gone out of your way to help us. Why?"

"The truth?" he asked.

"For a start," Augie chimed in.

"I already told you how much I appreciated what you've done for me, but what I was really hoping for was maybe getting into Security at the Union. I know no one can take Mike's place, but I thought you could use a little help. If it's no, I'll understand, and I won't bother you again."

The three of us looked at each other, smiled, and nodded, "Okay, Davy," I said. "Can you be here tomorrow?"

"Sure, Jesse," he answered. "What time?"

"About 11 o'clock, I want you to go with Larry in your car and show him where Tommy is. Okay? And remember, whatever you do, don't roll the windows down.

"I'll be here," Davy exclaimed eagerly.

"Okay, then," I said, "see you tomorrow."

When the door had closed, Augie turned to me with a questioning look. "Do you think we can trust him?"

'I think we can," Larry shrugged. "He's helped us a lot already."

"Okay," I said, "First, we bring him into the security, and

we will see how that works. If it's good, we let him into the business, but nothing about the 'family,' understand?"

"Okay, boss," they both nodded, "And one more thing, Larry, take your equipment tomorrow." We finished another beer, put out the light, locked the back door, and went home.

Chapter 91

Saturday

9/19/1968

WE PULLED INTO THE CAMPGROUND PARKING LOT AT ABOUT 10:30 in the morning. Facing the entrance, Augie turned and said, "I didn't think we'd let Larry come here by himself."

Lighting up a Salem and smiling, I answered, "It's always good to be on the same page. I think we can trust Davy. I just want to make sure everything's on the up and up."

"Isn't that Davy's car?" Augie pointed to the tan-colored Ford entering the campground.

"Follow him," I said, "but not too close."

Waiting for Larry and Davy to return, we sat in the back-room of Rollie's, having a beer and a smoke. Walking in the back door, Larry immediately went to the fridge and extracted two beers, giving one to Davy, then sat across from him.

"You know which trailer, right?" I asked Larry. "Because we'll probably be going in at night."

"Yeah, I got it," he answered.

"Okay now, Davy, we want you to report to the Union Hall on Monday morning. You'll be working with us from now on. I'll square it away with Frank."

"Thanks, guys. You won't be sorry."

"I hope not," I said to no one in particular.

With that settled, we locked up and went our separate ways.

Chapter 92

Monday

9/21/1968

"I THINK WE SHOULD CHECK TOMMY OUT FOR A COUPLE OF days before we do anything," Larry announced. It was Monday morning, and we had just sat down with our coffee.

"Fuck that!" Augie argued. "I say we go get him tonight and end this shit."

"What if his girlfriend is there?" I questioned. "Do we take her out too? Plus, it's too open there. What if we're seen?"

"Okay, boss," they both agreed, "but let' s make it quick."

"We'll start tonight after work if you want. You can call Jeannie and Barb. I'll call Molly."

"What about me" Davy inquired.

"What about you?" Larry answered.

"After all I've done, I thought I was part of the crew."

"You are part of the crew!" I said. "But this is personal."

"I know it is, and I still want in."

"Do you think you could pull the trigger," Augie challenged, stepping in front of Davy.

"If I have to," he replied.

"Wrong answer," Augie said, stepping away.

"You want in, then I'll tell you what; for now, you drive and stay with the car, okay?"

"Okay, Jesse, whatever you say."

We arrived at the campground at about 6:30 pm. Noticing Tommy's car parked next to the trailer, we retreated to the parking lot, where we had a good view of the entrance. There wasn't much conversation. We all just sat in the car and smoked a lot, each with his own thoughts; finally, we called it quits and left at 1am.

By the time Friday rolled around, we were convinced that Tommy spent most of the time alone, watched TV, or drove into Portage to eat. After dinner, we followed him to Hegewisch, where he picked up his girlfriend, then went back to the campground. They stayed there Friday and Saturday, then after dinner in town, Tommy drove her home.

With one last goodnight kiss, Tommy ascended the three concrete steps, turned left, and walked toward his car, parked at the curb. He was so engrossed in his memory of last night's adventure that he was oblivious to what was happening around him. Settling behind the steering wheel and still relishing the images of last night, Tommy didn't see or feel Augie sit up and put the muzzle of the silencer against the back of his head.

"Don't start it," Augie snarled. "Just move over,"

Looking into the rearview mirror, Tommy felt a cold chill run up and down his spine. "Augie?" he asked, already knowing the answer.

"You were expecting Billy, Victor, or maybe Frankie?"

"It took you guys long enough."

"We have a lot of time," Augie said. "Now shut the fuck up and move over."

Larry appeared, opened the driver's door, and slid in. "Hey, Tommy." He grinned. "How the fuck are you?"

"You get rid of one Pollock, and another one shows up."

Not even losing his smoke, Larry slammed his elbow into the side of Tommy's face, bouncing his head off the side window.

"Don't fuck'n make me tell you again to shut up you, Mother Fucker, or I'll blow your brains all over the dashboard."

"You're real tough, holding that gun," Tommy answered, trying to sound braver than he felt.

"About as tough as you did, holding that baseball bat."

"Fuck you, and Mike, he had it coming!"

With that, Augie slammed the Walther onto the base of Tommy's neck, rendering him unconscious. "Let's go," Augie said.

"Okay," Larry answered, pulling away from the curb.

Chapter 93

Tuesday 6:30am

9/22/1968

WHEN TOMMY CAME TO, HE COULDN'T TELL WHICH HURT more, his cheek or the back of his neck, lifting his head and looking around, and it came to him where he was. "We're at the Gun Club out by the lake," he said. As he tried to move, he could feel the handcuffs holding his arms behind him and his legs tied to the chair he was sitting in. Augie was seated directly across the table. Larry was standing off to his left. Despite the chill in the cabin, Tommy was sweating profusely and had already pissed in his pants.

"Hey, Tommy," I said, walking into his view. "Long time no see."

"You gotta believe me. I didn't mean it to happen that way," he pleaded. "I just wanted to fuck him up a little, that's all."

"Why?!" Larry asked. "He was a friend."

"Because he showed me up a couple of times."

"And for that, you fucking beat him to death, you Mother Fucker," Augie growled, rising to his feet.

Knowing he wouldn't be leaving, a strange calmness came over Tommy. There was no more pleading in his voice. His entire being felt at ease, serene, and peaceful.

"We used to be best friends, Jesse, remember?"

"Good friends, Tommy, but never best!" I shouted, slamming my hand flat on the table, my face inches away from him.

"To me, he was just another dumb Pollock who didn't know when to stay down," Tommy snarled.

As I straightened up, I noticed that now he had that trademark smirk spread across his face as if daring me to do something.

As I was talking, I motioned to Larry and Augie, who went and stood behind Tommy. They both stood there, holding their Walthers and their arms crossed. "You know what your problem is, Tommy?" I asked, taking my place next to Larry.

"You always thought you were better than anyone else,"

"When it comes to Mexicans and Pollocks," he said with gritted teeth, "you're dammed right! Do what you're gonna do, and I'll see you in hell!"

"You first, Tommy," we said in unison, then pulled the triggers. There was a soft *psst* as three slugs entered the back of Tommy's head. He gave one mighty jerk as most of his face and brain splattered across the table. As Larry undid the cuffs, Tommy's body slumped forward, and his face (What was left of it.) landed with a soft thud in the middle of his brains and a lot of blood.

Twenty minutes later, Davy dropped us off in front of Rollie's, then drove home. Augie, Larry, and I then proceeded back home to the suburbs.

Four-thirty am found me sitting alone in the darkened

kitchen. I had just started up another Salem when Molly walked in, turned on the light, and then sat opposite me.

"What's wrong, Hon?" she asked, her voice full of concern.

"I felt you tossing and turning." I looked at her sitting there with her hair disheveled, no makeup, shapeless nightgown, and slightly swollen stomach (she never looked more beautiful.)

It's over," I sighed, barely above a whisper.

"It is?" Molly sounded unbelieving.

"We found Tommy last night, living in a trailer at a campground in Indiana."

"I'm so sorry it happened," Molly intoned. "I know you two were close."

"Christ, Molly," I said, raising my voice. "At one time, he was my best friend."

"But this wasn't the same Tommy you knew back then," she said.

"I don't think I'm the same person as I was then either."

"What do you mean?" Molly asked.

"I feel like I don't know who I am, Molly. We've killed four people – five, counting Ricky Robles. What does that mean?"

"I never thought I could kill someone until what happened to Mike sort of pushed us over the edge. Every time I close my eyes, I see Tommy the way we left him. I just can't get it off my mind."

"I think," Molly said, "you did what you thought you had to do for Mike." With a calm voice, she paused, then continued, "I told you before that I would never question what you do or how you do it, but now with the baby, you have to promise me it's over."

I went to bed that morning, determined to keep my promise to Molly.

"That it was over." After all, we would be a family soon.

One thing that kept me awake for a while. That night was what Davy had said: "Why don't we start our own Security Company." (Something to think about.)

THE END

About the Author

Steve, the second youngest of eleven children, was raised on the Southside of Chicago. He graduated from Chicago Vocational High School in 1957. After graduation, he went to work for the Wisconsin Steel Works, where he worked for twenty-one years. In June of 1963, Steve was drafted into the Army. He spent two years in Germany as a radio Teletype Operator. After being discharged from the Army, Steve married Carman Suarez. They raised three children and eventually retired to Las Vegas, Nevada. Steve has always been an avid reader. South Deering is his first book.

―――――――

To learn more about Steve Esparza and discover more Next Chapter authors, visit our website at www.nextchapter.pub.

South Deering
ISBN: 978-4-82415-574-0

Published by
Next Chapter
2-5-6 SANNO
SANNO BRIDGE
143-0023 Ota-Ku, Tokyo
+818035793528

4th November 2022